# BRAVE NEW WANDA

LYNDA RUTLEDGE

# BRAVE
# NEW
# WANDA

*a novel*

WORDFARM
LA PORTE, INDIANA

WordFarm
2010 Michigan Avenue
La Porte, IN 46350
www.wordfarm.net
info@wordfarm.net

Cover Image: iStockPhoto

Design: Andrew Craft

USA ISBN 0-9743427-5-0
Printed in the United States of America

---

*Library of Congress Cataloging-in-Publication Data*

Rutledge, Lynda, 1950-
   Brave new Wanda : a novel / Lynda Rutledge
      p. cm.
   ISBN 0-9743427-5-0 (pbk.)
      1. Human reproduction—Fiction. 2. Biotechnology—Fiction. 3. Texas—
Fiction. I. Title.
PS3618.U83B73 2004
813'.6—dc22

                                                            2004005083

---

P    17   16   15   14   13   12   11   10   9   8   7   6   5   4   3   2   1
Y    17   16   15   14   13   12   11   10   09   08   07   06   05   04

# *Acknowledgments*

Wanda and I would like to express our appreciation for the support received from grants, scholarships, residencies, and awards given by the Illinois Arts Council, Ragdale Foundation, and Squaw Valley Community of Writers, and for the encouragement from friends and mentors at Sewanee Writers Conference and the Columbia College Fiction Writing Department who were there for her beginning.

You know who you are.

We'll never forget you.

# *Chapter 1*

*The New Mexico Whiptail lizard
produces offspring without the
benefit of sperm.*

—Wonderful World of Biology

*A* blond, moon-faced girl in cutoffs and boots hopped down from the hood of a rusting Cadillac, illegally parked behind the huge Dallas hospital. Blowing the bangs out of her eyes, she sized up the man emerging from the doctors' entrance, eyeballing him good.

"Hey, *MISTER*," she yelled, as he strode by. "Are you my fucking daddy?"

The man jerked his head around. "Ex-*cuse* me?"

She squinted. "Nose looks right. You double-jointed?" She hyperextended an elbow, making a bow back the wrong way.

The man quickened his pace toward his car. The girl followed, boots clomping.

Inside his Mercedes, the man punched the auto lock as the girl pressed her nose against the tinted window. Then, quickly, he pulled the car around her and away.

Stomping back to the Caddy, she reached up to pat the one-eared yellow dog poking its huge head through the rip in the car's ragtop.

"Don't you come near me with that nasty mouth of yours," warned the chubby old lady in a faded housedress, overflowing the driver's seat.

Cracking a knuckle, the girl gazed back toward the hospital doors. "You've got to talk that way, else nobody hears you. Don't you get cable?"

The old woman harrumphed, dabbing at her neck with a handkerchief. "If your mama, God rest her soul, could see you hounding these fine, upstanding men as if they'd thrown her down in the middle of Highway 80 and had their way with her, it would just kill her."

"She's already dead, Granny." The girl cracked another knuckle.

The old woman groaned. "Why do you believe that no-good stepdaddy of yours? Your daddy was your daddy! And if he ain't your daddy, then I ain't your granny, and nobody but your granny'd put up with you half the time, Miss Wanda Louise Ledbetter."

The girl screwed up her face. "Wanda—just *Wanda*, now, okay?" She pushed a stray clump of hair behind an ear just as the automatic doors of the doctors' entrance swished open. "Here comes another one."

"You said we was going to Poetry Cemetery, and this ain't it," the fat woman griped, swatting the big dog's wagging tail out of her face. "Now get back in this car right now! My feet are starting to swell."

An anemic siren filled the air. The girl turned to see a white security car, yellow light twirling, jolt over a speed bump and halt directly behind them, inches from the Cadillac's bent bumper. Two guards, one with a belly testing the limits of his khaki uniform, the other young and skinny as straw, hopped out of the vehicle.

"Young lady, what do you think you're doing?" the big guard called, straightening his Stetson to mean business.

The girl crossed her arms, moving nearer the overgrown yellow dog. "If you were a big-shot hospital official or even a real policeman I might answer your questions, but since you are obviously either a police force reject or a retiree without any real power, I don't see it's any of your business."

The skinny guard sniggered and stifled it with a cough.

Puffing up, the big security guard propped his hands on hips wide enough to still be moving, and growled: "Unless you've got a permit to park that hunk of junk here, you've got yourself a little problem."

"Oh, big woo," sneered the girl. Just then, another doctor exited the hospital. "Excuse me." She pivoted on a boot heel.

"Just hold your horses." The big guard grabbed her arm.

The dog bared its fangs.

The guard let go, thinking better of it.

One eye on the dog, he tried again, this time with a smile. "Now, honey. What business does a nice young lady like you have in a place like this?"

The girl stuck out her jaw, inched directly under the big dog's head, crossed her arms even tighter across her chest and said, "I'm here to find my daddy and no pisshead asshole sumbitch's going to stop me."

"Whoa—" hooted the skinny guard, "has she got a mouth on her."

The big guard scowled. "That's no way for a little girl to talk."

The girl popped out her chin. "I'm thirteen. In some cultures, I'd already be contributing new members to the tribal status quo." Her chin went higher. "And just so you know, I *also* happen to be in personal communication with the Governor."

"Hmmmpgh!" came a comment from the Cadillac.

Both guards leaned down to see into the car.

The skinny guard squinted. "Who's your granny talking to?"

The girl moved protectively between the guards and the old woman. "Leave her alone."

"Ma'am," the big guard called around the girl, "is this your grand-daughter?"

The old lady looked up. "Why, yes. She's really a nice girl when she's not being a toot. She's just been all pent-up since she shot Harley."

The guards popped to attention, yelping in unison: "Shot *who?*"

"Always had a mind of her own and a mouth to boot," the old woman rattled on, as both guards jumped back, scanning the scrawny kid for firearms. Standing there in her T-shirt, cutoffs and cowboy boots, she seemed presently unarmed, her jaw the only thing cocked.

The grandmother droned on: "I'd say, 'Louise'—that's my daughter-in-law, Wanda Louise's dead mama—'don't let that girl walk all over you or you'll live to regret it.' Well, looks like I'm the one living to regret it. I got to go to the bathroom."

The big security guard's ears perked up. "Ma'am, did you say the child's mother is dead?"

The woman sighed. "Died last Sunday. Strangest accident you ever saw. Didn't have her in the ground good before I'm being dragged down sixty miles of bumpy Texas highway to this fool place."

The guard frowned. "What about her daddy?"

"Dead, too. My sweet son—not even twenty-five years old. Bless his weak heart."

"He wasn't my daddy," snapped the girl.

The grandmother was still talking. "Men don't seem to live too long in our family. I've got three dead husbands myself. John Sr., my first, came back dead from the war. My second, Dewey, came back dead from the road. My third, Cecil, he came back dead from the cow pasture. Dead, dead, dead, dead. It just ain't safe out here. Now, Wanda Louise, I got to go feed the chickens."

The girl turned her face away from the guards to whisper, "Granny, you don't *have* chickens anymore."

The old woman gasped. "They're all gone, too? Well, that's just my point!"

With a bulky sigh, the big guard readjusted his Stetson, then leaned into the girl's face. "C'mon, honey. Your own grandma just said your daddy was dead. Why are you bothering these good doctors after they've put in a hard day's work taking care of sick people?"

The girl didn't budge. "Because one of them's walking around with my genes, that's why—and I'm not your honey."

The big guard threw up his hands.

The girl gazed past him and up at the twenty-story hospital building. "It happened here. And my research says it was probably, like, an intern. Somebody'll know where he is."

The big guard looked back at the grandmother. "Ma'am, what is she talking about?"

The old lady shrugged. "She's always been like that—a walking library. Real smart. But we love her anyway."

The big guard rubbed his face with both beefy hands hard enough to make his jowls jiggle. "Okay, back up. Which doctor is your daddy?"

The girl rolled her eyes. "The one whose sperm was inseminated in my mother; don't you know anything?"

The young, skinny guard was suddenly sputtering. "L-Leon! She's talking about that sperm bank up on the seventh floor! My cousin did it. Got paid a hundred bucks for jacking off to girlie magazines!"

"Well, duh," sneered the girl. "How dim are you guys?"

For a long moment, no one moved. The big guard stared at the trouble before him. Then calmly, evenly, he said: "You just go on home now, young lady."

"I'm finding my daddy," came her quick response.

The big man fumed, moved his belly around and fumed again. "You ain't going to leave." He said it as a sad fact.

Wanda Ledbetter raised her chin as high as it would go. "If I do, I'm coming back, sure as shit shines."

"See what I mean, officer?" came the grandmother's moan from the Cadillac. "Stubborn as stinkweed."

For a beat, the big guard fingered his belt, then he pulled out his walkie-talkie.

The skinny guard blew a whistle through his teeth, loud, long and appreciative: "A donor baby, back for revenge. And I thought this job was going to be boring."

# Chapter 2

*The European cuckoo lays its eggs in nests
of other birds and flies away leaving its
eggs to be hatched by others.*

—Wonderful World of Biology

Seven floors above, Dr. Charles Youngblood was wrapping up a consultation, speaking soothingly to the couple sitting in front of his big desk, holding hands, arms straining, straight as scarecrows. As he delivered the usual spiel, he made a mental note to remember to push the chairs closer together before the next appointment.

"Then we'd inseminate you with your choice of donation from our sperm bank catalog, matching physical characteristics as well as musical, mechanical, athletic abilities to your own."

Finished, he interlaced his fingers, sat back in his plush leather chair and waited.

"I don't know," mumbled the man, snatching a glance at his wife. "Another man's . . ."

The woman squeezed the man's hand.

"Some choose to view it as adopting with half the child's biological makeup yours," the doctor added helpfully. He squelched an urge to check his watch.

"It would still be ours, honey. We could keep the secret," the woman said.

"Who would this donor be?" asked the man. "Could he, you know, find us?"

The doctor smiled patronizingly. "He signs all rights away, and the records are permanently sealed. You'd probably be surprised how often this procedure is done."

The woman perked up. "How often?"

"Some estimates suggest as many as 500,000 possible donor births in this country since 1950." With that, the doctor smiled broadly, warmly, professionally, and got to his feet. "Ask my nurse Carla for some reading material, and call when you're ready."

The couple was hardly out the door when the phone beeped. He ignored it twice; it beeped again as a red-haired nurse stuck her head in the door.

"Dr. Crouch. On line 2."

He made a face, looking at his watch.

"I think you'd better take it," the nurse said and waited.

Not liking the strange look on his nurse's face, the doctor picked up the phone: "Yes, Bill. What can I do for you?" He listened for a moment and then sank ever so slowly back into his chair. "Well, it's possible . . . She's where?" He switched the receiver to his other ear as he heard the rest. "Yes. Fine. I'll look into it." He put the receiver back on its cradle in slow motion.

The nurse was at the window craning her neck toward the doctors' parking lot.

"Don't you have some files to misplace, Carla?" the doctor snapped as he strode over to the door and held it open for his nurse to walk through. Closing it behind her, he moved to the window and gazed down at the parking lot scene. Absently, he started to crack a knuckle and caught himself: Awful habit. Instead he grabbed the phone and punched in an extension number:

"P.R.? Patty Hightower, please."

★ ★ ★

Down by the doctors' entrance, the big security guard wiped at his upper lip. He squinted at the asphalt sizzle; he checked his watch again; he flexed his grip on his walkie-talkie. The young guard fanned himself with his guard cap. In front of them, Wanda passed by, and then passed by again.

Wanda's grandmother was now squirming in her seat, having watched her granddaughter pace like a fenced cat for going on twenty minutes. "Wanda Louise Ledbetter, my bladder's talking to me now! If I had Harley Dean right here, I'd wring his scrawny trucker neck," the old woman announced, having repeated the threat now more times than Wanda and the guards cared to count. "But first I'd make him admit he's a liar! That devil started all this."

Wanda kept pacing, mind revving thunder. Harley *had* started it all; she knew that. The dumb peckerwood had started most everything. Things were shitty enough living the whole last year in the doublewide mobile home out on the edge of College Mound with the stupid trucker—only someone like her mama would take up with a guy who looked like a junkyard cowboy Elvis. Lately she'd even taken to keeping her grandma's old .22 loaded and ready under her bed since her tiny room's particleboard excuse for a door wouldn't close half the time.

Yesterday, though. Yesterday had been the shittiest of all. Bad enough her mama was dead, Harley killing her as good as if he'd put a gun to her head. And bad enough she had to stand there in the poor section of College Mound public cemetery, itching in her old Sunday dress she'd just about grown out of, alone with the piss-head trucker since they'd run out of relatives and Harley'd run off all their friends. But then she'd actually had to ride back with Harley to that tin house on wheels as if he were family, with him already halfway to pickled. The moment she hit the front door, she'd stripped out of that Sunday dress, whipped on her cutoffs and boots, grabbed her mama's beat-up suitcase and started throwing all her worldly belongings into it as quick as she could, the .22 resting on her bed. Just in case.

That's when Harley appeared, standing in the rickety door in his Western-cut suit with the dive-bomb yokes, bolo tie pulled loose, spitting snuff into an empty beer can. "Whatya doing, sweet thang?"

"What's it look like, Brainiac," she'd snapped. "I'm gone."

She heard Harley smack his lips. "Well, now, you don't have to do that. We're still family."

The trailer was so small, she could smell his beer and snuff breath over her shoulder as she packed. She could have puked right there.

"C'mon, sweet thang, your mama would've wanted you to stay. Gimme them keys. You can't even drive."

Wanda pulled a drawer out of the plywood dresser and upended it into the old suitcase. "If you think I'm so young I'd believe such cock and bull, you're dumber than you look. And that's pretty dumb." She threw the drawer down and pulled out the other one and shook it out over the bag.

Harley sniffed. "You think you're better'n me, don't ya? You are such a little smart-ass. I'da whipped that out of you long ago if your mama would've let me."

Wanda turned her back on him, packing as fast as she could.

"You know, there's something real funny about you," he said. "Why, you haven't even shed a tear for your mama."

Wanda's fingers slipped off the drawer and it fell between them. She kicked it. "Shut up, Harley—*just shut up.*"

"Where you going? To your crazy grandmother's?" He spat into the can. Saliva and tobacco dribbled down his chin, and he swiped at it with the back of an unsteady hand. "Hell, girl, you couldn't even get that old woman to the funeral."

She grabbed up the stack of library books piled beside the bed and dropped them like bombs into the suitcase. "She's just not feeling good, that's all."

"She's *nuts*," Harley said. "Probably down in that fallout shelter right now, or out asking strangers for nickels. If Louise hadn't gone and died, the old lady'd been in a rest home by now."

Wanda whirled all the way around. "Take that back. Mama'd never do that."

"And if I have my way, she'll still get there, if she gives me any flak over the stuff Louise stored over there. I was her husband, you know; I got a right to anything of value."

"You're lying through your fat face!" Wanda yelled.

"Call the rest home. The old lady can't take care of you. You quit that packing now."

He touched her arm.

She jerked away so hard from his touch that she all but fell back on the suitcase. "You're n-not my daddy—" she yelled, stuttering with anger as she scrambled back to her feet. "My daddy's dead. And—and—he was a generous, kind, wonderful man who'd never put Granny *anywhere* but in her own house."

Leaning heavily back on the doorjamb, Harley snorted. "There you go again about that damn sissy daddy of yours."

"Don't you say anything about my daddy or you'll be flat sorry. I'll sic Wild Thing on you—"

"I'll cut off its other ear. The mutt's lucky I hadn't poisoned it."

"If my daddy was alive . . ."

"Shut up about your daddy! I'm sick of hearing it!" Harley yelled. "That wimp couldn't even get it up. You don't have a clue, do you?"

Wanda stopped dead still.

Harley leaned near, smiling smugly. "Louise told me about you. That wonderful *daddy* of yours ain't no more your daddy than *Jeezus H. Christ.*"

And then he had said it. Enjoying it, leaning close with his sideburns and his beer and snuff breath: "They bought a guy's sperm over there in Big D to make you, smart girl. Parkland Hospital, where Kennedy croaked. You're not even natural. You're like some kind of bastard, some baby Frankenstein. Louise figured that was why you were so 'funny.' Hell, no telling who your papa is."

*Liar*! Wanda had yelled. *Take it back, take it back right now*. She had grabbed up the .22 and pointed it at him to make him take back those awful lying words. *Take it back!*

He sidestepped like a Gulf Coast crab. She jerked.

The gun went off.

Boom.

And they both stared down at the hole in the tip of his dress boot, fancy silver tip blasted clean away, neither of them breathing . . .

. . . until a trickle of blood came oozing out the black hole.

Harley swallowed his snuff.

"You . . . you . . . *SH-SH-SHOT* me!" Lunging at Wanda, he tripped and fell face down in a howl.

Which gave Wanda a second's head start. Her fingers frozen around the .22, she snatched her bag, jumped over Harley, stumbled out the door and down the trailer steps. Whistling Wild Thing frantically into the car, she somehow started the old Cadillac and roared away, jolting and jerking toward the road. But when she looked in the rearview mirror and saw that Harley was hobbling toward his eighteen-wheeler, she almost panicked. Without thinking, she stomped on the brakes, swerved the car around 180 degrees and put all those years of watching TV to practical use. Careening the Caddy between the teetering Harley and his rig, she aimed the .22 at the big tires and blew through the nearest set with all the shots she had left in the little automatic, the sound drowning out Harley's rolling cuss and Wild Thing's righteous barking.

But as she drove fast, faster, faster away, straining to see the road over the steering wheel, she began to think hard. She wasn't thinking about Harley's toe. She wasn't really thinking about Harley at all. She was thinking about all the differences she'd noticed between herself and the little bit of family she'd ever known. She didn't look much like any of them. Nobody was blond, or hazel-eyed, and there wasn't a double joint in the bunch. Except for her mama's big ears, she could be a stranger. And what about how smart she was? "It just happens," she'd heard the guidance counselor tell her mama. "That's why we call it 'gifted.'" It must have been from her daddy, she had always thought.

Her *daddy* . . .

She careened the Cadillac toward town as echoes of Harley's words rumbled up like coming thunder in her bones. She could feel it in her chest, up her arms, into her fingers gripping the big steering wheel, quivering, coming fast.

At the town's one stoplight, she stomped both feet on the brakes, bouncing Wild Thing into the dashboard. Swerving the Cadillac over a curb, she came to rest behind the College Mound Public Library, eyes peeled for the town's lone cop, and rushed in the back door to the greetings of the librarians.

"Look who's here! Wanda Louise! How you doin', sugar?"

"Such a shame about your mother, sweetie. Anything we can do?"

Wanda made a beeline toward the catalog computer.

"Ethel, you ever see this girl read?" one of the librarians said to the other. "Photographic memory, like nothing I ever seen. And since I gave her that book on speed-reading, well!"

Wanda hit the computer search, her fingers now thundering blind.

The librarians shared concerned looks. "Sweetie? Can we help you?"

But the librarians kept their distance as Wanda located the thickest volume on human and animal reproduction the library owned, *The Wonderful World of Biology*, and checked it out. Then plopping down in front of the Internet computer, she searched, downloaded and printed out everything she could find about artificial insemination and quick links to stuff called "assisted reproductive technologies," jumping each time somebody came in the tiny library's door. Finally, grabbing up the book and the paper pile in her arms, she hurried past inquiring librarian eyes and out the back door.

Pushing Wild Thing over, she thrust her armful into the Caddy's backseat, started the Caddy with a jerk and lunged away down the closest country road. When she felt safe, she pulled onto a side road and began to speed-read the entire pile, committing it all to her photographic memory. She read and read, the facts jumbling and bumbling through her mind, as if even her thoughts would stutter with the weight of it all. Finally, when there was nothing more to read, nothing more to grab, nothing more of words to stop the thundering, she stumbled out of the car and fell back against its rear bumper.

Wild Thing hopped out of the car, sniffed at the air, then nudged Wanda's arm with a wet nose, but Wanda barely noticed. Holding her head in both hands, she clamped her eyes shut, trying hard to think straight: Things were shitty, all right. Things hurt you bad enough when you're just hanging around, just getting from one minute to the next trying to figure out why you're here and who sent for you and what the poot it all meant while you're stuck all day with kids dumber than dirt and teachers with run-down eyes, studying the geography of places you'll never get to go and the spelling of words you'll never use. Then your mama takes off with some no-good jerk she tells your secrets to and then dies. And then dies . . . And then goes and gotdam dies. And now you find out you might not be even the mess you thought you were.

Wanda took a deep, dull breath. It might have been a shitty life, but at least it was hers.

Suddenly, tears began pushing hard against the back of her eyeballs. And that got Wanda moving. Jumping to her feet, she decided right then and there she wasn't going to blubber. No sir. Ordering Wild Thing back in the car, she threw open the passenger door. There, on the floorboard, lay her mother's cowhide saddle purse, busted open, its insides spurting from it, having rolled finally from its hiding place under the seat where her mother must have shoved it one last time.

Wanda took hold of the saddle-horn flap with just her fingertips and turned the purse right side up, picking up her mother's runaway things: lint-covered Tic-Tacs, a rat-tail comb, her lucky Las Vegas lighter, a lipstick tube (Revlon Million Dollar Red), a pack of her stinky Virginia Slims and her old leatherette wallet, open to the picture compartment. Only there weren't any pictures. Except the one of some old-time movie star named James Dean that had come with the wallet, now so worn-out that the scratched plastic was stuck to the guy's face.

Wanda eased down onto the broken seat, running a finger slowly across the paper picture's face. You'd think her mama would've had one picture of her. Other mothers do that, carry pictures of important people, to show them off. Some stupid school picture or something. But all she carried around was a picture of this dead movie star, dead as her mama, dead as her daddy. No, *not* her daddy, not her *real* daddy . . . The tears pushed from behind her eyeballs again; she pushed back, staring soulfully at James Dean. Hey—*he* could be her daddy, for all she knew.

And then Wanda Ledbetter got stubborn, as only a brand-new orphan could upon hearing she might have an extra parent somewhere.

What would she do?

She'd get mean. Everybody thought she was a pain now? A difficult child? Well, hide and watch. Let Harley call the cops. She'd make a run for it, hit the road. Never look back, Jack. She was going to be too mean to live, that's what she was going to be.

But first, she was going to find her daddy.

Her real daddy.

She stood up straight and worked hard at feeling mean clear through.

Then, eyeing the streets for Harley or the law, she had driven back into town and over to her granny's house, where she talked herself blue making promises she never meant to keep in order to coax her granny, and her driver's license, onto the road toward the secret that lay somewhere in the Dallas hospital now covering the sky behind her.

★ ★ ★

Wanda stopped pacing. The parking lot smelled of hot tar and gasoline fumes. She took a big breath, glancing around her, security car on one side, dead mother's junk heap on the other. Swallowing back a sudden tremble of leftover thunder, she quickly crossed her arms, too mean to live once again. Then she turned her gaze toward the tall hospital building, as the two guards fidgeted near the security car and her grandmother mumbled in the Cadillac, everybody waiting for the next move.

"Yes, God's truth, I'd do it," Wanda's grandmother was saying. "I'd wring Harley's neck good for all this, that's for danged sure. But first I'd go to the bathroom."

# Chapter 3

*When the queen bee mates, she leaves the hive and unites
in flight with the male bees whose sole purpose for existence
is to service her. Those who are successful are immediately
paralyzed, fall to earth, and die.*

—Wonderful World of Biology

$\mathcal{P}$atty Hightower resisted a need to slam the door behind her as she walked back into her office in Hospital Public Affairs. Instead she closed the door civilly, then pivoted and kicked her plastic wastebasket the length of the room. Calm once again, she rubbed the toe of her expensive pump, then bent to pick up the wastebasket's contents before anybody saw the mess. She was doing this far too much lately. It was easier than crying, which was what she usually did when angry. It hadn't been a terrific day so far. Eric had just left the little plastic jar sitting on her briefcase. He hadn't even said goodbye. Just left the jar with the milky substance of life to be dropped off at the hospital lab and then "inserted," once and yet again, with Dr. Youngblood's enormous needle.

("A needle, huh?" Eric's business partner had joked in front of her at their last party. "So that's replaced you? Bet she hadn't even noticed the difference, ha ha. Better watch it. Beauty queens are used to having their way. And she knows I know the way. Ha ha.")

Ha ha.

Patty smoothed her skirt and forced herself back to what she had been doing before the trip down the hall, proofreading a batch of bulletins on her desk that announced the hospital's latest biotechnological funding. She fought a shiver, still feeling the cold stirrups on her bare feet, legs spread wide under the hospital sheet.

She crossed her legs.

Then she forced her mind away from where she'd just spent her twenty-minute break. Her office's being conveniently on the OB/GYN floor meant she'd hardly missed any work through all of these baby-making procedures. But it also meant she spent her day weaving through a never-ending flow of pregnant women. Plus it meant some strange moments professionally. ("Enjoyed the press reception the other night," she could still hear Dr. Youngblood saying so very chattily as she'd lain back on the examining table. "You did a good job. Pleasure to finally meet Eric, too." And then his look had gone so very, very doctor-detached as he peered up her, aiming the intrauterine needle at that elusive bull's eye Eric kept missing.)

Eric. She wished she hadn't pushed it this morning. They'd been trying this last-ditch procedure so long they seemed to be running on automatic. She wasn't even positive she was in her best fertile time today. But when your frequent flyer husband's in the air more than in you . . .

"That was crude, Patty—deliberately crude!" Eric had griped this morning when she woke to find him fresh from the shower, packing for another trip to Chicago, and had let that certain remark slip. "What's gotten into you lately?" he fumed, folding a T-shirt to store-shelf perfection.

"I can't seem to help it." She sighed, enjoying the view of her husband, all tanned, lean muscle, wearing nothing but his watch and his underwear. The undershorts looked new. They were blue. "Sorry. Will you be back tonight?" she asked.

"Probably. I'll call." He turned toward the closet to get dressed.

Patty hesitated, then held out the plastic medical jar. "Honey . . ." Eric's gait hardly slowed, but she didn't miss the slight hitch in his broad shoulders.

When she'd finished her shower, she'd found the full plastic hospital jar perched on her briefcase and Eric gone. She hadn't been able to finish her yogurt for staring at it, realizing it was the closest thing to real sex they'd had in months and months, so she had gone straight to the fridge and downed a honey bun. Then she'd gone straight to the hospital.

She hopped up out of her office chair, moved in front of the full-length mirror on the back of her door and tugged at her skirt—her tight skirt, thanks to months of fertility drugs. And honey buns. She began checking her face with expert fingers. She ran a fingernail over an eyebrow, she rubbed the edge of a lip where it needed lipstick. Then, staring dully at her beauty queen reflection, she took her thumb and forefinger and squished her lips thoroughly, puckering fish-faced, and held it. Making fish-lip motions. Just for the ugly heck of it.

Blowing out a sigh, she fumbled in her suit pocket for a tube of lipstick.

The lab slip for Eric's jar fluttered to the carpet. She scooped it up. Strange how life turns out. Things had started out so perfect. After their big North Dallas wedding, they'd chosen to wait to have children. They were happy, in glorious, glamorous 3-D love, weren't they? Then one of those days, they casually chose to have them. Were they happy? They were sad then puzzled then anxious then desperate—desperate enough to keep going through this, she thought, looking at the lab slip. But still in love?

Patty plopped back into her office chair, closing her eyes. She tried an old trick, one that usually helped through the humiliating procedures: picturing her maybe baby with a sweet little Patty face. But this time the image made her heart feel like it was cracking. She shook it away and strained to see Eric's face, dimpled Eric with the crooked smile, a look that used to make her dry-mouthed. But his face wouldn't come, either—only that slight hitch of broad shoulders. In fact, the only Eric she could conjure was the Eric of their expensive portrait that he loved and she hated. Posed, perfect, hanging shrinelike on their living room wall: Barbie and Ken done in oils. That was all she saw, that painted face and the little plastic jar. And all she felt was the disappointment she'd been denying for so long about her marriage, her life.

"You ask me, Eric boy's the problem," said her nurse friend Lucille on Patty's last sad-eyed visit to the hospital nursery. "And I ain't just talking body fluids." Lucille was a big, black blunderbuss of a woman known for taking no mess off no man. Lucille pulled one of the newborns to her shoulder and patted its back. "If that boy was bald and wore his pants under his beer belly, you tell me you'd still be around?"

"Lucille, are you calling me shallow?"

She'd leaned close; Patty breathed in baby powder. "You want to roil both of your good-looking genes into a Gerber baby, fine; but if you just want a baby, you don't really *need* him." She rolled her big eyes toward the floors above that held sperm banks and all things reproductively technological. "Make your mystery selection, sugar, then dropkick your football hero." Glancing past her, Lucille's face turned sour; Patty turned around. A doctor was walking by—Dr. Strake. "Now there's a man I can sure do without. Don't look, baby," Lucille sniffed, patting the newborn faster. "He's lucky one of them crazy pro-lifers hadn't shot him dead in the parking lot."

Patty's chill was back, and with it an old, scarred-up ghost guilt that was just now starting to haunt her.

She forced herself out of her thoughts and pushed her chair up to her desk, trying to get her mind back on the press releases she still had to write: a new stomach stapling tool, sex selection advances, an important urology breakthrough.

Instead, her eyes wandered to the snapshot of Eric on her desk. She'd call him on the cell phone he always kept in his suit pocket, near his heart. She'd make him talk. And if he wanted to quit this craziness, they'd quit. Because to be truthful, sometimes now when she looked at him, when he was there to look at, she could hardly remember why she had married him. It wasn't just that fine face. She was not that shallow. She just had to remember again. Tonight they'd have sex just to have sex. Make love, not babies. If they could get everybody and everything else out of bed with them.

"Ms. Hightower?"

Patty jerked, jostling the cup of coffee by her hand.

"Oh, I startled you," said her assistant. The girl fumbled with Eric's picture, wiping the splashed coffee off it, admiring it a beat too long and then remembering why she'd come. "Dr. Youngblood is on line 1. He said it's urgent."

Good grief, Patty thought, hadn't she seen enough of that man this morning? Or, more to the point, hadn't he seen enough of her? She sighed. Then she reached out and picked up the receiver.

★ ★ ★

Outside, the big guard took off his Stetson and wiped his forehead with his arm. He was sweating himself a puddle in the Texas swelter, eyeing his walkie-talkie as if staring would make it talk. Finally he punched it on. "It's Leon again. Ain't anybody coming?"

Wanda shifted her weight as she leaned against the Cadillac fender, arms still crossed, too mean to live. "Mention the words 'freedom of the press.' And my personal communication with the Governor."

Leon was busy nodding into the walkie-talkie. "Yessir. She'll be here. That's a promise." He put down the walkie-talkie and looked back at the girl. "Somebody's coming. Don't go off half-cocked now."

An old grumble and groan came from the car. "Wanda Louise!" the old woman snapped. "I hadn't piddled in my pants my whole adult life and I don't intend to start now."

The young, skinny guard was still fanning himself with his guard cap. "I could take her back up to the guard hut," he offered, pointing with the cap. "I could do that, ma'am."

"No-no," Granny all but sang. "I don't go good around strangers, thank you. You're a right well-brought-up boy, though. Hear that, Wanda Louise?"

Everybody stared at everybody a moment. The only thing that moved was the sweat forming on foreheads and the saliva dripping from Wild Thing's mouth.

Finally Wanda began to pace again, cracking her knuckles and pushing her hair back behind her ear like a nervous tic. Wild Thing hopped out of the car and followed her. Back and forth, back and forth.

The skinny young guard leaned toward the big guard and whispered, "Leon, the old lady asked me if I had any nickels, then she just looked them over and gave them back to me. What's that about?"

"Shut up, Jerry," grumbled the big guard.

Wanda and Wild Thing made a move for the car.

Leon came to attention. "Somebody's coming now."

"I'll be back in the morning," said Wanda. "I've got to take care of my grand-mother." She flung the passenger side door wide, just as the guard started to grab hold of her arm again, having forgotten Wild Thing's umbrage the last time. Wild Thing offered a bared-tooth reminder; Leon stepped back. "Somebody's coming!" he bellowed, pointing a sausage finger straight at her, cocked and ready to fire.

Wild Thing hopped in behind Wanda, and Wanda slammed the door. "Granny, time to go," Wanda grunted, nudging her big arm. "Time to drive. *Granny*—" she hissed.

"Drive? Well, all right, all right."

And away the Caddy roared, Wild Thing barking and the Caddy bouncing high over the speed bumps, narrowly missing a Chevy Blazer, a Lexus and a Dr. Pepper delivery truck, until they were finally out of sight.

"Okay, pull over, Granny, pulloverpullover!" Wanda gasped.

Granny swerved and popped the brakes a couple of times until the Caddy bopped a curb and ran one wheel up on it for a landing. She sat back, pleased with herself. "Well, now, that wasn't too bad. Maybe I should start driving again." Wanda rolled unsteadily out of the car, rushed around to the driver's side and careened them all away.

★ ★ ★

Meanwhile, back at the parking lot, Patty Hightower found the two security guards standing all by themselves in front of the security car.

Patty called as she made her way across the lot. "Isn't there supposed to be a girl out here? Leon, what is going on?"

Groaning hard enough to jiggle his jowls, the big guard took off his hat and gave the security car's fender a roundhouse whack.

# Chapter 4

*The male sea catfish cares for and carries
the eggs he has fertilized in his mouth.*

**—Wonderful World of Biology**

*S*itting in the glow of the motel desk lamp, Wanda poised her pencil over a small, spiral-bound notebook:

*Dear D—*

"Whatcha writing?" Granny asked, leaning over her shoulder. "Always scribbling in that little book of yours."

Wanda slammed the book shut.

Granny stepped back. "Well, excuse me. Didn't know it was private." The old woman went back to examining a pile of change on the desk, pushing it around with a wrinkled finger.

Pulling the small notebook to her chest, Wanda watched her granny as she raised her eyes from the coins, straightened the big hairnet that held her beauty parlor hairdo in nightly place, then moved stiff and slow as sorghum toward the bed. Wanda worried a little. "Granny, do you need anything?"

"I need a certain young lady to keep her promises," she answered. "And a bigger bed."

"I don't like sleeping with you either, you know."

Granny looked around. "You used to not mind. 'Course you weren't more than about forty pounds back then." Wanda's grandmother plumped the pillow with a couple of jabs and eased her big self under the covers. "All I want is for you to take me to the Poetry Cemetery like you said, and then I want us to go home. My chickens are going to miss a feeding."

Wanda felt a lump in her throat. "You don't have chickens anymore. Please? Okay?"

Granny's face went a little blank, confused, then straightened out. "Of course I don't. Isn't that funny?" She frowned. "Well, good riddance."

Wanda put the pencil and notebook down and came over to the bed, stepping around Wild Thing, who'd plopped down on the floor, one leg high, licking her privates, to straighten the covers under Granny's flabby arms. Her fingers lingered on the old woman's hand.

Granny grabbed Wanda's hand suddenly, urgently. "And good riddance to Harley Dean! Until that no-good came around, your mama was a decent, church-going woman. Your mama loved your daddy. I don't deny they had a hard time having you, lots of trips up here to this hospital. But they had you, didn't they?"

Then she let go of Wanda's hand just as suddenly as she'd grabbed it, and lay back, spent. Wanda sat down heavily on the edge of the bed and pulled Wild Thing's furry head close, stroking, squeezing her near.

Wild Thing moaned with delight.

"Your daddy loved you, baby." Granny murmured.

"I don't want to talk about him," Wanda said. "I never knew him and I don't want to talk about him."

"You don't talk about people, they go away, baby. I don't know anything about my people. All I got of them are headstones and hand-me-down names and this big German honker. Your mama never talked about her side of the family, as if they had the plague. But your daddy's and granddaddy's side, the Ledbetters, they were talkers. And even though they're gone too, I know all about them."

Wanda headed toward the sink, pulling off her cutoffs and boots as she went, her granny's voice following behind: "You are your daddy's girl and your daddy was the manager of the J. C. Penney catalog store and his daddy was a soldier and his granddaddy was a sheriff and his grandmama was a mail-order bride. From Boston, Massachusetts. And oh. There was this Texas *patriot* they were just real proud of, swore he rode into the Battle of San Jacinto with Sam Houston remembering the Alamo. Before that, it's for sure they all got off a boat somewhere, sometime, but they quit talking about 'em and they disappeared. So you talk about 'em, Wanda Louise. Because you are your daddy's girl. A Ledbetter." The old woman paused, sighing sad and full of memory, her big breasts heaving. "From the day you popped outta your mama, and your daddy bought that brand-new Cadillac, he loved you. And your mama loved him. And your mama loved you."

"And they all died happily ever after," Wanda snapped. "The end."

The old woman grunted. "Goodness, you've always been a tough one." And then she added sweetly, quiet enough to make Wanda glance around: "I used to listen to you in the night. Little cries that wouldn't wake up a flea."

Wanda turned sullenly back to the sink, but listening, listening.

"I said to myself, no one was going to have a hold on this one. This baby was singular."

Wanda fumed, self-conscious, fighting to stay mean. "You're rambling again, Granny. Changing subjects faster than a bumblebee farts—like Mama used to . . ." She bit off the end of the sentence.

Her grandmother crossed her big arms over the bedspread. "You're mad at your mama, ain't you, baby? You got a right to be. Maybe she'd have done better if she hadn't had to move you two in with me. But she'd get so melancholy, hugging that Bible, living like a chain-smoking Baptist nun. No wonder she went with Harley when he came tomcatting around. Going without loving for ten years'll make anyone that young melt like butter at the first sign of heat. She dropped that Bible, I tell you that."

Wanda cringed. "I don't want to talk about it. Geez!" She flipped on the faucet.

"Nothing wrong with talking about it. Not talking about it's what gets you into trouble. I suppose you think you know all about sex, too."

"I know enough, okay? I know where babies come from and all that crap." Wanda began brushing her teeth. Loudly.

"Who's talking about babies? We used to have 'em because we couldn't stop 'em. Now they can stop 'em and they're raising Cain about having 'em. Baby girl, there's more to loving than what gets left inside you."

Wanda swallowed a mouthful of toothpaste spit.

"If that's all it is, there's something missing no baby's going to fill. I loved your daddy, but I'd never trade having him inside me for having your grand-daddy inside me."

Wanda gagged and coughed. *"Gawd! Granny—!"*

"Inside me. Beside me. Made no difference. And you watch taking the Lord's name in vain." She eyed Wanda. "There's a world of things you don't know on this topic, Miss Smarty."

"Well, I don't want to hear it from my grandmother!" Wanda whined.

"It's my ovaries that are dried up, not my heart," Granny went on. "And if my ovaries were more important than my heart, then they wouldn't be what's dried up, would they?"

"Can we talk about this tomorrow?" Wanda begged. "*Please?*"

"Like Wild Thing here. She's a woman." Granny nodded at Wild Thing going around and around in circles, making herself a bed on the carpet. "It's the most natural thing at certain times in her life to just offer herself up, but if she ain't choosy, she's stuck with a whole litter of Heinz 57 mutts uglier than sin."

"*Boy,* I *sure* am sleepy—aren't you sleepy?" Wanda tried desperately. "We're getting up *real* early."

"You don't know what early is. On the farm, we'd get up at 4 a.m. I've been talking to Johnny 'bout this and he agrees with me now."

Wanda turned out the overhead light and felt her way over to her side of the bed in the small sift of moonlight coming in the window. She had hoped she could stop her grandmother talking before she got to talking to the dead again. "He always agrees with you," Wanda sighed. "I don't think your reception's so good. And you promised you wouldn't talk about talking to dead people."

Granny's voice faded almost transparent. "What we had, death can't just up and break. Love like that doesn't die just because one of you quits living."

"I know, Granny. True love."

"Don't make fun, sister," her grandmother warned, swatting at her under the covers.

Wanda jerked away. "Research says it's all just chemical, anyway!" she grumbled. "Preprogrammed by our genes to perpetuate the species. Lasts just long enough to mate and bear children."

"Stop talking nonsense! You ain't got the slightest notion what I'm talking about."

"I didn't say it! Scientists did."

Granny snorted. "Chemicals. Hmph. Those scientists should be making themselves useful curing cancer or my hemorrhoids. I'm talking about something special between two people. Most women think it's just gonna come riding by. Well, you can wait all your life, even marry what does come riding by and still be waiting. Such a link's a gift of grace from God. Stronger than the grave."

"Stronger than all your other dead husbands?" Wanda snapped.

There was a pause in the dark on that one. "Child. You are itching for a switching."

"Why'd you keep getting married, if you loved Johnny such a big deal?"

"I had to survive, didn't I?" Granny shot back. "I had your daddy to raise. That was how it was done then. You think I had a choice? Women today, they don't know what it was like back then. But I ain't talking about need. I'm talking about a little piece of God-love that makes a moment a true treasure, buried deep, rich enough for a whole lifetime." An old, full sigh filled the dark.

"Everybody dies," Wanda muttered. "So what's the use?"

Granny paused. The silence hung over the bed. It made the night air seem hollow, used up, personal. "Some pain's worth it." She fidgeted. "Now I'm feeling melancholy. Tell me about the swans again from that big library book of yours."

Wanda rolled her eyes. "I already told you a hundred times."

"I could be gone by the morning and then how would you feel? Tell me."

Wanda fidgeted. "Geese, Granny, not swans." Then she repeated it all quickly: "Greylag geese mate for life, sometimes half a century. He runs all the other males away and begins his dance, squawking and calling, stretching his neck to the sky. Until she joins in. And they live happily goosy ever after. Okay?"

"It's a rare thing."

Granny's voice had dropped so low, it drew Wanda's face toward her in the shadows. The old woman's eyes reflected in the moonlight were more clear and straight and intelligent than Wanda had seen in weeks. And it made Wanda very nervous.

"Baby," her granny murmured low and serious, "your mama and Harley—I know what they were planning. But lately my mind and my heart, they keep finding Johnny. And I want you to know my world, baby, before I die. And I want to go back and see my cemetery tree. You said you'd take me."

Wanda turned toward the window, to the broken piece of moon hanging there. "Don't talk about dying." The yellow dog came up and nuzzled under her hand.

The creaky old voice floated through the dark. "Latch the back screen door before you come to bed now. You hear?"

Wanda swallowed down a rising bit of fear that always threatened to take her over when her granny went off somewhere like that. But soon she heard her begin to snore.

As the moments passed and her granny was deep into snorting sleep, Wanda watched the piece of moon out the window and listened to the sounds of laughter coming through the wall, sounds like her mama and Harley used to make, quiet giggling, murmuring. She flipped on the table lamp and, with an eye back toward her sleeping granny, reached for her pencil and little book and began to write:

> Dear Daddy,
> Whoever you are, I'm going to call you that over Dear Biological Paternal Unit or Dear Genetic Donor or even Dear Father, because I choose to. Because I didn't ever get to call anyone that. Because I think everybody ought to have someone to call Daddy sometime. Even if the person doesn't deserve it.

Wanda eased off the lamp, nestled back into the cool sheets and opened the book in her mind: *Dear Daddy. Dear Doctor Daddy. Goodnight.* And as she floated toward slumber, up bobbed another of the library book facts she'd stored away . . . She fell asleep dreaming of daddy sea catfish, schools of them swimming her way.

# Chapter 5

*A sea horse father offers his open pouch to the female.*
*The female inserts her eggs and then he seals his*
*pouch and carries the babies until the young explode*
*one by one from the pouch and swim away.*

—Wonderful World of Biology

The next morning, Patty woke up scratching at the trim on the silk teddy she'd bought at Neiman Marcus on the way home from work. She was curled up in Eric's recliner, dreaming of the TV chattering, the phone ringing, their home fax humming, beeping to life. The early sun from her townhouse's balcony streaming hot on her face was the first clue she'd just spent the whole night there waiting for Eric to come home. She opened one eye and then the other to the video chatter. It was a *Good Morning* show host—her second clue. Unbending herself, Patty leaned over to switch off the chirpy TV woman and turned to gaze at the ruins of her candlelight dinner, one empty bottle of wine drunk alone, both candles melted down to the silver candlesticks. And she had the instant fear that is common to such situations, planes going down, car crashes, hit-and-run accidents, heart attacks, muggings. *He's dead somewhere,* she worried. *Dead and all alone.*

The teddy itched again. All that brocade stitched in the "right" places. She should have washed it first. She was trying to reach in to scratch where it itched when she heard the little beep of the fax machine in the study—she hadn't dreamed it.

The cat wanted in. Patty opened the balcony's sliding door for it, then stumbled toward the sound of the fax. Eric *had* left a message he'd be home, hadn't he? He's been in an accident, she just knew it. That's the way their luck had been going.

She reached for the fax.

Dear Patty,

She blinked, then squinted:

Dear Patty,
I'm not coming home. This isn't working. I hope we can be adult
about this.
Eric

She gaped.

She gripped the slick fax paper so hard she ripped it, sagging back against the wallpaper. Something icy walked up her spine.

*He . . .* f-f-faxed *me?*

Feeling as if the word was more than slightly scatological in this context, she almost laughed.

And then she had the instant wish common to such situations: planes going down, car crashes, hit-and-run accidents, heart attacks, painful muggings. Visions of him being good and dead somewhere. Dead and all alone.

Pushing up her spaghetti straps, she stalked toward Eric's walk-in closet and swung the mirrored doors wide. There before her was space, lots of space. Half his clothes were gone. She grabbed up their cordless phone and punched in his cellular number, picturing that pocket phone near his heart ringing loud enough to cause arrhythmia.

No answer.

She redialed: Chicago.

"Stozwitz and Little, Financial Analysts, Inc., Shari Shively speaking."

"I need to talk to Eric Little. This is wife. It's an emergency—"

"Frankly, he doesn't want to talk with you right now, Patty."

She stiffened: *Patty?*

"You were never right for each other," the secretary was saying, "You didn't understand him. All that pressure. It was too much."

Patty's heart stopped.

"Especially when there is nothing wrong with his manliness," the secretary's voice kept on. "I should know. And if he won't tell you, I will. I'm carrying his baby and he just asked me to marry him."

Patty made like a statue for a beat.

Then she pivoted, strode purposefully to the balcony, opened the sliding door, reared back and hurled the cordless phone in a nice, high arc that cleared the park hedge below, hurtling straight at a passing jogger. She gasped.

"Duck!" she screamed.

The jogger scrambled as the phone took a nasty bounce on the sidewalk and came to a rest in the thick Bermuda grass framing the path.

"I'm so sorry," Patty called. "I'm a very nice person. Really."

The man picked up the phone and wiped it off. "Hardly a scratch. Mine broke in two the first time I threw it." He chunked it up to her.

She stretched over the balcony to catch it.

"Nice negligee," the man added, leering. Hiding herself behind the phone, she took a quick step back inside to the sound of plates crashing to the floor. She whirled around in time to see the cat jumping off the smoked glass dinner table and curling up near the upside-down plates, wiping contentedly at its mouth.

Patty gazed through the glass table at the cat and saw, instead, her own reflection. She saw herself in the new silk teddy, standing over the wrecked meal. The cat purred, and she suddenly saw Eric in his new blue underwear, standing over his secretary.

The teddy itched again. With a flick of a spaghetti strap, she tore out of it.

And as she stood there on the cold linoleum, naked in all the ways it's possible for a person to be, the crushed phone in her fist rattled and branged, scaring her airborne.

She fumbled for the Talk button.

Dr. Charles Youngblood's voice bellowed over the cracked earpiece: "Where are you?"

"I can't come in today." She swallowed; her head was swimming laps around the room.

"That girl is back. You *have* to come."

"I . . . I think I'm going to be sick." Patty ran for the bathroom, knelt at the throne and let it come, the mobile phone skidding across the bathroom tile.

"Get it all out. Feeling better already, right?" came the doctor's frantic, muffled voice bouncing off the grout. *"Right?"*

★ ★ ★

In the hospital parking lot's morning sun, Wild Thing raised her big, round head and sniffed the young guard's skinny butt.

"Yo, dog. Cut that out!"

"Control your mutt, young lady," the big-bellied guard ordered, standing in front of the old Cadillac's grillwork, arms crossed across his vast chest.

Wanda sat on the hood, arms crossed as well, chewing the heck out of a piece of gum. She made a smooching sound and Wild Thing roamed back to her. She uncrossed an arm just long enough to give the dog's head a pat. "Doesn't this hospital have any other guards besides you two? Geez."

A late-model BMW came to a rolling halt in an empty space across from them. Inside, Patty Hightower sat for a moment in the air conditioner's blast and vaguely inspected herself to make sure she was fully dressed, shoes matched, buttons buttoned, belt attached, zippers zipped. Then with a great swallowing effort, she focused. Making an absent pass over her hair, she flipped on her professional smile and detached herself from the vehicle.

Straightening her skirt, she headed, smiling, smiling, toward the scene ahead. "Hello," she called toward an unkempt girl in T-shirt and jeans and in desperate need of the basics of personal grooming. "I'm Patricia Ann Hightower."

The girl hopped down from the hood of an old Cadillac. *Don't Mess with Texas*, said the girl's thin T-shirt. Patty put out her hand. The girl didn't take it, pulling her crossed arms ever tighter. The T-shirt rode up.

"She says her name is Wanda Ledbetter and that's her grandmother inside the car," grunted the big guard, gesturing enough to disclose growing half-moon sweat rings.

"Howdyadew," sang the old woman.

"Who are you supposed to be?" said the girl.

"I'm the hospital's Public Affairs Director, Miss Ledbetter."

"What's that?" Wanda asked. "A fancy name for P.R. mouthpiece?"

Patty's professional smile went stiff. "What can I do for you?"

"I'm here to find my fucking daddy."

Patty's eyebrows raised a full centimeter.

"Watch your mouth, now!" the big guard warned. "You could take a lesson from her. She's been a Miss Texas. Ms. Hightower, the girl thinks her daddy might have . . ."

Patty said, having mustered her smile again, "Thank you, but let's let Miss Ledbetter . . ."

"My name is Wanda," Wanda said, pushing her hair behind her ears. "You're giving me the creeps with this 'Miss' stuff."

"All right, Wanda, what . . ."

"You're going to try to sweet-talk me, right? Send a nice, pretty smiling lady down here to gain the dumb kid's confidence, then talk her out of making waves. I know how it goes," Wanda said, nodding knowingly. "But just so *you* know, I'm in communication with the Governor. So I'm not taking no gotdam guff off nobody."

"Wanda Louise Ledbetter!" snapped the grandmother. "Don't pay her nasty mouth any mind, Miss. This blaspheming thing's just hit her since she put that bullet in her stepdaddy."

*Bullet*? Patty's smile slipped a little. And then it fell right off the face of the earth. She made a small, delicate tent over her nose and mouth with her hands and composed herself again. Then she took her first real good look at the scene in front of her—from the girl's bargain barrel T-shirt to her skinned-up boots to the green gum she was smacking, over to the trashy car and the old wasted woman in a wrap-around housedress, hanging a fat arm out the driver's side window. And she just stared blankly at it all.

Until she felt warm breath on the back of her knee. Moving upwards.

Patty gasped, grabbing at the back of her short skirt.

"Wild Thing, stop that!" the girl ordered.

Leon the guard sidled up close to Patty's ear. "You want me to interrogate her over this shooting thing, so maybe we could call the police in on this?" he whispered. "That'd get rid of her." His breath smelled like bacon and eggs. "Just give me the word." With a knowing nod, he moved back beside the girl.

Patty smoothed her skirt, took a big, deep, thoughtful breath and gazed at the messy girl, stifling an urge to offer her a hairbrush. Instead she heard herself saying, "How would you and your grandmother like to get some coffee?"

The girl wrinkled her nose.

"A Coke, juice, whatever," Patty pressed. She looked at the old woman. "Mrs. Ledbetter, is it?"

The old woman smiled. "Gladys Jean Ledbetter Giddens Birdsong. Name's as long as my life. So just call me Granny. I don't much answer to anything but that anymore, anyways."

"Granny, then. Would you like a bit of breakfast?"

"Why, yes, I certainly would, thankyouverymuch. You're mighty kind."

Before the girl could object, Patty began giving instructions. "Leave your car under that tree for shade. And Jerry will guard the dog, won't you, Jerry?"

The young guard's face went south. But in a moment, Wanda, her grandmother and Patty—the urchin, the shuffling old lady and the beauty queen—were parading through the cool hospital lobby and into the cafeteria line. Within another moment, Wanda's grandmother had piled her tray with food and homed in on a large round table. And Patty noticed for the first time the old woman was shuffling along on a well-worn pair of elastic houseshoes.

Buying a chocolate donut and a Dr. Pepper as an offering to the girl, Patty touched nothing else but a big cup of black coffee, her stomach still queasy. She edged the donut toward Wanda as they sat down across from each other. Wanda was eyeing her through scraggly bangs; Patty sipped her coffee and tried not to notice.

Meanwhile, Wanda's grandmother, hunched over her food, began humming to herself. Patty watched the old woman upend the bowl of cereal. She *had* planned to appeal to the grandmother. "Granny?" Patty began.

Wanda interrupted. "Leave her alone, okay? She just goes off sometimes."

Patty pulled her eyes away from the old woman and focused them on the girl, who was already focusing her eyes on Patty.

"So." Wanda narrowed her eyes. "You were in beauty pageants and that sort of crap?"

"A long time ago." Patty tapped her cup with a long fingernail.

Still staring, Wanda cocked her head in thought. "You remind me of this girl back in school. Cissy Purvis. Little Miss College Mound Rattlesnake Roundup two years in a row. Everybody sucks up to her. Even the teachers. She got breasts last year, bleaches her hair, wears lipstick already."

Patty didn't know whether to check her hair, her lipstick or her breasts. "Oh, well, I'm sure you'll turn out to be just as pretty when you grow up."

Wanda made a horsey sound through her nose. "Who says I want to? That girl is *dumb*. Dumber than a box of rocks."

"Yes, yes, well . . ." Patty realized she was stammering. Forcing herself to stop, she took a long, irritated swallow of her coffee.

Wanda took a long, squinty-eyed suck of her Dr. Pepper, then belched. "Phe-eww—went up my nose." She squinted again at Patty. "Hey, are you about to puke? You look like you're about to puke."

"I'm fine."

Wanda leaned away from her. "All it takes is hearing it, and move over, I'm hurling too."

"I'm *fine*—" Patty repeated, taking a big breath, forcing herself calm. *Focus now,* she told herself. *Get this over with and you can puke to your heart's content.*

"Wanda, I need to ask you a question."

Wanda spat her gum into her palm and looked around for someplace to park it. "You want to know where my parents are, right?"

Patty nodded.

She stuck the gum on her cup lid. "My mama's dead. Died Sunday. If you want to know what happened, everybody said it was an accident. I don't agree. But that's another story. As for my daddy, he's the one I'm trying to find."

Patty paused. "I'm so sorry. How about your legal father? Whoever raised you."

Wanda's eyes went dead. "No man ever raised me. And my stepfather's limping his way to hell, I hope. If you mean the man who everybody says is my father, he's dead, too."

Patty mumbled another regret.

Wanda shrugged it away. "Seems like men just screw things up when they're around, anyway."

"You're not supposed to know that yet," Patty said under her breath. She glanced at Wanda's grandmother. The old woman was poking at several raisins she'd dug out of her muffin. "So it's just you and your grandmother?"

The girl stuck out her chin. "If she's my real grandmother." She pulled her straw out of the plastic cup top, then jabbed it squawking back in. Then she did it again, and again.

"That's got to be tough," Patty murmured.

Wanda sat back in her chair. "Is this where you try to bond with me so you can talk me into going away?"

Patty arched an eyebrow at this hard-shelled kid: "I'm trying to help, Wanda." She heard the slightest of sighs in the girl's head-down fume, then watched as Wanda started the straw squawking again, only faster—in, out, in, out—until suddenly she stopped and said:

"You always this nice? Sometimes, don't you just want to rear back your head and cuss till you croak?"

Patty's face flushed, flames flaring high and hot up her cheekbones. She resisted an urge to rub at an oily sensation on her fingers. An oily fax sensation. Instead she clenched her jaw and said to the girl with the bangs in her eyes: "Life just stinks sometimes, doesn't it?"

"Yeah." Wanda rubbed her nose with a knuckle. "Shit happens. Life's a bitch and then you die. Have a nice day."

Patty burst out a laugh at the old joke she'd never thought funny before.

And it made her feel half-alive for the first time that morning.

"Had a T-shirt that said that," Wanda explained matter-of-factly. "Never wore it. Granny didn't like such language on clothing for people in the fifth grade. She went to church a lot."

Patty breathed in deeply, wanting to hold on to the nice feeling. *Exhale. Concentrate on breathing,* she told herself. *Relax.* "You go to church?" she asked absently.

Wanda gave another shrug. "Used to. When we lived with Granny. Then Granny started watching stupid church on TV, those guys with woodpecker hairdos I bet even Mother Teresa would want to slap."

*Exhale. Inhale.* Patty was thinking. *Exhale. Better. Much.*

Wanda put a pinch of donut into her mouth. "Sunday school wasn't half bad."

Patty was feeling better by the moment. She'd loved Sunday school. Brave Bible characters. Little old ladies patting your head. Lots of singing. "Did you sing those cute songs?" Patty smiled wistfully. "You know, like: 'I've got the joy of Jesus down in my heart/And if the devil doesn't like it . . .'"

"... he can sit on a tack, right. We sang that one. Tacks and joy and precious me—but shit still happens. They don't tell you that in Sunday school."

"No," Patty was forced to agree, her nice Sunday school feeling snatched away. "They don't."

"The United States is number one in the world in people who believe in God," Wanda suddenly quoted. "Also number one in murders. Guess that means there's lots of murderers out there who believe in God," She took a suck of her soft drink and reached for another pinch of donut. "Whether I believe in God, I hadn't quite decided. Did I mention that I've been in communication with the Governor?"

Patty sighed again. "I'll keep that in mind." She glanced over at the old woman, who was still working on her pile of raisins. Resting her fingers alongside her temples, she forced herself once more to focus: "Wanda, do you have any proof about your biological father being a donor?"

That, for the first time, turned Wanda quiet. She let go of the donut and pushed it away. "You ever hear anything that made so much sense you knew it was true?"

Patty studied the girl's face. "But why do you want to know this man? You're smart. You have to know that his donation was just a way for your parents . . ."

Wanda popped her cup down on the table. "Why do they call it a donation when they get money for it? It was his sperm, okay? His twenty-three
chromosomes. Half of my forty-six; half of me! If I were adopted, nobody
would mind me looking for him." Wanda leaned across the table. "I'm *not* an
orphan! I got a father out there! I'm walking around with his genes. I feel like
some ghost's got his fingerprints all over me and it just seems fair I should get
to see those fingers." Wanda had to stop to swallow, feeling something catch.
"Just seems *fair*."

Patty paused. "But what if he doesn't want to know you exist?"

Wanda started jabbing her straw again, in, out, in, out, the plastic squawking
louder and louder. "Well . . . maybe I just want him to know. He had a choice.
I want one, too." With that, the straw went silent. And Wanda went suddenly
eyes-down quiet with the sad feeling that came stomping in behind those words.
She ripped the gum off the cup's top and popped it back into her mouth with
a sullen chomp. "It's not like I'm asking him to be a sea catfish or anything."

Wanda's grandmother had just finished wiping her mouth back and forth
with her paper napkin and gazed around at the two sitting at the table with
her as if they'd just arrived. "Is she giving you a hard time, Ms. Hightower? It's
in her nature. You gonna eat that donut?"

And then to Patty's surprise, this tough-talking girl slid the donut toward
her grandmother and then began wiping up the crumby mess around the old
woman's plate. As if it were the most natural thing for a tough-talking girl to
do. Patty began turning her coffee cup around in a circle, around and around,
watching, strangely touched. She raised both hands to her temples and rubbed
them around and around. Then she dropped her hands and got suddenly to
her feet.

"I've got to be crazy, but let's just ask. C'mon—before I change my mind."

# Chapter 6

*The aphid gives birth to live young without mating. She makes copies of herself.*

—Wonderful World of Biology

*S*even floors up, Patty left Wanda and her grandmother standing beside the Xerox machine in the filing area of the OB/GYN doctors' offices. Her fingers playing across the controls, Wanda leaned against the machine, thinking of bugs and doctors as Granny landed in a rickety secretary's chair and worked to get comfortable.

There was a window across the room, and Wanda inched toward it as if it were the edge of a cliff. She peeked out. She had never been so high. She spied tiny cars and bug-little people, here, there and yonder—then gazed way beyond, the line between the earth and the sky looming farther away than seemed possible. She squinted, wanting to see more, much more. She saw everything, noticed everything, and she was going to know everything. Hide and watch, she told the horizon.

Along the wall beside the windows were diplomas and certificates, dozens of them, and she moved over to consider each closely, photographic memory clicking away at dates and places: T. THOMAS BOWMAN, Medical School of Grenada, Residency, Parkland Hospital; DR. G. GORDON STRAKE, Baylor Medical School, Residency, Johns Hopkins Hospital; CHARLES A. YOUNG-BLOOD, Loyola Medical School, Residency, Parkland Hospital.

"Hey!" she called to the plump receptionist filling her coffee mug across the room. "Where are all the women doctors?"

"Who are you?" the receptionist asked.

"WANDA L. LEDBETTER."

The woman disappeared around the corner. And just as Granny had finally gotten comfortable in the secretary's chair, a gray, pinched-face nurse, wound as tight as her hair, came out of nowhere to shoosh them out of the inner offices. Granny grunted as Wanda pulled her up, led her through the door into the waiting room to the nearest sofa and eased down beside her.

The room smelled of nerves. It was full of women with long faces flipping through worn magazines, all waiting to hear their names called by nurses with pleasant voices. *Like the kind used to calm large animals,* thought Wanda. Her elbow was pushing against a popping-pregnant woman who was sweating and jittery. The woman flapped her magazine closed, jerked her purse open on her big belly and began rummaging. She came up with a pack of Kool Lights and some breath mints.

"Studies show a significant percentage of smoking mothers produce cross-eyed babies. Just so you know," Wanda volunteered.

The woman rolled an eye at Wanda.

For extra effect, Wanda demonstrated the look.

"Wanda—" Patty was standing in the inner office door, motioning them toward her. Wanda helped her grandmother up once more. Granny's grunts made all the nervous women look up from their page-flipping.

Granny waved.

They followed Patty around a corner and into an office as ornate as the outer offices were sterile. With another huff, Granny settled herself into one of the studded leather chairs in front of the oak desk, while Wanda pushed her hands deep into her jeans pockets and studied the pictures on every wall. Boats. They were all boats. Big ones, small ones, old ones, fancy ones—everywhere. There was even one on the big desk. One of those ships in a bottle. And beside it was a photograph of a woman and a boy about Wanda's age hanging off the edge of a sailboat, both looking more than a little green. Wanda moved behind the desk to a bulletin board running over with snapshots of grinning babies, birth announcements and thank you notes: *Thank you, Dr. Youngblood. You've helped us make a miracle! God bless you Dr. Youngblood. You're invited to our son's baptism. You've answered our dreams, Dr. Youngblood, thank you from the bottom* . . . Wanda made a face, moving on to another row of diplomas, and proceeded to read every date, every title—everything.

While Wanda was circling the room, Patty was pacing, watching the girl curiously, wondering if she was about to lose her job on the same day she lost her husband. A few minutes ago, she had still been numb enough not to give a rip either way, but that was a few minutes ago. Maybe this wasn't the thing to do right now.

But although her professional instincts were signaling hasty retreat, she didn't move. And when Wanda finally plopped down in the other high-backed chair beside Granny and rested one of those scruffy boots across the chair's arm, Patty came up behind the chair and began drumming her long fingernails on its high-backed top. In that way, the three waited.

The door slowly opened; the redheaded nurse Carla popped in, took a good long look, smiled at Patty and then disappeared, closing the door behind. A moment later the door burst open and in strode a tall, lean doctor, handsome in a rather stringy way, with his head down, nose in a report. He had already aimed his bottom at the seat of his chair before he noticed that his office was full of women. And they were staring at him. He froze in mid-sit and reversed course, straightening himself up to his tallest. "Hello," he said, smiling his best professional smile. It came out looking rather fractured. "I'm sorry. My nurse *Carla,*" he spat out the name, "failed to mention I had visitors." As he adjusted his horn rims, his eyes landed on Patty, and narrowed.

"Dr. Youngblood," Patty began, taking a big breath, "these are some people I'd like you to meet."

The chipped smile did not waver. "Ms. Hightower, may I have a word with you? Outside?" He glanced back pleasantly at Wanda and her grandmother. "Excuse us, please. This won't take but a second." His eyes commanded Patty into motion. At the last minute, he glanced back to see the ragamuffin girl had taken the cork out of his ship-in-a-bottle. "Don't touch that!" He rushed over and recorked the bottle. Then he remembered to smile. "Please—it's a one-of-a-kind creation. Just have a seat. We'll be right back, all right?"

Wanda waited until the door was closed, and pulled the cork out again.

On the other side of the door, Dr. Youngblood moved into Patty's face. "Have you lost your senses?" he whispered. "What are they doing in my office?"

"She's an orphan," Patty explained. "All she's got is that old woman who's not ... altogether all together. What would you do if you were her? Maybe you could talk to her."

"Talk with her? That's the *last* ..."

The red-haired nurse passed slow as a slug.

"Do you *mind*, Carla?" Dr. Youngblood scowled.

"Could she be a donor offspring?" Patty pressed as Carla turned the corner. "No one would tell her a thing like that if she wasn't. Not right after her mother died."

"Are you *hearing* yourself, Patty?" Dr. Youngblood spat, straining to keep his voice down. "Do you have any idea how this will look for the hospital if she presses this? Even if she *is* a donor offspring, that action was a secret decided and committed to a long time ago by her parents. Not us. It's not our affair. You and Eric surely have discussed donor insemination, by now—what if this were your daughter? This is not like you at all. Are you still ill?"

Patty stiffened. "I'm fine."

He made a circular gesture around her. "You don't look exactly your usual . . . self."

Patty began primping ever so slightly, almost hearing the words *beauty queen* at the end of his sentence. "I'm fine. I just thought . . ."

At that, Dr. Youngblood lost all composure: "You're not *supposed* to think!"

Patty couldn't quite believe her ears. "Excuse me?"

Dr. Youngblood threw up his hands. "What do you think your job is here, Patty? Policy making? Social work?"

Patty bristled. She forced herself calm: "I *know* my job, Dr. Youngblood. But she's not going away."

"Oh yes she is, because that is your job!" he said. "Are you experiencing a premenstrual hormonal surge? Perhaps we should reconsider the dosage of your fertility drugs if it's affecting your work."

Patty gaped at the man, suppressing an urge to show him a hormonal surge that'd rip that pompous look right off his face. Instead she gritted her jaw at every stupid, sexist, adulterous Y chromosome on the planet and said, calmly, evenly: "My hormones are *just fine*, Dr. Youngblood. This girl is a human being, and I thought—that is, I *considered*—that you, as a human being, might find some way to rectify this situation for all concerned. After all, we are a humanitarian institution." And this beauty queen *does* have a brain, you jerk, she almost added.

Dr. Youngblood fumed. "First, I'm just doing *my* job—protecting my department and its rules. Second, she's probably wrong. We wouldn't have inseminated them."

"Them," Patty repeated.

"Her parents. They wouldn't have been admitted to the program." The doctor's whisper stretched into a hiss. "Do I have to say it? Even back then, we had a policy about the couples' financial situation, for the child just as much as the ability to pay. They're white trash, Patty."

Patty frowned. "Maybe they weren't 'white trash' back then."

He whirled around to see Wanda in the open office door. The chipped smile reappeared. "Perhaps you and your grandmother would be more comfortable in the waiting area."

"You were here in 1989," said Wanda, eyeballing the doctor up and down. "The diplomas say so."

He waved the way with an arm. "It'll just be for a moment."

Wanda's eyes narrowed, snakelike. She turned back slowly to her grandmother. "C'mon, Granny." She helped the big woman up out of her chair.

Her grandmother groaned. "Make up your mind. I'm beginning to feel like a dang ping-pong ball, Wanda Louise."

Dr. Youngblood, his smile now all but frozen in place, waited until Wanda and her grandmother had left. Then he eased back inside the office, held the door until Patty followed and shut it with an emphatic click.

Wanda deposited her granny on another couch in the waiting room and stood there as her grandmother struck up a conversation with the woman next to her about the magazine article she was reading. Wanda read it upside down. Something about testing your husband's aptitude for fertility, or fidelity, one of those f-words. And by the time her granny had the woman digging in her pocketbook for a gander at her change, Wanda made a bathroom excuse, told her grandmother several times to stay put and moved quietly through the outer door.

Two nurses behind the receptionist window watched her go.

"That was her, Stella," Carla whispered to the other nurse, the gray, pinch-faced woman, the kind of old-style nurse who wore her calling tight, like the bobby-pinned nurse's cap she still wished she could wear.

"Thirteen years ago," Carla was saying, "Dr. Youngblood was here. But so was Dr. Bowman. And, of course, Dr. Roddy himself, and you *know* about Dr. Roddy." Carla smiled. "Oh my, this is going to be interesting, isn't it?"

The older nurse's eyes continued to gaze toward the thirteen-year-old girl as if she were a dreaded drink of bitter medicine, long after Wanda had slipped from view.

# *Chapter 7*

*W*anda slowed in front of the elevator, shuffling her boots ever so quietly, to stare at the weird name of the floor.

**7th Floor**
**Reproductive**
**Endocrinology**

That's all the sign said. So she began to roam, people going back and forth in front of her, some in white coats, some in normal clothes, fading in and out of rooms with little red or blue or yellow flags above their doors. Everyone was smiling, pleasant and polite, even the guy coming out of a little room with a plastic jar in his hand.

*Whoa,* Wanda thought, watching the guy suddenly duck his head, dropping the hand with the little container to his side, all but tucking it behind his thigh as he scooted around her. Wanda thought that was weird, so she walked over to the door to read the small sign hanging there. "Collecting Room," it said.

Wanda's boot heels dug in: *Collecting Room.*

In her mind she watched the door open thirteen years ago. Another man, a double-jointed, hazel-eyed, pug-nosed, blond-haired intern, was coming out and down the hall carrying a container to hand in to some smiling white uniform, who delivered it to where her mama lay flat on her back in a little hospital gown.

Wanda looked back; the sheepish guy had disappeared. So with another look this way and that, she edged the door open ever so slightly and peeked in.

What did she expect? Couches, dirty magazines? To catch a guy in the act? Not that it would bother her, of course. She'd seen a guy's pecker. Besides the guy just left . . . right?

She opened the door a little wider, fumbled for the light switch and flipped it on. The room was nothing more than a closet: a metal chair, a metal trash can, a box of tissues, a sheet music stand holding a dog-eared magazine—

—and a very, very creepy feeling.

She backed out.

"Can I help you?"

Wanda grabbed her heart. A pleasant nurse was coming straight up to her.

"Bathroom?" Wanda managed.

The woman pointed. "Back down this hall, turn to the left, then turn to the right. Can't miss it."

Wanda made movements in the direction of the pointing finger until the nurselike person melted into one of the little rooms, then she did an about-face. That's when she heard a swoosh.

There, in front of her, silver swinging doors eased open on slow automatic. Across both doors were small red letters now parting, swinging away from each other:

**NO ADMITTANCE
CRYOBANK
HOSPITAL EMPLOYEES ONLY**

From the doors appeared two white-coated men immersed in conversation. As they passed, Wanda slipped behind them and through the space just as the doors closed again. On the other side, though, was just another bunch of doors. *Now what?* she thought. Then she heard a crash and went toward the sound. Peeping through the door's glass window, she saw another young white-coat guy, his hands in heavy-duty oven mitts, kneeling over a round cylinder of sealed vials that seemed to have just hit the floor. Fog was swirling around him from a big steel barrel beyond. His left mitt was holding two unmarked vials, his right was grasping at two labels that had fluttered to the floor.

*Shit*, the man's lips read. *Shit shit shit.*

Then the lab technician jerked his head back as if someone had called his name, and uttered another curse. Flustered, he held the two vials over the marked slots, switched their positions and switched them again. Then, looking over his shoulder, he just popped them in, picked up the rack, shoved it onto a counter and scurried away.

Ten years from now, a son born to a couple who'd carefully chosen a sperm donation from a donor with a doctoral dissertation on Renaissance drama will surprise his parents with a predilection toward tractor pulls and mud wrestling.

Wanda pressed her nose flat against the glass. The fog in the empty room wafted toward the door. From the pictures she'd seen in her research, she knew exactly what she was looking at. She tried the door. It opened. She slid inside and over to the counter. Gingerly, she put out a finger and touched the vials. They weren't cold yet, so she picked one up and held it to the light—it was full of a yucky, milky substance. *Kind of egg-whitey,* she thought. She also thought about how weird boys are made. How weird that they can pump this out of the same hole they pee from. And how weird that it can make babies. How could such stuff do that? How could it have made her? She began to replace the vial in its tray, knowing the butter-fingered white-coat would be back any second.

But then—instead—she wrapped her slender fingers around it, held it tight and slipped back out both doors into the hall again.

"Hey, there, Sunshine. What're you doing in here?"

Wanda levitated. An old black guy in industrial blue work clothes and a big, loud belt—the kind with lots of keys jingling from it—stood close enough to grab her. She moved back, shoving the vial deep into her pocket. "You lost?" he asked, resting a hand back on a floor polisher. "You look lost to me."

"Wanda!"

Wanda groaned. It was the hospital mouthpiece beauty queen woman, and she was coming fast.

"Well," said the janitor as Patty rushed up, "looks like you're found."

Patty was fuming. "I figured I'd find you somewhere like this. Let's get you out of here."

"That's the sperm bank, isn't it?" Wanda said, pushing her bangs out of her eyes and keeping her hands away from the stolen contents of her pocket.

"I don't know what you saw." Patty guided Wanda's shoulder down the hall, embarrassed by the loud clomping of the girl's dirty cowboy boots.

"I know what a sperm bank is: 'A liquid nitrogen tank which suspends life at -400 degrees.' And that's your masturbatorium," she said, pointing to the collecting room.

Patty stiffened. "Watch your language."

Wanda shrugged. "It's not my word; I read it. What's the music stand in there for? They need both hands free?"

"Good Lord, Wanda." Patty took hold of Wanda's elbow to hurry her.

"It's not as if I hadn't seen one, you know—a penis."

"Yes, well," Patty mumbled, "sometimes that sort of thing is . . . necessary."

"For medical purposes," Wanda said.

"Yes, that's right."

"Purposes like me."

Patty wasn't going to touch that one. She looked left and right as they passed office after office, moving Wanda along faster. Wanda just talked faster. "This is the whole place, huh?"

"What did you expect?" Patty snapped. "Decanting rooms? This is just a medical facility, Wanda, not 'Brave New World.'"

"Huh?"

"Never mind."

"You got any sperm like that Nobel Prize sperm bank they have in California? My IQ is pretty high, they tell me."

Patty nudged Wanda around the corner.

"I *know* you're trying test-tube babies—in vitro fertilization, right?"

"We have a program," Patty admitted impatiently.

"Ever had a live birth? That's what you're supposed to ask. In case you're basing it on just pregnancies or embryos, that sort of advertising ploy. Lots of bucks to be made."

"Some might misrepresent, but we certainly don't," Patty snapped.

"How about surrogating or embryo banking or egg donation? I figured out that a kid could have about five parents that way: egg donor, sperm donor, womb donor and the couple who pay for it all. It'd be a mess at Christmas."

Patty rolled her eyes. "Good grief, Wanda! Where are you *getting* all this?"

"I have a photographic memory. I read it, and it stays." Wanda paused. "Trouble is, I don't forget anything either."

A doctor was coming toward them, a bit too curious for Patty's comfort. Patty flashed a beauty pageant smile at him until he passed, while Wanda was craning her neck to see into the passing rooms. "Do they do abortions up here, too? Pretty weird if women are going nuts trying to have 'em right across the hall where they're sweating bullets to get rid of 'em."

Patty flinched.

"You think they could, like, get together on this and swap out . . ."

"*Wanda!*" Patty heard herself yell. Glancing around, she regained her composure and then added, calmly, intensely: "You don't know what you're *talking* about."

Wanda frowned. "Geez, what's eating you?"

They were now in the common area near the floor's elevators, and Patty let go of Wanda's elbow, wishing she could rid herself of this whole thing just as easily. "Listen. If you want me to help you, drop the attitude, okay?"

Wanda looked as if she were considering this idea for a moment, then: "Do you do sex selections?" Patty sighed. She glanced around; she checked her watch. She moved out of the way of a wheelchair zipping by.

"In India, during a period of 8,000 abortions, 7,999 were girls," Wanda rattled on.

*Dear God, make it stop,* Patty thought.

"I could be any of those, you know . . . eggs and sperms and test tubes, all that crap. My mama might not even be my mama."

Then Wanda's voice dropped, as she added, almost to herself: "But at least I ain't in India."

The sound of Wanda's voice softening so dramatically turned Patty's head back around. The girl had wrapped her arms around herself, her tough, sad eyes fixed somewhere a long way from this hospital hall. That's when Patty noticed Wanda's arm. There was a bad bruise on it—in the shape of fingers. It looked very new.

A current rippled up Patty's spine. "How did you get that bruise?"

Wanda covered it defiantly. "I swapped a toe for it."

Patty opened her mouth. But she couldn't think of anything to say to that and found herself just staring at the girl. Standing there in the middle of the busy floor, staring. Again. Not sure what to do with the dozen wrenching emotions this child and this morning were putting her through.

So with an exhausted sigh, Patty zeroed in on a nearby soft drink machine, stuck her hospital card into a slot, punched a couple of selections and held one out to Wanda.

Wanda didn't take it.

Patty held it out again. "C'mon, let's sit down. I need a sugar jolt." Wanda looked back toward Dr. Youngblood's office. "Your granny's fine," Patty assured her. "Having a great time talking everybody's ears off."

"And checking everybody's change," Wanda mumbled.

"Yes. What's that about?"

Wanda made a face. "You wouldn't understand." Lightly she touched the bulge in her blue jeans pocket where the vial of donor semen was stashed. Worrying that Patty had noticed, she quickly took the soft drink. She watched Patty sit down at a table near the machines, wanting for her to do the same. Someone bumped Wanda in passing. She looked back at the stream of people now moving past her in the common area. Feeling a little claustrophobic, she moved to the big windows along the farther wall and looked out. The view turned her silent. So many people, so many houses, so much everything. Looking at the little bug people way down below, Wanda thought about how small she'd seem to them looking up at her. And then she glanced down at the parking lot—and there was Wild Thing! The skinny guard had just given her a drink of water from a bucket, and Wild Thing was shaking off the extra from her jowls, making the skinny guard jump lively. Wanda leaned on the window and almost smiled. "You like dogs?"

"I have a cat."

"You know how I got Wild Thing?" Wanda said over her shoulder. "She'd gotten herself caught in a coon trap in the pasture behind Harley's trailer. I think she's one of those half-wolf dogs."

"I don't doubt that a second," Patty answered.

"Howled all night long till I just had to go out there. Sounded like my name, you know." Wanda put her hands over her mouth: "Waoooooooooonda."

And then Wanda grinned. It was the first time Patty had seen the girl do anything but frown. "That explains her poor ear."

"No, it was her tail that was caught; I wrapped it up. Like that Aesop's fable, you know? The lion and the thorn? She adopted me after that. Kept bringing me dead things. I think she thinks she's a cat."

"I'm glad to know you read something more your age," Patty commented.

Wanda looked offended. "I read them when I was five." With a last look out the window, Wanda moved back over to the table and dropped into one of the metal chairs, smile gone. "Dr. Smiley Face isn't going to help me, is he? He was here then. He knows." A quick, sick look passed over Wanda's face, like she'd just discovered she'd swallowed a fly. "Is he double-jointed?"

Exasperated, Patty answered: "What makes you think I'd know that?"

"I heard. He's your doctor, isn't he? You're trying to have a baby, too." She said it as a fact.

Patty blushed in spite of herself. She *hated* to blush. "Anybody ever tell you it's rude to talk about such things with complete strangers?"

"How do you find out the truth, then?"

Patty paused on that one. She took a deep breath. "Wanda." She leaned across the table toward the girl. "This is the truth. All the assisted-conception donor inseminations done thirteen years ago were done by one man, Dr. Harold Roddy, before formal hospital insemination guidelines, which means any records of such procedures would be considered his personal property, yet still confidential and off-limits by the nature of the agreements signed."

Wanda's eyes had not blinked through the whole explanation. "Where's this guy?"

Patty sighed. "Dead."

"*Dead?*" Wanda's jaw dropped.

"And," Patty added, "I was told he destroyed his records, as promised."

Wanda stared into her soft drink can at the little bubbles dying away. Then she sat the can on the table and shoved it away from her.

"Wanda, I'm sorry."

"Dr. Smiley Face told you all that, didn't he?"

"Yes, Dr. Youngblood explained that's the way things were back then," Patty said. "I'm sorry."

"Quit saying you're sorry, okay?" Wanda spat out.

"I'm just trying to be nice, Wanda."

Wanda narrowed her eyes at the hospital beauty queen. "I don't trust nice, okay? The nicer people are, the more they don't listen. How do I know if all this stuff you're saying is the truth? You have to do whatever they say. That's why you're sitting here in the first place. You're trying to shake me off—just like Wild Thing did that stupid guard's water!"

Wanda jumped up and headed back to the window to stare down at her mama's Caddy. Her dead mama who had been here. She *had* been here.

Watching the snit Wanda had pulled herself into, Patty just wanted to go. Now. What else was this girl expecting of her, anyway? She had her own problems. Big ones! She'd done all she could, hadn't she? Especially considering Dr. Youngblood and her job.

Patty rubbed her face. *I'm just not thinking straight,* she realized. This was Eric's fault. Eric of the unswerving, self-absorbed self-assurance. Eric the high-roller who never knew a moment of self-doubt, who made choices every day like he made change. Who was always in control. Who always did the right thing. Until today. "May his self-assurance wither until his secretary can no longer fondle it," Patty muttered. She looked at her watch, got to her feet and looked at her watch again. Wanda's x-ray eyes roamed back to take her in.

"Listen," Patty responded, trying to dodge that look, "I don't know what else to say. I have to get back to my office. I'm really sor—" She stopped herself. "I just have to go. Take my advice and go home. There's nothing else. C'mon. I'll go with you to get your granny."

"I can get her myself." Wanda marched ahead, down the hall to Dr. Young-blood's office, leaving Patty trailing behind.

Seconds later, Wanda had grabbed up her granny and pushed past Patty, who was now holding open Dr. Youngblood's door.

Dr. Youngblood came around the corner and slowed at the sight. "They're leaving?" he asked Patty.

Patty nodded.

He smiled at her, touching Patty's arm as he walked past. "Good girl."

Patty froze. "What did you say?"

"I said, 'Good job,'" he called back as he disappeared inside.

"No, you didn't," Patty mumbled. "You said, 'Good girl.'"

And something sharp, something kicked out of joint so very early that morning, finally wrenched loose. She thought about the fax, about Eric, and that was enough to make her flush livid. Then she thought about Dr. Youngblood, about all the comments she'd endured about her beauty and her brains and why she'd gotten this job, and she flushed blood mad. She thought about all the press releases she'd written, all the positive spins she'd created—and how deep down it bothered her, these lessons in rationalization, persuasive expository, creative writing. And she thought about that touch on the arm.

And, perhaps for the first time, she realized just exactly how good a girl she'd been. "Public Affairs Director." No, Dr. Youngblood, she didn't have a public relations degree; she had a journalism degree. Not Fashion Merchandising or Elementary Education or Hotel Hospitality, like her friends. *Journalism.* "That will sound wonderful for the pageants, dear," her mother had said. Which had almost made her change it. Often she'd wished she had, the old pompous psych game of truth, justice and the free-press way popping into her head at all the wrong times. And god knows the journalists she knew were the biggest jerks she'd ever met. Pushy, self-righteous, obnoxious, self-serving bunch of opinionated megalomaniacs who never got a quote right.

But nobody, *nobody,* ever called *them* "good girls."

Her fingernails dug into the door she was gripping. She felt like ripping it right off its hinges. She felt like ripping select parts off selected members of the male sex. She felt like ... like ...

Patty glanced back at the girl waiting for the elevator with her grandmother. This scraggly, thirteen-year-old motherless child who was probably smarter than she was. Who was having about as much luck with men as she was. Who deserved better.

Just like she did.

Suddenly Patty pivoted and marched over to the girl and the old woman just as the elevator doors whooshed open. "Come on," she said, taking them both by the arms, "I need to make a phone call. But not here."

★ ★ ★

Several walls away, Dr. Youngblood was pushing open the door to his private office to find another doctor leaning against his desk, arms folded, waiting.

Startled, Dr. Youngblood cursed under his breath. He jerked his head back toward the hall. "Thank you, Carla, for telling me Dr. Bowman was waiting!"

"Rumors are all over," Bowman said.

Youngblood fell into his big chair, sighing. "There's a teenager saying she was a product of a donor insemination done here in 1989, Tommy. Wants to find her 'father.'"

"The *donor*?"

Youngblood nodded. "She's gone, so it could be taken care of, but ..."

Dr. Bowman looked away, passing a hand through his slick black hair. "This is why we added that exemption document—to keep anyone from claiming child support if the donor was discovered."

The two doctors caught each other's eyes and quickly glanced away.

Bowman leaned against the desk a moment, then shook his head. "Remember Roddy? Cruising the halls telling us: 'We need fresh, boys! You're doing it anyway. Donate for science and $25!' The old alky," he muttered.

Youngblood intertwined a steeple of fingers and touched them to his lips.

Bowman sighed. "Why did I choose this field? Infertility patients—I swear most of 'em are so desperate, if we told them to cut off their big toes and transplant them between their legs, they'd ask when." He ran his hand through his hair again. *"Damn."* Then with a faint wave, he was gone. "Keep me up on it."

Youngblood sat still a second, his fingers still touching his lips. Then he leaned forward, flipped through his Rolodex, reached for his speakerphone and punched, hard, the numbers on the card.

"Law office of Tyler, Ridley and Anderson," the voice answered. "May I help you?"

★ ★ ★

Meanwhile, inside Room 211 at the Motel 9, Patty unhooked the latch, turned the deadbolt, then opened the door of Wanda's room. There in front of the door stood a slim, rumpled man about Patty's age in a polo shirt, a skinny tie, jeans, a well-trimmed goatee and a pair of dirty basketball shoes more expensive than the sum of the rest of his outfit. He took a long, deep-water look at Patty, then gave her a sweetly wicked grin. "Patricia. How long has it been?"

"I hear you've been busy," Patty said, her grip on the doorknob tightening. "Two wives? Or is it three?"

The man stopped smiling. "I see you've put on a little weight. Is it nine pounds or ten?"

Patty caught herself about to tug at her tight skirt and shot him a look that would wither wood.

"C'mon, Patricia. Let's be nice," he said. "I've been working on what to say to my first love, and you're screwing up my romantic scene."

"Your first love, my *ass.*"

"Sparkling repartee, just like old times. Speaking of your ass, how's your husband? An investment broker, I hear?"

Patty crossed her arms, high and tight. "This is business, Griffin. I may have a story for you."

He cocked his head. "You're giving me a story?" Wild Thing pushed past Patty and sniffed his crotch. He jumped back. "What is *that?* Yellow Fang?"

Wanda moved around Patty. "She won't bite. Unless I want her to."

He stuck out his hand for her to shake. "Then I sure want to be your friend. Griffin LaCour, *Dallas Morning Tribune.*"

Wanda pumped his hand once, chin high: "Wanda Ledbetter, Donor Offspring."

Griffin looked from Patty to Wanda back to Patty, the wicked smile now deep and wide. "I think I like it already."

# Chapter 8

Dear Daddy,

You might read about me in the papers today, page 2. I've got this idea that maybe you'll pick up the paper over your cereal bowl and you'd say, oh my god, oh my god, that's my daughter. Look at her. Look at that pug nose. Look at those double joints. She's got my mother's eyes! And you fold the paper and stick it in your back pocket and you jump into your Jag and you race to the Motel 9, thanking the artificial insemination gods for selling your sperm long ago in your immature, irresponsible youth and hustle me off to live happily ever-you-know with your All-American family.

Guess I've been watching too many "Father Knows Best" reruns, huh. Guess what'd you really do is have heart palpitations. Funny, though. I'da thought I'd want you to keel over in your oatmeal. But seems like now somehow you're more real to me than I've got any business letting you. Thing is, I think you'd like me. I mean, when I want to be liked, most people like me . . .

"Hey, kid, that cur dog of yours is pissing in front of the office. I told you if it causes a problem you're outta here. Get back, you mangy thing, you!"

Putting down her notebook, Wanda looked up from where she sat against the newspaper vending machine to where the greasy office attendant had already vanished back inside. And there stood Wild Thing wagging proudly over a wet spot near the front door's welcome mat. Wanda started to say something to the dog, but instead her eyes went back to the headline in the *Dallas Morning Tribune* she'd just bought:

## GIRL, 13, SEARCHING FOR DONOR INSEMINATION FATHER
by Griffin LaCour, Special to the Tribune

She didn't like the picture. Looked like a stupid school picture, every zit like a felt-tip pen smudge. Making an unconscious swipe at her bangs, she reread the caption under it:

*Orphaned donor offspring Wanda Louise Ledbetter wants
only to know her last living blood relative*

Just *Wanda!* She sighed. Screwing up her face, she reopened her notebook, touched the tip of her pencil to her tongue and added:

*If you see me in the paper, and do remember, don't fall over dead, okay? I'm a little low on relatives lately.*

*Your daughter whoever you are,
Wanda*

Her hair kept falling in her face. With her eyes never leaving the page, she pushed the hair into a ponytail, using a rubber band she'd found by the newspaper dispenser. Then with a last dark underline of her name, she closed the little book and stared down at the worn James Dean movie-star picture she'd taken from her mother's billfold. She ran a finger over his face. Picking it up carefully, she got to her feet, folded the newspaper, and stuffed it and the little notebook in the front of her jeans. And with a quick check of the vial of donated daddy stuff in her front pocket, she eased James Dean in beside it, grabbed up Wild Thing's improvised rope leash and started back to the room.

Her granny was peering out the half-opened doorway, making nervous gestures with her handkerchief. Wanda pulled her shirttail over the newspaper.

"There you are, Wanda Louise," she whispered loudly. "I think it's time to leave. It's loud and it's stinky and I think there're Messicans next door and while

I don't have anything against Messicans in general, these I do not like at all." The phone was ringing. "And that thing won't quit making that racket. What are you hiding there under your shirt?"

Wanda lunged for the phone.

★ ★ ★

Eight miles away, in his well-appointed home on Turtle Creek Boulevard, Dr. Charles A. Youngblood's kitchen phone was also ringing. Having just poured artificial sweetener on his Raisin Bran, he started to go ahead and take a bite, his eyes glued to the newspaper, heat rising up his neck. He needed to remain calm; he needed to eat something. But try as he might, he wasn't one of those people who could ignore a phone. Even on a morning like this.

"Hello—" he sighed into it.

"Charles Allen."

He cringed. "Hello, Mother. How are you this morning?"

"What's this about that girl in the newspaper?"

Dr. Youngblood moved the long cord around the edge of his kitchen table. "Mother, I don't have time to talk. All I've been doing is answering this . . ."

"This work you do, it worries me."

Youngblood sighed. "I don't have time for one of your philosophical ozone talks, Mother." He turned the page of the paper, spotting an article about an in vitro fertilization in Nebraska:

### ALL IN THE FAMILY—THREE SISTERS AND A BABY

*Three sisters create one child: One sister gave the egg,
one gave the womb, one gave the husband*

"Maybe this girl's come for you, Charles Allen. Like some angel unaware. I brought you up to be a good Catholic," his mother's voice droned on. "Now, may the holy saints forgive you—you're playing God?"

He slapped the paper shut. "You cannot take that stance, Mother, because then all medical care is an intrusion and every cure is playing God."

"Don't you twist my meaning, Charles Allen. Curing isn't creating."

"My patients want children, Mother. We're helping them. I'm proud of that."

"And if you're so proud, why do you hide the records?"

Dr. Youngblood drowned one of his Raisin Bran raisins with the back of his spoon. "I concede the whole matter might be handled better. But that's a small thing considering what we might achieve in the whole field."

"Oh, so it's not *all* for the sake of the patient," she crowed. "I suppose you're going to tell me that puttering around with life is fine because it's there?"

Youngblood finally gave up on the Raisin Bran and dropped his spoon: "As a matter of fact, yes. We're unlocking nature's secrets one by one as if it's natural to do so."

"Well, tell me, Mr. Natural, is it natural to pump a woman with drugs enough to make octuplets, then suggest she get rid of a few to give the others a better chance? What's it called? 'Pregnancy reduction'? Bet you didn't think your mother knew about that."

He began rubbing a temple. "You're about to get around to abortion, Mother, so goodbye now." Seven a.m. and he already had a corker of a headache. He took the phone from his ear and got to his feet, the chair making a raw sound on the linoleum. His mother's voice was still spilling out of the earpiece as he headed the phone back to its wall cradle: "Have to go. It's been such a nice chat," he said toward the mouthpiece.

"You help that girl, Charles Allen. She could be your miracle."

"I don't believe in miracles."

"Oh? Not even the miracle of birth? Then you need a miracle, son. Now finish your Raisin Bran."

Dr. Charles A. Youngblood set down the phone, rubbed his chin hard enough to hear the stubble and then sat down to try once more to get a spoonful of cereal in his mouth.

But the phone rang again. Resolutely, he started the spoonful to his mouth anyway.

It rang again.

He dropped the spoon into the milk, got up, lifted the receiver and slammed it back down before it could ring again. Then he picked it back up. And began to dial.

★ ★ ★

At that exact moment, six streets over and one story up, another phone rang. It had just drummed Patty Hightower out of a very nice dream about swimming with a whole family of dolphins. Her waterbed was moving.

"Hello," Patty mumbled, cotton-mouthed.

"Patty. Charles Youngblood. What . . ."

Instantly Patty's brain kicked in. "You have reached the Hightower/Little residence," she quickly droned. "We can't come to the phone now, but if you'll leave your name and number, we'll get back to you. Thank you." She made an attempt at a beep sound, which actually came out rather well.

"What the hell happened! How did the papers get to her? See me as soon as you get in the office."

The phone clicked off. Patty pulled herself back against the headboard and stared at the sunlight streaming into the room. Shafts. Pointy, bright, persistent shafts.

The phone rang again. She switched on the answering machine and was pleased at how much she had sounded like it.

"This is Dr. Crouch. Just seen the morning paper. Call me immediately."

The phone clicked off.

Then rang again.

Patty still hadn't moved, leaning back against the headboard. The cat jumped up on the bed and rubbed against her.

"Patty, darling? My goodness, where ever could you be so early? It's Mother, honey. I have news. Chalice Hathaway called for your number. She wants you to judge the next Miss Texas Tot pageant! Don't forget my charity dinner next week, now. I want to show off my two celebrities! Give a kiss to dearest Eric!"

Patty fell sideways on the bed.

Click.

Brrnng.

Beep.

"Patricia, it's Griffin. How's my Deep Throat? Isn't this fun? I always said this is where you should be. I've found out that the kid could sue, perhaps even set legal precedent. Call me."

Patty didn't move. The light flickered as something flew past the window.

The phone rang again.

After the beep, though, there was a pause.

"Patty . . ." The deep voice faltered, then straightened out. "It's Eric. I'll be by this evening to pick up more of my things around seven. We should talk."

Patty lunged for the phone.

★ ★ ★

Back in the Turtle Creek Boulevard house, Dr. Youngblood stared at the phone he had just returned to its cradle, his hand still on the receiver. Today would be a good day to go sailing. Way out. Where the water was the bluest and not even the land was in sight. The idea depressed him, standing there in landlocked Dallas. He was definitely going to move to the coast. Galveston. Corpus Christi. Why, maybe even San Diego. Miami. Or an *island*. Too much land around him in Texas. Too much Texas. Too much earth.

He sat back down slowly and took a yogalike cleansing sigh, imagining clear, calm blue water, then speared a spoonful of cereal, the quest once more being to get a couple of spoonfuls of cereal down before he had to leave. He had it halfway to his mouth when the phone rang again. One ring, two rings, the spoon suspended between bowl and mouth. Three. He dropped the spoon back into the bowl with a splash. "Yes!" he yelled into the phone.

"Charles."

"Hello, Lorraine," he said with a resigned sigh.

"I remember thirteen years ago, Charles. You helped put yourself through that last year of medical school donating. It was our first big fight."

"First? How can you remember back through so many memorable ones?" Dr. Youngblood dropped his voice. "Don't worry. There are no files to prove anything. I called our lawyer and revised my will. No 'offspring' of mine by anyone but *you* can receive more than one dollar from my estate, just in case of the wild possibility that . . ."

"It better be, Charles. You can't do this to me and Charlie."

★ ★ ★

At the Motel 9, Wanda had just finished her lunge for the clunky phone and had gotten an earful of dial tone. She fell back on the bed. "Damdamdam, Granny! Why didn't you answer it?"

"Watch your mouth, young lady," scolded the old woman. "Phones are rude. Now show me what you're hiding under your shirt."

Wanda slowly pulled the paper from under her shirt and handed it to her.

Her grandmother eyed her, then eyed the paper. "Hmph. The newspaper." Shuffling around Wild Thing, already asleep in the middle of the room, she took the reading material into the bathroom for her morning constitutional.

Wanda sat down on the floor beside Wild Thing and waited for it.

A minute passed, then two. Back open came the bathroom door, and Wild Thing came to doggy attention as a very ungrannylike granny came waddling out with big cotton panties around her ankles, eyes big as dinner dishes. Then the shrieking began.

"Oh no oh no oh no no no!" she cried.

"Oh rorr rorrr rorrrr!" Wild Thing howled an octave higher.

It continued long enough that Wanda began to worry. Granny's eyes scared her. They were glassy, unfocused, terrified. Wanda took a deep breath, helped the old woman back into her panties and straightened her nightgown, waving a whining, sniffing Wild Thing away. "It's no big deal, Granny, I promise!"

"Harley will find me now!" Granny cried.

*Huh?* Wanda thought.

"He'll drag me off to that rest home! I'll die first. I'll just go ahead and be with God and Johnny."

Wanda felt a rawness in her belly as she watched her granny act so nutty, more nutty than she'd ever seen. It was getting worse. "Granny, I never saw the guy read a paper; hell, I never saw him read, period."

Granny wasn't listening. "Harley will laugh his fool head off when he sees you telling the world his stinking lie. And then he'll take everything away from us!"

"That'll be a neat trick, Granny, since we don't have anything." Wanda got her big granny into a sitting position on the edge of the bed and tried to get her to focus her eyes. "Harley's not going to find us."

And then snapping back from wherever she'd gone for that stablike moment, Granny did focus those eyes, right on Wanda: "Well, it ain't any better for you, sister. You shot him, you know."

Wanda hadn't thought of that. The law reads the paper. She had a sudden vision of roadblocks and the lone College Mound policeman, gun raised and pointed like ol' John Wayne.

"It's just like my dream," her grandmother was murmuring. "We lived by a pond with ducks and catfish and two nice swans. And Harley's there with people in white. Digging up my yard and my house and the cemetery tree and running off the swans. Going after my treasure."

"Calm down, Granny," Wanda whispered. "Please?" *Please, please, please,* she thought. Picturing the county sheriff standing in front of that roadblock on Highway 80, Wanda hesitated, then added: "It's okay. We . . . just can't go home for a while."

"We got to go home before Harley steals everything! Got to! Got to!"

The phone rang again. Making sure her grandmother was balanced on the edge of the bed before letting go, she grabbed for it. "HELLO!"

"Hello, is this Miss Wanda Louise Ledbetter whose story was in the paper today?" The voice was squeaky, cracked and muffled. Wanda got a mental picture of someone holding a handkerchief over the receiver, spy-movie style. "Hello?" it repeated.

Wanda stood up straight. "Who wants to know?"

"You don't need to know my name. I think I have information that you'll want."

Wanda's eyebrows went up, then one curved down. "Hey. Who is this?"

"I'll meet you at the Denny's around the corner. You take a lovely picture." The phone clicked silent.

Wanda was suddenly very worried. How did she know where they were staying? She turned back to her paranoid granny, who was sitting on the bed now, rubbing something ferociously around and around in her hand. "Wanda Louise? We can't stay here anymore. Harley's coming and those Messicans next door, they . . ."

Wanda reached out and grabbed both the old hands in hers. "Granny, I've got to go for a little while first, okay? I'm going to lock the door behind me. Wild Thing will chew Harley's butt off and enjoy it, okay? Okay?"

"I've got to go, Wanda Louise! Oh, sweet dear Jesus mine!"

"Take a nap or something, okay?" Wanda begged. "Then I promise we'll go home and by the cemetery, okay?"

Granny hadn't heard a thing Wanda had said, now that she was off in the other place where Wanda knew she could not follow. And that made Wanda feel pain in a place deeper than blood and bone. She squeezed Granny's hands tight, and at her touch, her grandmother's old hand opened, palm up, to show a coin: a buffalo nickel.

Wanda gaped: *Holy moly shit*—she'd found one. The last time Granny had found a buffalo nickel Wanda still had a piggy bank and pigtails. She just closed Granny's hand back around it and lectured her again until she lay down on the bed. Then Wanda touched Wild Thing softly on her big snoozing yellow head and eased out the door.

# Chapter 9

"They're waiting on it, boy. I'll be back in five minutes."

*Charles Allen Youngblood paced in the empty examining room with the magazine and the glass vial Dr. Roddy had just shoved in his hands. He wanted to leave, to forget the whole thing.*

*But he was going to be late for class.*

*So he unzipped his pants, reached in and . . .*

*. . . the elevator doors whooshed open.*

Dr. Charles A. Youngblood, standing alone in the hallway, smoothed his hair, straightened his tie and pulled himself out of the thoroughly unpleasant memory with a reflex check of his fly. He stepped onto the empty elevator. When the doors had all but closed, he remembered to punch the basement button.

When the doors whooshed open again, several hundred feet lower, he stepped off warily. He'd just spent the last thirty minutes trying to get his computer to access files from 1989, and all it would do was direct him to Room 2 in Records. A quick call told him that Records had no idea where Room 2 was, that all precomputer files were held in the basement. Perhaps in Room 2.

Well, there wasn't a Room 2. There weren't any rooms at all, from what he could see. The place was just one big gloomy warehouse space with filing cabinets from here to there, lit only with sporadic fluorescence. He straightened his tie again, then edged over to the first row of filing cabinets and began checking for some clue. Soon he realized you had to find the right department, then you had to find the right year, then you had to find the right doctor . . . He quickened his pace. He didn't have time for this.

When he finally found all three in the same place, he felt a sort of dark triumph, yanked at the filing cabinet drawer—and cut his forefinger wide open on its metal edge. With a loud curse, he stuck the bleeding digit into his mouth and looked around to see if anyone had heard. Then using his intact hand, he flipped quickly through the offending drawer to the place where Dr. Roddy's gynecological files from thirteen years ago should be.

There. Good.

ABCDEFGHIJK L Lanier, LaRue, Langley, Lidle.

He backed up. Looked again where Ledbetter should be. Then flipped ahead. Loman. Lyon . . . Nothing.

He backed up again. Taking his bleeding finger out of his mouth, he began searching with both hands. It should be here. If the woman was a patient, it had to be here. These were hospital files, not personal ones. And the hospital had records of every procedure—*that* was policy. He waved the stinging finger in the air, then had to put it back into his mouth for another suck; he was getting blood on the manila folders.

"What are you doin' there?"

Dr. Youngblood got up so quickly he made himself dizzy. He was being eyed by an bony old black man in an industrial gray uniform with an annoying number of jangling keys hanging from his belt. Standing up as tall as he could, he automatically straightened his tie once more, getting blood from his finger on his white collar. "I'm Dr. Charles Youngblood, Reproductive Endocrinology. And who are you?"

"Nasty cut," the man grunted, rolling a pair of catfish eyes over the doctor. "You just got blood on that expensive 100 percent pinpoint oxford cotton you got there. Ain't ever going to come out. Let me get you a Band-Aid."

Holding a thumb over the cut, Dr. Youngblood adjusted his glasses. "No, no. I'm going straight back to my office. I was just looking for an errant file."

The old man whipped out a Band-Aid from his back pocket. Dr. Youngblood looked at him oddly; the old man shrugged. "Happens a lot down here. I could spend my day filing down the sharp corners of these old cabinets." He had stripped the paper from the Band-Aid and was now holding it up for the doctor to take.

Dr. Youngblood put the Band-Aid over the small gash and pressed. "There seem to be some files missing from thirteen years ago. Gynecological. Would they be somewhere else?"

"You're standing at it. But since they don't put this old stuff on computer, what do you expect? A piece of paper can be just about anywhere, right, Doc?"

Dr. Youngblood applied more pressure to the bandage. Then, mumbling a thanks, he backed away from the old man and vanished up the elevator.

The old man, without looking, shoved the filing cabinet shut with a kick, then ambled back into the shadows to the music of jingling keys.

★ ★ ★

The breakfast rush had just about died down at the Denny's around the corner from the Motel 9, so the waitresses in their parlor-maid uniforms had had plenty of time in the last twenty minutes to chew over the pale, hollow-cheeked, chicken-necked, black-coiffed, dark-glassed woman in black sitting in the far booth, her back against the wall.

"Would you get a load of her," one of them whispered, hand on a hip.

"I hadn't seen makeup that thick since my mama used to put Max Factor pancake powder on with a shovel," said another. "What's with the glasses? She blind?"

"Naaah."

"The cape is nice. I heard they were coming back in style."

"It's ninety-eight degrees outside, Velma."

"Maybe she's a celebrity."

Another waitress sniggered. "Right. Mel Gibson left me a ten-spot just this morning."

"You know who she looks like?" one of them decided. "Cher."

"Yeah. Back in the Sonny days."

"But Cher wouldn't be caught dead in those clothes."

"What do you think, Lola? She's your customer."

Lola plopped down an order pad and straightened her apron with a little jiggle twist of her hips. "I think if Cher doesn't order something soon, I'm getting the manager. If she just wants water, there's a garden hose out back."

Just then, Wanda Ledbetter eased inside the glass doors and looked around. She noticed the gaggle of waitresses staring at a woman in the far corner booth—a weird, chicken-necked woman in black, wearing big, dark, wraparound sunglasses . . . who was waving at her.

Wanda wanted to leave. She leaned back against the glass doors and swallowed, fighting the urge to run. But she had to know, she had to. So she forced herself toward the weirdo woman, scooting to the booth as quickly and as inconspicuously as possible considering that everyone in the place had at least one eyeball attached to her back. Once there, though, she couldn't make herself sit down; she just stopped in front of the table, staring at the woman's brown eyebrows above the black sunglasses. Then taking a big breath, she stuck out her jaw and forced herself mean all over, too mean to live.

"Wanda Louise Ledbetter," the woman whispered.

Wanda stiffened. "Who the piss are you, anyway?"

The woman eased back into the rolled vinyl booth, patting the seat beside her. "I'm the one with your future in my hands."

Wanda didn't move.

"Sit down, darling. You're attracting attention."

*Me?* thought Wanda. But she sat down—on the opposite edge.

The woman smiled knowingly, like some juiced Cheshire Cat, Wanda thought. And she had lipstick on her front tooth.

The woman dropped her voice dramatically. "I represent a group who call themselves . . . the Sperm Warriors."

Wanda didn't respond.

So the woman repeated herself: "Sperm Warriors, like Greenpeace. The Rainbow Warriors? Much better model than the pro-lifers, don't you think? Image is all," she explained, nudging her big black hair a little to the left.

"That's a wig, isn't it?" Wanda said.

The woman rearranged its long locks over her bust. "It's a disguise, darling. All of it is, the glasses, the cape, the leotards, even the padded bra. Tomorrow no one will remember anything but how odd and black-clad I was—the covert principle being reverse invisibility, you know." She scrunched up her pointed nose. "It's better for both of us if you don't recognize me and I can go on with my underground but increasingly important activities."

Wanda blew out a sigh. *I should check myself for weirdo magnets,* she thought.

"Now, Miss Wanda Louise Ledbetter of mobile-home College Mound, Texas."

Wanda did not like the sound of that at all. "You know something or not? If not, I'm outta here."

"We Sperm Warriors are all just like you, Wanda Ledbetter—donor offspring. And we have banded loosely together to help others who find out they're donor children. Do you want to know why?"

"No."

The woman paused dramatically. "Because it's all but impossible to uncover your biological father in this country once you find out the Big Secret. The rights of the parents and the rights of the donor, *ha!*" The woman pounded the table; Wanda levitated. "What about *our* rights, little sister? Genes are forever!"

*I'm not your sister,* Wanda thought to herself.

"Ah, but we *could be* sisters."

Wanda's head snapped up.

The woman in black smiled beatifically. "Who knows? That is just the point. I could be, we all could be related and we'd never know."

Wanda looked at the woman as if her head had rotated backward, but made very sure she wasn't thinking it. The woman straightened the shoulder pads under her cape and began to rummage through the big, black leatherette bag on the seat beside her. "I'm here, Wanda Ledbetter, because we saw your story in the paper and have sent it across the nation to inspire others to go public to force the issue into the open." She pulled out a crumpled brown sack, then set it aside.

Lola the waitress swung up to the table. "Will you be ordering anything now?"

The woman in black threw her hand over the bundle as if guarding it from the waitress's eyes. "Just bring more water. Maybe with just a pinch of lemon to soften the awful tap taste." The woman sniffed righteously.

Lola snorted. "Well, how 'bout you, precious?"

Wanda realized the waitress was talking to her. "A Dr. Pepper," she mumbled.

"Now, where were we, darling?" said the woman in black.

Eyeing the sack, Wanda eased her hand into her front pocket and closed her fingers gently around her stolen sperm vial. "You know who my daddy is or not?"

"Probably."

Wanda froze. She hadn't expected that.

"You and I, Wanda Ledbetter, we're legally illegitimate. Of course, who cares about that anymore?" The woman shook her black fake head tragically, then pulled a piece of paper from inside her cape. Wanda's eyes went to it. "Except the courts. Mothers filing paternity suits against doctors when no-good husbands run off; offspring falling in love with somebody who turns out to be a half-sibling. Now, that's a heartbreaker." The woman shook her head again. The wig wiggled. Her hand tightened around the piece of paper; Wanda squirmed, her eyes now stapled to it.

"Of course, to be fair . . . in the case of hereditary diseases, some offspring are tickled purple to know they're donor babies. But it's *not* like adopting. Oh no. Not unless you tell the child from the beginning." She sniffed, dabbing at the sweat under her fake bangs. "And do you want to know who's *really* to blame, Wanda Ledbetter?"

Wanda shot the weirdo woman the evil eye.

She waved the paper-stuffed fist at Wanda. "We are—all of us! Our raping of the environment is polluting the sperm count out there and it's going to get worse—50 percent it's down in the last fifty years! Steroids in the meat, pesticides in the fruit, toxicity in the air!"

Wanda felt a sick warmth flowing over her body, her cheeks flushing, her head dizzy. She pulled her hand out of her pocket and started worrying her paper placemat, tugging at the meanness, trying hard to find it and pull it back over her.

"Secrets, secrets. Women want to shop for sperm like they shop for shoes." The woman wagged a maroon fingernail at Wanda. "I mean, who can keep a secret like that for life? Please! I can't even keep Christmas presents a secret till the end of December!" She paused. "Am I telling you too much too quickly, darling?"

"I just want to know about my daddy!" Wanda spat out. But the woman was talking again. Wanda, though, wasn't catching it, her babbling nothing more than sound now in Wanda's ears. Her insides were tingling. Little black lines were forming in front of her eyes. She closed them; the lines turned white.

"Oh, poor dear. This is all too much for you. I do go on."

Wanda opened her eyes, sat up straight and forced the meanness into her jaw, jutting it way out. But she couldn't quite get the sassy remark off her tongue and out her lips.

The woman glanced down at the paper in her hand as if just remembering it and dropped the sweaty scrap of paper on Wanda's ruined placemat.

Tingling now all over, Wanda touched the damp scrap by its edges and began to open it slowly.

Inside was scrawled a man's name.

The two sat in silence, a pregnant pause floating between them, Wanda staring at the paper, the woman savoring the drama. And when the woman started up again, it was in a voice full of pomp and drama:

"If you were conceived thirteen years ago at Parkland Hospital, Miss Wanda Ledbetter, then we think your daddy is a man named Dr. Harold Linus Roddy, well-known to us because he was the original doctor daddy here in Texas. However, Harold Linus Roddy was a boozer with a deep need to perform, so to speak. Unable to turn down a patient but also unable to remember how many he'd inseminated with his own sperm, he just kept right on . . ."

Lola came strolling back up at that moment, and the jaws of the woman in black clamped shut. Lola plopped the drinks down along with the bill. "One Dr. Pepper, one tap water with lemon."

When Lola was out of earshot, the Sperm Warrior started up exactly where she left off: ". . . Resulting in what we have estimated to be over sixty possible children born from thirty years of inseminating his 'sweet girls,' which is what he called his female infertility patients, if that patronizing sexism doesn't make you want to urp your muffins. I mean who'd the old reprobate think he was—Methuselah replenishing the earth? Only when he got too old did he begin paying medical students to help the cause. It's highly possible you're one of his progeny. The bad news is he's dead as a dirt clod and his personal files have disappeared." She gave her black synthetic locks a frustrated stroke.

Wanda's eyes were soaking in the handwritten name. The scribble. Black letters shaping a man, a daddy, in her head.

*Dr. H. L. Roddy.* Doctor daddy. Dead doctor daddy.

Wanda felt as if she might vomit; the raw heat turned sideways. "Was he double-jointed?" she mumbled.

The woman in black leaned across the table, down to business: "Now listen, dear little Wanda. Here's our advice: First thing you got to do *before anything* is find some proof that your mama underwent assisted reproduction via donor at Parkland. That you can do by going to the storage files in the basement of the hospital. The hospital files, of the procedures themselves, can't be destroyed, and there should be some paperwork to prove the insemination even without his records. We'd do it for you, but you have a better chance by yourself. If you do find anything, then you give it to us or that reporter. And we can all play detective. But first," she was suddenly whispering, "if you find your mother's insemination file, look for this one clue to whether Dr. Roddy was your donor. Look for a little mark, a happy face—his own personal sperm mark—in the right-hand corner on her last insemination. If it's there—he's your daddy."

Ceremoniously, the woman placed the brown paper bundle she'd been guarding in front of Wanda. "Here's a candy-striper outfit. Wear it down to the basement like you're on an errand of mercy. Which you are—for yourself, Wanda Ledbetter of College Mound, Texas." Wanda closed her fist around the piece of paper in her palm and focused on the sack. "You find anything, you wave it in their faces. And if you got a happy face, at least you'll know. If not, well, you'll be like the rest of us, still searching for the jerk who jerked off for pocket change to make us." The woman's voice dropped. "Or learning how to stop searching."

The woman seemed spent, sagging back against the booth. Then, reaching an arm across the table, she placed several of those maroon-nailed fingers on Wanda's hand. "You always have us, darling, if you want us. Second Tuesday of each month, number's on this sack. Now, I'm late for my protest rally."

The caped woman got to her feet, whisked the cape over a shoulder, pulled her black bag under her arm and took a few steps. Then, looking back at Wanda, she arched a brown eyebrow. "I know what you're thinking."

Wanda gazed at the goofy woman.

The woman took a step back toward Wanda. "That I'm a bit strange." She grinned. "Well—that's what happens when you don't know where your sperm's been. Ha! Just a little donor offspring humor. Good luck, little brave sister. We'll be watching."

Wanda dropped her eyes. She didn't watch the woman in black rush across the restaurant. Or slide out the door. Or vanish down the street. She couldn't take her eyes off the sack.

"Hey, precious." Lola came up close. "You all right? That woman hurt you? I can call a cop."

The wet pressure behind Wanda's eyeballs was there again, hard. Way too hard. She pushed it back with every last drop of meanness she could muster. And jumped up and ran out the door.

★ ★ ★

Just then, around the corner, Patty Hightower raised her fist to knock on the door at the Motel 9.

"Who's there?" a creaky voice demanded before she touched the door.

Patty paused, fist in the air.

"I said, who's there! I got a gun!"

Patty froze, her eyes popping wide: *Gun?* She scooted out of the line of fire. "It's Patty Hightower, Granny! I bought you breakfast at the hospital. No one answered when I called and I was on my way to the hospital so I . . ."

The door slowly swung wide. In Granny's hand was a loaded newspaper. Patty breathed again as Wild Thing came out wagging her tail, recognizing this woman whose ankles smelled of cat.

"Wanda Louise said she'd be back soon and we'd go to the cemetery," the old woman announced, lowering the newspaper.

The grandmother was a mess. She had on one house shoe and one sandal. Her face was haggard, her clothes askew. And gone from her eyes was the sharp glint Patty had noticed there yesterday. "Harley could come. He might have seen the paper and he could come. It's just like my dream. He kills the swans and digs up my house and my tree with people in white all around, then hauls me off to the rest home. But I'm dying first."

Patty rested a hand on the woman's forearm. "Nobody's going to hurt you."

"Are you selling farm eggs? My chickens are off today."

Patty suddenly noticed the gun on the bed. A real gun. She did not like guns. She didn't even like fake guns. Smiling warily at the old woman, she took a step back toward the door, but then stopped herself. The old woman thought she was selling farm eggs, and she'd hate herself if something bad happened. So steeling herself, Patty asked, "Granny, is that loaded?" She pointed gingerly over the big woman's shoulder to the rifle lying peacefully on the flowered bedspread.

"This thing?" Granny grabbed it up and popped it open, showing her its empty barrel. "Naw. Shells are on the back porch. You think I'm crazy? You tell Wanda Louise it's time to go now."

Patty squeezed the old lady's forearm again, making sure not to touch the rifle. And with a promise to be back soon to check on her, she stepped over Wild Thing, who was back asleep in the middle of the floor, and descended to the parking lot full of big trucks, souped-up, broken-down Chevys and Fords, and one junker convertible Cadillac. She stood a moment beside it, glancing back up at Room 211. Then she got in her BMW and aimed it away, toward the hospital.

# Chapter 10

*Wild Greylag Geese mate for life. The male squawks*
*and preens, the female joining in the dance,*
*stretching necks to the sky, a ritual bonding them*
*together against the dangers of living.*

—Wonderful World of Biology

Wanda's grandmother didn't notice the red light she'd just run. Nor the curb she drove over, nor the way the cars around her were parting like she was Moses and they were the Red Sea. She was thinking about more important things. Things that couldn't wait for a thirteen-year-old to quit running around and keep her promises. She was thinking about Harley and rest homes and swans and Johnny and the Poetry Cemetery. That's why she had to go. Had to get to the tree. She'd seen Harley in that dream as clear as day, and he was up to no good. She had to check her treasure. It'd been too, too long. She'd spent the morning worrying herself into a tizzy, even going so far as getting the .22 out of the Caddy where she saw Wanda hide it. And after that hospital egg woman had pounded on her door, well, she couldn't stand the worry one second longer. She'd gone looking for the back porch where she always kept the bullets for the .22. And when she couldn't quite find the back porch in the motel room, it was too much. Who took the back porch? Harley? No, no, she had to go. Had to go now!

So she grabbed her big purse and the big dog, left the motel door swinging wide and climbed in under the Caddy ragtop's flapping smile of a tear.

And off they went. She and Wild Thing were cruising down the blacktop, wind so wild that Granny's beauty shop cotton-candy hairdo was whipped in a glob onto the side of her head and Wild Thing's jowls were flapping whether she stuck her doggie head out the rip or sat listening to the sound of Granny's voice yelling over the whistling blast.

"And another thing, I ain't going to no rest home. I ain't ready to do any resting," she was hollering. "Rest homes. Might as well call 'em waiting homes, parking lots for undertaking parlors, 'cause nobody comes out of 'em alive. Church women visiting, talking to you like you lost all good sense. Dragging in those snotty-nose Sunday school kids to sing off-key, like you've gone tone deaf, too. Thinking you're so far gone they've made your day. Huh." She jerked her head over at Wild Thing. "You hear that, Harley!" Wild Thing perked up. "And another thing, you better not have touched that tree or those swans! And the joke's on you! They're geese, you dumb peckerwood, they ain't swans! You listening?" Wild Thing's good ear stood up. "I'm packing heat, Harley. Don't tempt me, now. *Oh* yeah. You ain't messing with me." She turned toward Wild Thing and punched the air with a pudgy finger, swerving across the road. "You hear me, you dimestore devil! I'm on to you!"

Tongue hanging out long enough to be blown back onto her jowl, Wild Thing watched Granny gyrate and grumble, liking the rumbling sound so much that she joined in. Growling and whining and whimpering happily, she plunked her paws on the Cadillac's armrest and poked her nose through the hole in the ragtop, sniffing at the passing smells. There was always something interesting blowing by, when the winds were blowing this fierce.

And so the two rode south, back along the wide Texas highway, Granny steering steady and focused now—a woman on a mission. Until finally, this side of Waco, the Caddy and the woman and the dog cut off the highway onto a country road leading down the Brazos River, and in a few minutes they skidded to a dusty halt. They had landed halfway up the yard of a run-down, boarded-up church standing sentry before a patchwork cemetery: a cow pasture of graves framed by four large, drooping trees someone had planted in each corner of a quiet, stone-surrounded acreage a century ago.

But Granny didn't see the boards on the once-white clapboard church. And she didn't see the way the trees were drooping past their prime, or how badly the little cemetery needed a good country cemetery cleaning. She rose from the Cadillac seat seeing bright stained glass illuminated from within the church, and beyond, a revival tent pitched in the pasture near the farm pond full of ducks and geese and snakes. She felt Johnny Ledbetter's rough cowboy hand in hers, steering her around the snaky bank in the dark. And she felt the cool of the evening after everyone had gone, the warm rush that good, loud, pulpit-pounding preaching stirred in her and the hot flush that having handsome Johnny Ledbetter so near thrilled through her ... That night, the night before he left, a lifetime too soon.

But he was there now. She saw him, oh she saw him, smiling down.

"You in that army uniform, Johnny Ledbetter," she murmured up to him, "proud as a peacock." He had walked her through the cemetery in the warm night, as the last of the cars, headlights streaming, pulled away from the place, and it was as if he was also gone. And she could not bear it. Granny sighed and smiled as sad and sweet as forbidden fruit.

Until she remembered how with a laugh, in that grumbling preacher clown-frown, Johnny Ledbetter had begun that song, that Song of Solomon that they would read during church when no one was looking, reading enough to know by heart. "Scripture flowing from those big lips of yours as if you'd swallowed the whole book of the Bible," she said out loud. "Remember, Johnny? Remember?"

*Yes, Gladys,* Johnny answered, *I remember.*

And before her eyes, she saw herself still holding his hand, moving through the churchyard, past the marble markers, toward the cemetery tree—hearing on the lazy night air his sweet mocking false bass voice:

*Come! ARISE! Oh princess of Lebanon!* he commanded, and she laughingly obeyed. *Come! Beautiful princess! My fair one, my dove. How beautiful are thy feet in shoes. Kiss me with the kisses of thy mouth; thy love is better than wine. Thy lips are like a scarlet thread and thy mouth is lovely. With one jewel of thy necklace thou hast ravished my heart—*

And she remembered the pause, the power of the words to change his voice in the dark enough to make her blush as he repeated, now quieter—*thou hast ravished my heart. Thou hast made my heart beat faster with a single glance of thine eyes* . . . the rumble now dying down to a murmur, a melting, halting: *The curves of thy hips are like jewels, thy lips, milk and honey* . . . And the deep voice was once again enveloping her, entering her. As they leaned back against the hollow of the tree, she heard him repeat the sacred words as if hearing them for the very first time, his voice like fingers shallow on her neck singing on and on the power of Solomon's song:

*Thy kisses are like wine that goes down smoothly. Thy breasts are like clusters. A garden locked art thou, oh princess, a spring sealed up. Let my left hand be under thy head and my right hand embrace thee* . . . *my fair one* . . . *my beautiful one* . . .

Hushed in the shadow, she could see him sadly sigh and then finish with a whisper more mellow than molasses, *My beloved one* . . . And then, his big cow-herding hands surrounding her waist, she could feel him slowly, gently press his face, his chest, his body against hers, against her treasured tree and the nearby cool of the marble. And she could not remember if the next words of her memory came from her beloved's lips or from her years of rereading the Song of King Solomon, chapter and verse. But that afternoon, standing there in the sun a half-century later, she heard them come from his whispering young mouth as they moved against the tree and against the stone *in the secret place of the steep pathway* . . . his words soft as a breeze, under the night camouflage of the branches. *Let us go early into the vineyard. And there I will give thee my love. Open to me, my bride, my dove, my beloved, my perfect one—oh, let me see thy form.*

*Hurry.* Hurry. HurryHurry

And from Granny's old lips rolled the rest of Scripture she'd locked away long ago:

"'I open to my beloved; oh my beloved, for thee.'"

Under the hot summer sun, Granny moved across the old cemetery to the tree as through a dark dream, the big ranch hand warm in hers, murmuring, "There, Johnny Ledbetter, there." Her summer dress had slipped down and they had moved together, moved and moved and moved under the moon and the swish of the leaves, and she felt the heat of his breath on her neck and she had stretched it wide to catch it all. She felt his slender hips pressing near and her heart beat faster with a single glance of his eyes, as with his left hand under her head and his right hand embracing her, he had embraced slowly, slowly all of her. "Over me, beside me, inside me. Near. Dear Lord, near to touch souls," she murmured. "We slipped together that moment, open to each other, and then you were never gone from me, through everything. You were there, sweet Johnny, my sweet Song."

*Hurry my beloved. And be like a young stag. Put me like a seal over your heart. For love is as strong as death.*

Wanda's grandmother reached out and touched the tree near the stone fence, the old tree, so alive and vibrant still, then turned back to Johnny and leaned to kiss him, to hold him to her.

Growling, Wild Thing bolted away and plopped down a few feet from where Granny stood, then cocked her head curiously back at the old woman. That is, until the yellow dog caught a new smell in the air and in herself. It was clear and heavy and unmistakable, and written in her doggy being. A call. And without a look back, she was up on all fours and trotting high-tailed away, toward the irresistible male scent coming fast her way.

As Wild Thing vanished into the trees, a moment of lucidity came over Granny.

With a sliver of staggering clear-headedness, she saw she'd just kissed the dog. Then she turned those clear eyes on the tree and saw that her beloved tree with the deep hollow and the sweet vibrant branches was dead. And she reeled against it, reeled slow and sad, her eyes closing against the blinding sliver of truth as she slid down to its gnarled roots, her hands over her face, her mind reaching back for Solomon's Song sung by her Johnny.

Oh sweet Lord. Where was she? What was happening? She looked down at her hands, rough, liver-spotted, wrinkled. Whose old hands were these? She saw the years rush in on her and remembered the living that had made them so. And yet these memories, here, under this tree, these were still so much with her . . . such stunning remembrance over all others, perhaps most cruel. She squeezed those ruined hands to her breast, then stretched them out, trying to reach far back, oh, come back, please.

And then they were clutching her chest as her heart jumped, slowed, then jumped again. A pain.

And there, from a long way away, came the faint answer of a sweet deep voice: *It goes down smoothly for my beloved . . .*

*Flowing gently through the lips of those who fall asleep.*

*Hurry, my beloved. Hurry . . .*

*For love.*

*Love is as strong as death.*

# Chapter 11

The stick tree wasn't much shade. But since it was the only living thing between here and there—here being the parking lot and there being the hospital's side door—Wanda Ledbetter found herself standing under it after walking the half-mile from the Denny's, shifting her weight back and forth, one boot to the other, both hands clutching the weird woman's brown paper bag. She had rolled its top up and down so many times it was in shreds, she was thinking so hard.

*Dear Daddy . . .* she thought.

*Dear Daddy, it could be like this, see. You went to pick up your baby. And it was switched. Years later you find out your daughter is not really your daughter, but that I am.*

*Or maybe there was a terrible accident. I got lost in the woods. A kindly farmer found me and raised me. Yeah.*

*I'd be like that. That's all—not like her. I'm not a piece of weirdness. I'm not going to end up wearing wigs of the stars. Promise. So if you're dead, well, okay. But if you're not . . .*

She opened the tattered top of the paper sack again and looked at the striped jumper she would normally not be caught eaten by wild dogs in. But this time she pulled it out, yanked it over her head, smoothed it over her own clothes, and looked down. The thing hung off her like a potato sack. *Great,* she fumed. *Just great.* Good thing Dubby Mayhew couldn't see her now; she'd never live it down. She took a deep resolute breath. *Dear Daddy, here I come.* And she took off toward the door.

★ ★ ★

Across the parking lot, Nurse Stella Peabody had just pulled her Oldsmobile sedan into a parking space, turned off the key and picked up the morning newspaper from the seat beside her. As the air conditioning dissipated in her closed-up interior there away from the elements, from the world, the prim woman straightened her bright white uniform's collar, then adjusted her glasses to look once again at the picture of the girl she'd seen in Dr. Youngblood's office yesterday, this Wanda Ledbetter. The child's sweet, troubled face made her flush with unwanted feeling, remembering.

Like echoes, she heard her own long-ago words: "Dr. Roddy, I don't feel quite right about this."

"Now, Stella, not to worry. It's just semen, after all."

"I just feel I should express my reservations."

"Just sperm, my dear."

Then she heard the words she didn't say, the ones she tried to say: *Just sperm? That sperm is you, Dr. Roddy. That sperm is old as the earth, part of creation, part of an ongoing, undeniable link. You are part of all you create now and forever. Don't men know that?*

"Doctor, what I'm trying to say is . . ."

"Now, now, Stella. Trust me. What else can I do? I must help these sweet girls. A married woman must have a child, mustn't she? You must promise to keep these a secret, dear. For them. We are doing good."

The nurse felt an old burning in her heart. It had not diminished with the years. Things had changed at the speed of rockets all around her, but not that feeling. The inside of her Olds was growing saunalike in the reflected Texas sun, and her upper lip had begun to perspire. She dabbed at it and caught a glimpse of herself in the windshield's bright morning-light reflection. Her face was gray, even with the new Mary Kay makeup her neighbor was now selling. Goodness, how silly—why had she bothered? She had always felt old. One of those women relieved to reach middle age. She was comfortable with her life now, after all these many years: her life of service, her service her life.

That life had always been here at Parkland, and for most of those years, before the hospital had grown so large, so high-tech, so impersonal, it had been with him. Years so wonderfully warm, structured, predictable, secure, and then

. . . Only when she had begun to cover so much for him, so much at the end, did she wonder if she'd done the right thing.

*But—I did!* She argued with her reflection. He was a fine man! A kind, generous, loving doctor—the kind she'd become a nurse to serve. The old-fashioned, dearly dedicated kind who felt responsible for all his patients as if they were family, who was with you in birth and in death, who knew your name, your parents' names, your childr . . . Stella stopped, biting the word off. It wasn't his fault, his weakness. Alcoholism is a disease; they've proven that. He *was* a fine man. They don't make them like him anymore. He cared so much. Too much.

She put her hand up to the burning she felt in her own heart, then gazed down at Wanda's newspaper photo. *Why can't things be simple again? Why are things today so odd, so foreign? Like that business there in the front of the hospital, for example.* She sighed sadly, gazing at the far-off scene: All those people there making noise, carrying poorly lettered signs and making nuisances of themselves, why, even yelling offensive things at a person like herself they don't even know, who's given her whole life to helping people. *And oh, my goodness gracious,* she gasped, *looky there! Look at that candy striper across the way!* Now that is something she just could not understand. Parkland's candy stripers had been such good girls, always smiling with an encouraging word. But today's girls are so unusual that she just felt confused. Good girls with their piercings up one side and down the other? With little rose tattoos on their ankles and goodness knows where else? Like that little candy striper over there, wearing her neat, striped jumper with a pair of dirty cowboy boots? Stella shook her graying head and felt older than she could ever remember, watching the small blond girl clomp into the hospital. Into her hospital.

*If only things were simpler,* she thought.

Things were simpler then. "They were, weren't they, Dr. Roddy?" Folding the paper neatly, she glanced back at her reflection. Then she opened the door to meet the morning heat.

★ ★ ★

" 'Brave New Wanda,' old boy!"

Griffin LaCour, who had just settled into his chair before his computer in his newspaper cubicle, felt a sharp, stinging pop on his right shoulder. He jerked around. A slick man of silver-haired age, in a suit so expensive it could have walked in on its own, settled a hip down on a corner of his desk.

"Ex*cuse* me?" grunted Griffin, irritated.

"Good show, that," said the man, rocking a loafered foot. "Royally undercovered here across the pond, this 'reprotech' area and all its ethical sinkholes. Just wanted to deliver a personal 'attaboy' as you Yanks say; thought you deserved it, Griff old boy."

"'Brave New *Wanda*'?" Griffin scowled.

The man framed the air with his hands, moving left to right. "'Brave New Wanda.' That's our series headline. There will be a series, eh?"

Griffin tried not to rub his shoulder. "Well . . ."

The man waved Griffin's objections away. "Think of the possibilities, LaCour (French descendance, is it?)" The man leaned closer. Griffin got a noseful of his cologne. "Our Brave New Wanda finds her biological father and presses for the rest of the secret records, for how many other times the bloke donated, eh? Then you count up how many little pooper siblings she has, and Brave New Wanda has herself a Brave New Family, see it? We cover the reunion, the legal chaos. The possibilities are endless, Griffith! We'll have more attention than you can shake a twig at."

"Stick," Griffin muttered. "And it's Griffin."

The man's hands were shaping headlines again:

"SPERM BANKING: Choosing Children from a Catalog.

"THE SECRET—Those Who Couldn't Keep It.

"SURROGATING—Do Rich Exploit Poor for Use of Wombs?

"GENETIC SCREENING—Would You Flush an Embryo If You Knew It Would Be Crippled, Blind, Ugly?

"EMBRYO BANKS—Freeze-Dry Your Family for the Future.

"CLONING—How Long Till There'll Be Another You?

"Connect that with these screaming abortion types and watch the show, eh? Big as Texas, Griffith. We'll grab these dogies by the horns and wrassle 'em to the ground, eh? Head 'em up, move 'em out! Rawhide!"

*Oh yeah, eeee-haw,* Griffin thought, unable to decide whether this guy was being insulting or just stupid.

The Brit was on his feet and already stepping away, but not before he popped Griffin yet again on the shoulder. "I sniff Pulitzer land. By the by, I've alerted my people about Brave New Wanda." He winked. "Media consultants, you know."

Griffin looked confused. "What are you talking about? We're the media."

"It's a new age, old boy."

Griffin leaned over his desk. "You mean. . . ." He stopped to make a putrid-smell face. *"Public relations?"*

The Brit flashed a smile that made Griffin think of pacts with the devil. "Ring me when you've got today's 'Brave New Wanda' copy, eh?" And with another attaboy pop on the back, he disappeared.

Griffin rubbed his shoulder. Another reporter, young, black, and as clean-cut and starched as Griffin was rumpled, sauntered up with a fistful of messages. "Wonder where Wonder Boy got his journalism degree—Carnaby Street, what?"

Griffin gaped past the reporter. "Who *was* that guy?"

The reporter leaned on Griffin's desk. "Where've you been? That's our new editor-in-chief prophesied for so long, going to save us from that other paper across town. From the London tabloids, what I heard."

"London, my ass," Griffin said, rubbing his shoulder. "Bet he's from New Jersey."

The reporter stood up, straightening his tie. "Well, word is, if he doesn't do what he's here for, we'll all be gone. What the hell. Who reads today, anyway? I'm starting to talk in word bites myself, I swear to God." He almost forgot to hand Griffin the pile of memo notes. "Here. The receptionist asked me to throw these on your desk with the others. You're the only guy I know that turns off your voicemail. At least read the top one. It's from me. We're down a player for the game tonight and I'm working, so if you don't show up this time, they'll crucify me for recruiting your sorry heathen ass as our sub." He popped Griffin on the same shoulder and left.

Wincing, Griffin jerked his shoulder out of the line of fire. He picked up the stack of new messages: He had a softball game tonight. His cleaning had been ready for thirty days and they were no longer responsible. His last ex-wife's lawyer called. Complaints about his column were up: six death threats for "Gun Control for Joe Bob," nine death threats for "Football, the National Church of Texas," and no death threats for "Texas Debutantes, the Gaudy, the Passé and the Ugly," but the Princess Pecan of the Court of Fruit Trees has her Debs for Christ chapter praying for his soul, and the Princess Yellow Rose of the Flower Court of Tyler has the hots for him.

Griffin chucked the rest of the messages onto his desk. They landed on the morning edition, and he whisked them aside to check out his story. His eyes fixed on the photo—the scruffy kid's ponytailed, chin-up sullenness. *This didn't feel right*, he decided. The phone rang. Still staring at Wanda, he fumbled for the receiver: "Griffin LaCour, Tribune."

*"Lawrence P. Feldman here. Entertainment law. Have your 'Brave New Wanda' materials in hand. See lots of possibilities. Books. Film. Got her number?"*

Griffin's second line was beeping; he popped it on. "LaCour—Tribune."

*"Mr. LaCour, this is Dr. Y. J. Tittle of the Tittle Foundation. We are a psycho/medico/sociological research organization founded by the scion of a wealthy Ft. Worth founding family very interested in the future. Perhaps you've heard of our extensive research in developmental psychology as it relates to anthropological/environmental/eschatological pop culture phenomena?"*

"No."

*"This D.I. child you've uncovered, we believe she would be a perfect candidate for our ongoing environment versus genetics research. A few tests, a little observation. Both her and the donor father, as soon as your investigation uncovers him. And of course, there's a generous finder's fee . . ."*

"You've got to be kidding." He hung up. The phone line immediately beeped.

"LaCour—"

*"Summer Jacobs with the Sherry Berry Perry Show, New York. We've just been handed a release about your Brave New Wanda article this morning. And we have a slot open the girl would fill perfectly on next Monday's show. She'd be appearing with a San Francisco single mother and author of* Pregnancy the Turkey Baster Way. *We were hoping we could get the father to reveal himself to her on camera. Do you know how our people can contact their people?"*

"Hey, LaCour!" the reporter in the cubicle across the aisle from him was holding out his phone. "It's for you!"

Griffin clunked the receiver down on his desk, stepped over and grabbed the reporter's receiver. "What!"

It was one of the editors from the city desk: "There's a demonstration brewing out front of Parkland, probably a pro-lifer. We've got a reporter on it. But word from On High is to inform Mr. Griffin LaCour about anything over there. Consider yourself informed."

# Chapter 12

$\mathcal{S}$tuffed inside one of Parkland Hospital's elevators, Wanda tried not to squirm. A wheelchair was butting up against her knee, and a woman who looked green enough to puke was breathing on her shoulder. Somebody had fried bacon for breakfast. Somebody else had done laps in their perfume. Somebody *else* had bladder problems. *Lord, it stinks in here,* Wanda thought. She cracked her knuckles, tugged at her potato-sack jumper and tried not to breathe, imagining the disease germs surely floating all around her. She looked up. The woman in a lab jacket across from her was staring. Wanda looked away, then looked back. The woman was still staring, eyeing her up and down.

"Take a picture, it'll last longer," Wanda snapped. Now everybody else was looking at her. "Mind your own beeswax, okay?" she said to the crowd.

With each stop, the crowd thinned from around her, until finally she had the elevator to herself at the very top floor. She eased over and looked at the buttons. Considering this was only her second-ever elevator ride, her first being yesterday, it was monkey-see, monkey-do time, she told herself, as she put out her finger and hit the button marked B.

Basement?

She hit the basement before her stomach did, and while she was waiting for it, the rest of her wasn't doing so hot, either. For there, through the doors, was something right out of every slasher movie she'd ever seen (which was pretty much every one made): a very large, very dark windowless warehouse full of rows of metal filing cabinets out to yonder, lit only dimly with fluorescent lamps every few rows and quiet enough to hear your own heart thump. Which Wanda's was suddenly doing. Big time.

The doors began to close, and she jumped through them, catching her candy-striped skirt in the crack. She yanked; it ripped free and she reeled back, landing flat on her fanny.

For a second Wanda just lay there, spent. Then, grunting and rubbing her elbows where they'd hit the concrete, she pulled herself to her feet and inspected her torn skirt. *Great,* she grumbled, *just great.*

Wiping her nose with the back of her hand, she mustered her bluster and began to inch slowly into the darkness, her boots scuffing loud and lonely on the concrete floor. She roamed from one low-hanging lamp's rectangle of light to another, eyes bugged out, waiting to be grabbed by someone wearing a hockey mask. But by the time she realized she was a little lost, she wasn't thinking any longer about hockey mask spooks. Now the vision was of the Sperm Warrior woman with a mouthful of vampire teeth, black cape flowing, poised for a lunge from the inches-away dark.

Basement of the Living Dead.

That stopped her. You can be too mean to live and a vivid imagination will still get you every time. But maybe such visions of Hollywood hockey mask fiends and Sperm Warrior vampires were easier to worry about. Because way in the back of her mind Wanda knew that the ghost she was really thinking about, worrying about, trying not to see around each corner there in the dark, was her chain-smoking, trucker-loving mom.

Her not-living-dead mom.

Who was real. Who was sealed tight inside a box under the ground. Never. Never to come up again.

And with that image, an image only the daylight had kept from her thoughts, she froze, falling back against one of the cabinets, breathing big and slow. Squeezing her eyes shut, she tried not to think about the horrors of where her mama really was now—and what her mama really was now—tryed not to think at all.

But in the personal dark behind closed eyes, imagination does its most vivid work. Instantly she popped her eyes back open, socket-wide, searching the shadowed light, frantic for anything to look at, to think about it, anything, anything but her embalmed mama, low in the ground.

That's when her eyes picked up the numbers on the cabinet across from where she stood. And numbers on the one next to it. And the one next to that and on into the dark . . . numbers in order of years, departments, doctors. . . .

With a thick, hot rush she was suddenly on the trail, pumped with courage and hope and mission, forging past Draculas and chainsaws and mummified mothers. Faster and faster, she moved through the shadows. Where was it? *1985, 1986, 1987, 1988!*

There! *Gynecology, 1989.* She felt a quick gasp of triumph as she yanked at the file drawer.

And slashed her finger wide open on the metal edge.

Wanda yelped, jumping back from her attacker. With a swing of her boot, she kicked the gotdam thing shut so hard it rattled. Then she crumpled into a heap, sucking fiercely on the stinging finger, and from behind her eyeballs, the old, wet pressure came rushing up so quick there was no stopping it, not this time.

So Wanda cried. For the first time since her mother died, the tears came hard, heaving, stinging as much as her finger. And she sat rocking back and forth on the cement floor, one boot stuck out from under her jumper, as the angry, hurt, lonesome tears filled her eyes, rolled down her cheeks and stuffed up her nose. Just like they're supposed to.

"Hey! Who's there now?"

Wanda scrambled to her feet, wiping furiously at her wet face with her forearms, and tried to disappear back into the shadows. A man who jingled was coming at her. A familiar man. As dark as the place.

"Well, now, what we got here?" The man reached up and pushed the low-hanging lamp forward, spotlighting her where she stood. "Well, hi there, Sunshine."

Wanda sniffed defiantly and stuck out her jaw. "I'm not crying."

"No, you ain't crying. You're bleeding. Anybody can see that." He pulled out a Band-Aid, ripped off all its paper with long, crooked fingers and held it out. "Life's just the drizzling shits sometimes, ain't it."

Wanda didn't move.

"Reason enough to bleed any day, you ask me. Go on, take it."

She grabbed it and whipped it around the slice.

"You lost again? Boy, am I getting the visitors down here this morning. Going to have to break out a new box of Band-Aids."

The cut was stinging worse; so were her eyes. She pawed at the left-over wetness and said with a blustering snarl: "You're not going to call that ol' fat security guard or anybody, are you?"

The janitor snorted. "Now why would I do that? That man's got a B.O. problem. Takes me a day to fumigate every time he shows his lard-ass down here. It ain't as if I can open a window down here."

Wanda eyed the man and his keys and his gray uniform, inching back for a getaway.

"Where you going, Wanda Louise?"

She stiffened. "How'd you know my name?"

"You look like a Wanda, but I just don't think the Louise suits you much."

"That's what I've been telling ..." Wanda stopped herself and squinted hard at the old guy.

He put out a long, skinny arm and leaned it against a cabinet. "Guess I should be honored. I've been reading that paper from front to back every morning for forty years and I never met anybody in it."

With one little final defiant sniff, Wanda crossed her arms. "I hadn't done anything, you know."

"You looking for something in particular, Miss Wanda Ledbetter?"

"Naw, just looking around," she blustered, glancing around for the elevator. "I gotta go."

"Maybe I can help you. Come into my office over here and let's see." He began moving down the aisle, motioning back with his hand. "Come on now. I ain't going to bite."

Glancing back at the filing cabinet, she followed, slowly.

The old man was talking over his shoulder. "So, your mama *and* your daddy's dead, huh. How about a stepdaddy?"

"Shot him."

"That right." The janitor didn't even blink. "He live?"

"Unfortunately."

The janitor snickered. "I know what you mean. I got a few relations I'd like to shoot myself. Our family reunion—whooo, we could take it on the road." He entered a little closet under a heating vent. "You know, today's been nice. I don't get to talk to too many people round here. My maintenance engineer colleagues, the whole lot of them must have stopped growing brain cells about the time they started growing hair in new places. 'Course if this was TV, the distinguished elder statesmanlike African American that I am, I'd be running the place. But as it is, well, you make it through the world using the best you got. Me, I got a gift for hospitality."

Wanda stuck her head into the little closet. The janitor pulled a three-legged stool from a peg off the wall, set it in the narrow doorway and patted it as he plopped down into his own rickety chair in front of a cast-off desk.

"Now, let's get down to your business," he said.

Wanda narrowed her eyes. "What do you know about my business?"

"You rest yourself, and we'll talk about it."

Wanda eased onto the stool as the man selected a small key from his belt and inserted it into a lock on his beat-up desk. "I read the paper real early. Crack of dawn, birds still sleeping, sometimes standing there when they throw the paper." Then he pulled a file from the drawer, chunked it on the top and popped it with a knuckle. "This what you're looking for?" Wanda jumped to her feet. "I remember that Dr. Roddy. Big old white man. Lots of teeth, gummy smile. Smelled of disinfectant and alcohol, as I recall—and I don't remember it being the rubbing kind."

Wanda's eyes were glued to words on the outside of the file. *Gynecological*, it said, and: *Mrs. John Lee (Louise) Ledbetter, Jr.*

She eased over to it, touched it and then, with a glance back up at the old man, slowly opened it. Once it was open, though, she began flipping hurriedly through its pages, scanning each sheet of the official pieces of paper, wishing for something, anything she could understand. Until she found a word she knew well: "insemination." *Consultation, procedure, intrauterine needle, supplies, lab fees: Artificial Insemination—Donor. October, November, December.* And then, last: *January, 1989,* three inseminations: *1/5, 1/7, 1/8.* Holding her breath, she flipped to the next page: *Delivery,* it said. *September 9, 1989. Healthy infant girl. 9 lbs. 3 oz. Dr. Harold Linus Roddy, attending physician.*

Gripping the folder hard enough to crush it, Wanda was now rushing back through, looking closely at each page, each and every one. But there was no happy face anywhere.

"So what do you think, Wanda Ledbetter?"

Wanda didn't move.

"They must have wanted you pretty bad to go to all this trouble, don't you think?"

"They didn't want me," she mumbled. "They wanted it."

The janitor frowned at that, studying the girl's face so long the silence came back. Wanda again heard her heart beat. Thumping, bumping up her throat. She swallowed it down and, in a voice as weak as water, said: "Why do people have to let you down?"

"Ah, Sunshine," the old man answered, "it's their job. Why else would we need God?"

"I don't need God," Wanda grumbled. "I don't need anybody."

"Sure you do; you just don't know it yet."

With a rattling groan, the janitor got to his feet, closed the file and said, "Now. I'd hate to lose the high-prestige position I enjoy here at this fine hospital facility, so let's keep this to ourselves, okay? As for you, seems like you got to decide what you're going to do next. Me, I got to put that folder back in its rightful place ... here in an hour or so," he added, fussing loudly now with other papers on his desk and turning his head away several pointed times. "That *is*, I suppose, if it's still on my desk."

A little dazed, Wanda finally understood, reached for the file, lifted her jumper and stuffed it inside the waist of her jeans. She looked back at the janitor, started to say something but wasn't quite sure what. This man was not the same kind of old as her grandmother. She was pretty sure she liked him.

"There now," the janitor said. "That smile turns you into a real pretty young lady. Thought it might." He smiled back at Wanda. "By the way, my name's ..."

"Roscoe!" came a big voice from the elevators.

"That's my name," he said, glancing past her. "Well, little sister, someone must have spotted you. That's lard-ass Leon. I'll stall, and you get. Soon as I find my Lysol spray."

With a last smiling glance back at the janitor, Wanda scooted into the shadows, waited until she saw the big guard pass, then ducked into the elevator doors just as they were closing and punched blindly at the buttons.

"Hey! Hey!" the blubbery guard sputtered, slipping and sliding and wiggling, attempting a 180-degree turn back toward the doors.

As the doors closed, the last sound she heard was the whishing of a spray can.

# Chapter 13

The doors popped back open so fast, Wanda jumped.

She was staring into the first floor lobby, and there, through the front glass across the lobby, she could see outside. All she had to do was walk off the elevator, out the front doors, through all those goofy people shouting and making faces and blocking everybody's way, and she'd be gone with the file. With her eyes on a platinum blond banging the security car with a big sign, she took a step.

And a little boy jumped in front of her, hit every one of the twelve floor buttons of the elevator, then ran off to the sound of a high-pitched, had-enough mother's voice. "Stop that, you little demon!"

Wanda stepped quickly out of the elevator just before the doors closed on her, and several things happened at once.

The second elevator opened.

So did the stairwell door around the corner. And from it came the huffing-puffing, porker-faced security guard Leon. Wanda leaped onto the second elevator, ducking down behind a large attendant and a rolling bed containing the oldest man Wanda had ever seen. As the doors were shutting, the fat guard craned his thick neck, trying to see into the shrinking elevator opening. Then he turned around and heaved a great, sweaty sigh as three other security guards stomped up to him.

The elevator moved. Wanda came out from behind the attendant and found herself up close and a little too personal with the ancient man barely making a outline in the white sheets of the bed. Over, under and around him were tubes, bottles, straps, pumping things in and siphoning things out—all showing more life than he was. His mouth gaped wide and black. His chalky cheeks, eye sockets, neck were sunken hollow. Wanda had a sudden thought of a peeled onion. "He alive?" she whispered to the beefy attendant.

"Sure he is," said the attendant cheerily. "You're still kicking, ain't you, Mr. Frudigger?"

A sort of watery moan came wafting out of the cavernous mouth as the doors opened and out the two rolled. The doors closed.

Settling back against the elevator wall, Wanda checked her growing stash of hidden booty: stolen vial in her front pocket, hospital file safe against her zipper. Then resolutely, Wanda stepped toward the console and popped the seventh floor button hard.

Soon she was walking again on the floor housing the collecting room, the −400-degree sperm bank, Dr. Smiley Face's office, and halls and halls of little rooms with plastic flags above them. Fairly confident she'd shaken the jiggling guard, she rearranged the hidden file to keep it from pinching her belly button and began strolling down one hall of flagged doors to another and another, looking for the one place she hadn't been yesterday on the whole floor: the office of Patricia Ann Hightower, beauty queen mouthpiece.

She'd gone down the last of the hallways and was doubling back to find a directory when, at the end of a hall, she saw Leon the guard coming her way. She whirled on a boot heel.

To her left was a door. To her right was a door.

*Which way?* Blindly, she grabbed the right knob, threw the door wide, ran in, slammed it shut behind her—

—and froze.

Because there lay a woman with her legs spread apart, knees toward heaven, and a white-coated man sitting in front of them with his hand stuck up into her darkness.

Wanda shrieked.

The woman screamed, popping her knees together.

The doctor yelped, almost falling off his stool.

And the nurse, who had been standing sentry in the corner, swooped toward Wanda.

"You got your hand up her!" Wanda yelled. "He had his hand up her!" She stared down at the metal stirrups now exposed on both sides of the table as the woman and her sheet shrank back. "Like some mama cow!"

"I'm examining her!" the doctor yelled over the woman's howls.

"For what! Hoof and mouth disease?"

The nurse—now with a handful of Wanda's candy-striper jumper in her fist—was doing her best to rid the tiny room of the girl. But just as she was trying to open the door, it exploded wide again, making everyone fall back. The doctor grabbed for something to break his fall and, unfortunately, found only the bare woman's sheet, whipping it half out of the woman's grip, her lower darkness exposed once again to the new visitor:

Leon.

The woman screamed again, this time pulling the sheet over her head as Leon, mouth dropped onto chins, eyes big as cow paddies, mumbled profuse apologies while trying to back out of the room. Somewhere during that time, the nurse relayed her hold on the candy-striper jumper to the guard, and before Wanda knew what to think, her boots were tap-dancing on Leon's size 13 EE's in the hall with the door's slam echoing down the hallway.

"He had his hand up her!" Wanda yelped. "You saw it!"

"I didn't see nothing!"

Wanda scowled. "Like hell you didn't. Your eyes are still full of it, you pervert. Get your hands off me!" Securing the hidden file with both hands, she started screaming in the same pitch and ferocity with which she'd heard the naked woman so effectively bellow.

Leon let go. "Stop that!" he hissed, glancing around.

"You 'examining' me, too? Well, my hooves and mouth are fine. See?" She opened her mouth and stomped down hard on Leon's hoof.

The big guard jumped back, snatching her vertical. Stifling enough anger to turn his jowls purple, he yanked so hard Wanda's boots almost came off. And that did it. Wanda was forced to kick him right where it truly hurts.

She laid the big guy out flat.

Trying not to hold himself, Leon cussed words a whole lot worse than she ever used, Wanda noted. But quicker than any fat person should ever be able to move, he was back on his feet and had her pressed to the wall with as much of his girth as he painfully could get to obey him. He thrust his flaming face into Wanda's. "Okay, kid! I ain't gonna lay another finger on you, so long as you walk nice and proper until we get where we're getting. You try anything funny, though, and I'll be all over you like a stinkbug on doo-doo. You got that?"

"Fine," agreed Wanda, adjusting her jumper to protect her secret stashes.

The big guard muttered something into his walkie-talkie, nodded a second, then led her straight down the hall to exactly where she was trying to go in the first place:

The office of Patty Hightower, Public Affairs Director.

Once there, though, Wanda didn't much like what she saw. Patty was standing there, all right, but she had her arms folded, looking stressed-out and even a little mad. She didn't even say hello. Pushing her hair out of her face, Wanda frowned at the sight, confused, until the door opened behind her and in strode three men in suits, looking pretty stressed out themselves . . . with eyes only for her, it seemed to Wanda. She fidgeted under their gaze. One of the three she knew—that Smiley Face Dr. Youngblood. But the other two were strangers, one an old guy with male-pattern baldness and an air of authority, the other a nervous toady type hovering near the bald guy.

Then one more joined the group. *Uh-oh.* Wanda recognized him: The pervert doctor from the examining room, still dressed in his limp white jacket. And his slicked-back black hair. Who was now pointing at Wanda. Rudely, Wanda thought.

"You got her!" the pervert doctor said to Leon.

"He had his hand up that woman!" Wanda hollered back. "What kind of pervert place is this?"

Patty sighed quietly, gazing from Wanda to the doctor and back again. She took a guess at what Wanda had seen, trying not to see the whole thing through a thirteen-year-old's eyes. "Wanda," she said evenly, "that's the way that women get examined for health reasons. You haven't read about that?"

"If I did, it didn't come with pictures."

"It's okay. You'll have to do it too, someday."

Wanda snorted. "Not in this life. Aren't there women doctors who can do it? How would you ever know if you had a sex fiend feeling in your privates?"

"Oh, for the love of . . ." the pervert doctor howled.

"Calm, down, Dr. Bowman!" barked the bald man.

Wanda noticed that Dr. Smiley Face was staring at her. "Hi, Wanda, remember me? Dr. Youngblood? What are you doing in a candy-striper outfit?"

The pervert doctor was now looking at her sideways. "Don't tell me this is her!"

Dr. Smiley Face nodded.

"Leon," snapped the bald man.

"Yessir, Dr. Crouch?"

"What has this young woman been up to in our candy-striper uniform?"

Wanda tugged at the jumper as Leon spilled his guts.

"Hey. I was coming here, all right?" she added. "If Son of Flubber hadn't decided to play the Terminator."

Patty took a step toward her. "Wanda, why did you do all that?"

"It wasn't *my* idea. The Sperm Warrior lured me to Denny's with a spy-movie phone call, then gave me this jumper from some Amazon kid and told me where to find out about my mother and my real daddy."

"Oh, please," said the pervert doctor.

"Tommy . . ." said Dr. Youngblood Smiley Face in a smooth, soothing voice. Then he leaned his big, so-smiley-you-wanted-to-punch-it face into hers.

Wanda took a step back.

"You were in the basement?" he asked. "So, young lady, did you find anything down there?"

"You don't have to answer that." Wanda turned toward the voice coming from the doorway—the reporter. "They'll probably try to scare you with breaking and entering charges if you tell them anything worth knowing."

"Who let the press in here?" whispered the bald guy to his toady. Wanda decided she didn't like him. She turned back to the reporter, who'd already moved into the middle of the room.

"The First Amendment let me in," Griffin went on. "This is the public affairs office. Wanda's got a right to know, and so do the people."

"Stick a pin in it, LaCour," said the pervert doctor. "You guys are so pompous."

The toady guy cleared his throat. "Mr. LaCour, this is a private conversation."

Griffin leaned back on Patty's desk, not going anywhere. "Prominent legal counsel has informed me Miss Ledbetter has a very good case if she chooses to sue."

Wanda was suddenly revved. "A woman in Illinois sued her doctor for child support when her husband swore he didn't know about the donor insemination," she announced.

The doctors all turned to look at her for a beat.

"Why don't you tell her what she wants to know?" Griffin went on. "Seems like you already have enough problems right now, what with the demonstration downstairs."

"Demonstration?" interrupted the bald man.

"Out front, sir," mewed the toady assistant. "I was about to . . ."

The bald man sighed. "Pro-life or pro-choice?"

"Should we put a guard on Dr. Strake again?" offered Leon.

But just then the door opened again, slowly, squeaking. The noise made everyone turn around. And there stood the young skinny guard, his uniform wet all across his scrawny chest.

"Leon," moaned the damp guard. "They broke my walkie-talkie."

"Oh god, they're throwing blood again," said the bald man.

"That's not blood," said someone. "It smells sort of musky, sick sweet . . ."

Every adult in the room came to attention, staring in stunned silence.

Then one of the doctors finally roared: "They're throwing *THAT*?"

The toady assistant came up close to sniff. "That's what it is, all right."

The reporter laughed, the bald man moaned, and the skinny guard just stood miserably with his arms out from his body, while Patty gaped at the males surrounding her. "That bothers all of you more than blood?"

Wanda looked from one to the other, trying to figure out what was going on.

"Where are they getting it?" the pervert doctor asked.

"Getting *what*?" Wanda demanded.

Coming close to sniff for himself, Griffin retorted: "Well, one idea comes to mind."

"We have had some specimens come up missing, sir," the toady guy said, rubbing his nose as he moved back from the damp skinny guard. "But not enough to make this much of a splash. So to speak, sir."

"They'd have to have their own sperm bank to get that much," said Youngblood.

Taking a look at the demonstration down below, Griffin laughed again. "Or have lots of volunteers standing by."

Dr. Crouch, the bald guy, gazed down at the protesters. "What kind of protest *is* it, then?"

The skinny guard shrugged. "They keep yelling, 'I want my daddy. I want my daddy.' Finally, this crazy lady threw this on me."

Wanda perked up. "Chicken-necked? Long black wig like Cher?"

The skinny guard made hairdo gestures over his head. "More of a Marilyn Monroe."

"More like a Madonna," observed Griffin from the window. "In black shades."

"That's her," announced Wanda.

"Hit me with a sign, too: 'Sperm Warriors on the Warpath.'" The skinny guard pouted as he made a few futile swipes at his shirt.

The bald man fumed, moving away from the window, "Let me get this straight. They're protesting our sperm bank?"

"It's your secret files, Crouch," Griffin answered. "You told the paper you don't have them or are forced by some sort of quasi-law not to reveal them. They don't believe it, nor do I."

Irritated, the bald man turned on Patty. "Ms. Hightower, we asked you to control this whole incident before it got to this sorry state. You have let us down thoroughly, I must say." Patty began to respond, but he silenced her with a hand. Then he looked right at Wanda: "Young lady, there are no records to prove or disprove your claim. It's a moot point. So there you have it. You may not like it. But it is the truth. And there's nothing more to say."

Nope, Wanda decided, she really, really didn't like this guy. Giving him her best evil eye, she reached her hand inside her jumper and considered whipping out the file, then thought better of it.

"I have a few questions," announced Griffin.

The bald man started for the door. "Ms. Hightower is available to answer your questions, Mr. LaCour."

Griffin stepped in his way. "It's hard to believe you don't keep records on the modern donor inseminations."

"Bull insemination has more record keeping than human insemination in the United States," announced Wanda.

Everybody turned toward her again.

"And how accurate is your bank?" Griffin pressed.

"A white woman using what she thought was her dead white husband's sperm from a New York sperm bank gave birth to a black baby," announced Wanda.

Everyone turned her way for a beat yet again.

"And what about the powerful fertility drugs you use in many of your procedures?" Griffin went on.

"One lady died of her ovaries bursting after taking a bunch of those drugs," added Wanda. "And the World Health Organization says there's a cancer epidemic coming."

"What *are* you two? A tag team?" Dr. Pervert T. Tommy Bowman finally howled.

"And tell me, Dr. Crouch," Griffin went right on, "what happens if you produce a defective baby?"

"Reports state in vitro babies are three times more likely to die in the first three months of life," quoted Wanda. "And five times more likely to . . ."

"God Above, can we turn this child *off*?" wailed Dr. Bowman.

Dr. Crouch held up a hand to silence everyone. "Mr. LaCour, if a child is not healthy, we care for it, but ultimately they take it home. That's what parents do."

"C'mon, Crouch," Griffin said. "Aren't you pandering to the desperation of these couples?"

The bald man's whole head flushed red. Throwing up his hands, he took several steps back toward Griffin. "What would you have us do, Mr. LaCour, halt progress? Stop the future? If we tried, those very couples would be the ones suing for their right to these procedures!"

"Of course, haha—" the toady assistant interrupted, as he finally succeeded in getting the door open behind Griffin. "This is all off the record, Mr. LaCour, haha."

The two stepped through the door and away as Dr. Crouch, now calm, called back: "Please take the rest of your questions up with our Public Affairs Director. Good day."

Griffin turned toward Patty. She did not look him in the eye. Wanda noticed this and did not like it at all.

Patty began enunciating in her best professional voice. "I'll send you all the press releases on our various infertility treatments and assisted reproductive procedures, Mr. LaCour."

"What about this young girl, Ms. Hightower?" Griffin responded, enunciating rather professionally himself. "You know she can sue to find out if the records do exist."

Patty rubbed her temples. "Yes, well, I hope she would not, but . . ."

Wanda began popping her knuckles as she watched Patty drop her hands, wrap them around a convenient pile of folders and hug them to her chest. And to make matters worse, Tommy Bowman, pervert doctor, was coming her way. Wanda took a step back in case she had to do more place-kicking.

"Look, child," he said to her, now doing his rendition of Dr. Smiley Face's nicey-nice voice. He held out a hand as if to touch her.

"Hey, back off," Wanda warned. "I know where those hands have been."

"Oh good *grief!*" he groaned, taking hold of her arm. "Don't you understand? If you *are* a donor baby, you should be *thanking* us. You wouldn't even *be* here if it weren't for us."

Wanda winced, her knees buckling a little; he was touching the Harley-fingered bruise.

"Dr. Bowman!" Patty yelled.

He cut Patty off with a wave of his free hand, his hot breath blowing into Wanda's face. "So why don't you go home and enjoy the life we gave you, how 'bout it!"

At that Patty dropped the folders on her desk with a loud whop and grabbed Wanda's arm from Bowman's grasp. "And why don't *you* go sit on a *tack—how 'bout it?*" she blurted, leading Wanda out the door.

"Yeah," Wanda called back. "Sit on it."

As Patty rushed Wanda into the hall, they pushed past two nurses loitering unusually close to Patty's office, nurses Wanda recognized from Dr. Smiley Face's office. The older one was staring a hole through her.

★ ★ ★

Once inside the elevator, Patty blew out a big breath and laid her head back against the wall. She glanced down at Wanda, who was fingering her bruised arm. "You okay?"

Wanda stared back at Patty, almost smiling. "You told him to sit on a tack."

"And I'm going to hear about it," Patty muttered. "But if the devil doesn't like it—" At that she actually laughed. "God help me, I hope he didn't go to Sunday school."

Yanking the candy-striped jumper over her head, Wanda tossed it down with pleasure. Then she realized the file was showing. For a second, her fingers poised on the file, she considered giving it to Patty.

But then she flipped her T-shirt over it before Patty saw.

When Patty did look back at this girl beside her, whom she'd just yanked away from a group of people who paid her salary, she wondered if she was losing all good sense. She had another urge to take a hairbrush to the girl's flyaway mess as she watched Wanda cross her arms over her chest, intense and secret once more. A wave of sadness rolled over Patty at the sight. She began to try again to make Wanda understand the futility of her quest. But Patty could think of no words except the useless ones she'd already used. So they rode the elevator in silence.

Finally, just before the elevator stopped, Wanda said, "Would you give me a ride to the motel? Granny and Wild Thing are probably worried."

A vision of Granny and the gun popped before Patty's eyes. "Of course."

There was a pause. Then Wanda mumbled, "Thanks."

Patty gazed down at Wanda. The look the girl was now giving her was so full of guarded appreciation, and even, Patty thought, a little momentary trust, that she was a bit taken back. "You're welcome," she answered.

The elevator opened. They stepped into the lobby.

"Patricia—" a voice came from the stairwell.

"Leave it alone for now, Griffin," Patty called as they moved out the doors into the heat and the picketing fray.

Wanda began scanning the weirdos for her special one. Griffin, out of breath, finally caught up.

Just then, a camera flash blinded them.

"Okay, LaCour. I got your 'Brave New Wanda' shot," said a male voice somewhere behind the white spots before their eyes.

Wanda blinked. "What did he call me?"

A well-modulated female voice from behind them said, "Hey, isn't that—?"

In Wanda's face was now a microphone wielded by a blow-dried, over-dressed Asian American newswoman. "Wanda! Tiffany Yu, Channel 2. How would you like to be on television? Get that camera over here, Randy!"

Griffin suddenly attached himself to Wanda's elbow and began steering her in the opposite direction. Wanda, tired of people grabbing her, yanked it back and stood rock-solid still, daring anybody, including the reporter, to touch her.

Patty, Tiffany and the Eyewitness News cameraman caught up.

"What's your problem?" Patty hissed, moving into Griffin's face.

"I've got to get another exclusive with her," Griffin explained. "Please. I have to."

"Get in close, Randy, nice tight shot of the girl and me," Tiffany ordered, jockeying for telegenic position. "Wanda, you might want to scootch over."

"I mean it, Griffin," Patty snapped. "Not now."

Griffin pressed.

Patty threw up her hands. "You haven't changed a bit, have you?"

"*THIS* is Tiffany Yu here at Parkland Hospital . . . mmphgpph. This *IS* Tiffany *Yu,* here at Parkland; This is *TIFFANY* Yu hmmph, hmppggggh. Ready, Randy?"

That's when Wanda spotted her Sperm Warrior coming her way.

The woman in cheap sunglasses and bouffant platinum wig rushed from the middle of the crowd. Right toward Wanda—

And right by her—to squirt a pouch of globby-white substance all over Griffin LaCour's shirt.

"*Sperm has a name!*" she yelled, clear enough for a good quote, and ran back into the throng.

Griffin reeled back, almost falling over the curb.

"Did you get it?" Tiffany screamed at the cameraman. "*Fan*-tastic!"

Staring down at himself, Griffin wiped his hand across the mess. Then he touched a finger to his tongue.

"*Oh good Lord, Griffin!*" Patty yelped, then rushed Wanda away.

Griffin smacked his lips and sniffed: "Sugar. Hmmph." Then he sat down heavily on the curb.

★ ★ ★

Seven floors above, Nurse Stella Peabody adjusted her trifocals as she watched the fracas through one of the floor-to-ceiling office windows. But she only had eyes for Wanda.

"A beautiful child, a troubled child," she murmured, her hand at her throat. "Oh, Dr. Roddy."

# Chapter 14

$\mathcal{W}$anda reared back and kicked the motel office chair. "What do you mean you don't know?" Patty yelled at the motel manager.

"Lady," said the greasy man, "you tell that kid to quit kicking everything or she'll be paying for damage. Look, I ain't my customers' keeper, okay? I just said that I saw her and that big dog leave about an hour ago. And the maid found the door wide open. You're lucky there's anything left. I was about to take it all myself as payment for the bill."

"I hid the keys!" Wanda said for the third time. "I swear I did! I did!" She rushed out the door. Patty turned to follow.

The manager grunted. "Hey, what about the bill?"

Patty swiveled, rummaged in her purse and thrust some money into the man's hand. His fingernails were dirty. "I expect you to leave the room alone."

She found Wanda kicking at gravel, pacing back and forth in front of the BMW. "We'll find her," Patty said.

In a few minutes they were on the same highway that Granny and Wild Thing had cruised down earlier. Patty drove just a little bit faster than the speed limit would allow. She tried not to keep looking at Wanda, but it was impossible: the girl was a bundle of fidgets—cracking her knuckles, drumming her fingers, pushing her hair back whether it needed it or not, eyeing each new stretch of ditch that whizzed past.

Finally Patty sighed. "Listen . . ."

"She can't drive," Wanda blurted.

"Excuse me?"

"Plowed through the back of the garage and landed in Mrs. Yoakum's tomatoes last year and almost lost her license, so she quit."

"Well, who . . ."

"Me, okay? Me." She glanced at Patty. For a moment her face opened up, showing all the worry and guilt and pain she was carrying around. Then she jerked the look back behind jutted jaw.

They drove another few silent miles, Wanda checking each stretch of ditch for upended Caddys and low-lying grandmothers, until she collapsed still against the seat's leather tucks and rolls. Patty gave her a good look out of the corner of her eye. A patch of lost hair fell over her baby face; a small hand rose to push it back. Patty suddenly noticed Wanda had freckles. As if they only appeared when this child/woman was still. For some reason, that made Patty very self-conscious. Here she was driving down the road, out in the middle of Texas nowhere, with a girl she hadn't known long enough to even notice the child had freckles. She'd noticed a head of hair in need of a good styling, a wardrobe in need of a good shopping and a poor little orphan country girl in need of an attitude adjustment. She hadn't looked close enough to see freckles. Yet here she was, AWOL from work, driving into the sticks without a clue where this girl was taking her or why she was letting her do so. Yes, Patty decided, it was definite now. She *had* lost all good sense.

Wanda moved just enough to pull a small spiral notebook from her back pocket. She put it on her lap and placed a hand over it.

"Is that a diary?" Patty tried, unable to tolerate the silence a second longer. She got chatty when she was nervous, and now she was nervous: "I had a diary, too. It had the tiniest little key, as if you couldn't just pop the latch open. Which I'm pretty sure my mother did on a regular basis. I wrote about boys usually." She paused. She tried again. "Boy crazy. That was all my girlfriends and I talked about. Boys."

With her free hand Wanda popped the car's electronic window button up, down, up, down. "You mean sex."

Patty chuckled. "Sex? Lord, no. True love. Prince Charming. Romance. Definitely not sex." Squelching a sudden thought of Eric, she realized she hadn't thought about him in a nice long time. "I've got a feeling you know more about everything than I did at your age," she added, glancing at Wanda.

"You know what I know?" Wanda popped the car window shut with a decided electronic suck. "Everything is fucked up."

Patty sighed. "Wanda, you really shouldn't use that language."

"Why not?"

"Because," Patty answered, "nice people don't."

"I don't want to be nice. I never want to be nice. All nice gets you is some boring suck job like yours."

Patty sighed. "I'm glad I've impressed you."

"Besides," Wanda went on, "cussing is just cultural anyway. People who go live in other cultures report that they don't even get their new language's dirty words."

Patty shook her head. "You are something else."

"And there isn't a dirty word alive that's more revolting than sex," Wanda added.

Patty cocked her head Wanda's way. "Everybody thinks that at first, but you'll do it."

"Maybe if I were hermaphroditic like a fire salamander. They reproduce just fine all by themselves."

"That I'd like to see," Patty retorted.

Wanda heaved a sigh bigger than she was. "It's just that I'm sick to death of hearing about sex. The same time I'm finding out how my mama *didn't* do it to have me, I'm hearing all about how my grandmother *did* do it. My grandmother! Geez! She's turned into a dirty old lady!"

"Oh, Wanda, I doubt that."

"Swear to God. All of a sudden she's telling me in vivid detail about this night she had with 'Johnny.' And I'm talking vivid. Doing it under trees, dresses slipping down. The guy's supposed to be my grandfather, but still, you think that's natural? Telling your granddaughter things like that?"

Wanda began cracking her knuckles again, gazing back out her window. "Maybe she is nuts. She's been down in that stupid fallout shelter more than her house. Half the time she's off somewhere in her mind, talking to a dead guy, asking for nickels. And *now* she's run away." Her knuckles were all cracked out, but Wanda kept right on. "She's probably always been weird, but what did I know? Normal would have been weird at my house."

Patty suddenly thought of Granny sitting in the waiting room at the hospital browsing through the change in a woman's outstretched hand. "Why is your grandmother so interested in spare change? I mean, if you don't mind my asking."

Wanda cut an eye her way. "Promise you won't tell?" It was a look that wanted to talk but worried about who was doing the listening.

Patty promised.

"Buffalo nickels," she murmured.

"But they don't make them anymore. Not for decades."

Wanda shrugged. "They remind her of this Johnny who died in the war way back. Says he looked sort of like the Indian on the front. That guy must have been *ugly*."

"Well," Patty commented, "then she must have quite a collection by now."

Wanda shrugged. "If she does, I never saw it. She'd come in to my room when I was a little kid to kiss me goodnight and check my piggy bank, swear to God. Mama'd come home from her job as checker at the Piggly Wiggly and she'd quiz her about sighting buffalo nickels. I thought it was a game; I even *helped* her." They passed a big truck. The trucker leered down at them, waving, making puckering motions and swirling his tongue around. Wanda showed him he was #1.

Seeing that, Patty had a sudden stab of jealousy. For just a moment, she wished *she'd* been the one in the car with the moxie to shoot the bone at the sleaze.

A green Texas interstate sign flashed by:

**COLLEGE MOUND**
**3 miles**
**NEXT EXIT**

Behind it, along the fence line, First Baptist Church, Red's Liquor Store and Ray's Chevy House welcomed them with a row of signs in various degrees of disrepair.

Wanda settled back in her seat, on familiar ground now, and let her eyes blur at the passing land, the patches of brown, green, gray. The land looked different than it did yesterday. Was it just yesterday? She closed a hand protectively around her little book.

"This exit?" Patty asked.

Wanda nodded. And then, in a voice thin and weightless, she muttered, "She's not really my grandmother, you know."

At the sound of that, Patty reached out and squeezed Wanda's hand, a comforting, momentary reflex. She'd done it before she realized what she was doing and now fully expected Wanda to jerk away; she didn't.

"She's all right," Patty said, hands back safely on the wheel. "We're going to find her."

Wanda slid her fingers along the leather upholstery of her seat, stealing a tough glance at Patty. "I'll pay you back. I'll pay you all of it back."

---

IF YOU LIVED HERE YOU'D BE HOME NOW AND
TAKING HOME THE BEST BBQ IN TEXAS!

★ ★ ★

# BUBBA LIKES IT!

LONE STAR BBQ THIS EXIT

---

Patty veered the car into the College Mound exit, passed the best BBQ in Texas and turned down a winding two-lane road leading through pasture and mesquite trees. She felt a pair of eyes now firmly fixed on her.

"Just so you know," Wanda informed her solemnly, "the moment we hit the city limits the law will be looking for me . . . because I shot Harley. Probably an all-points bulletin. Just so you know."

Patty didn't like the sound of that. ". . . About this shooting thing," she began.

Just then Wanda stiffened: "Turn here!" Wanda pointed down a dirt road. "And go slow but don't stop! Granny's got the .22."

Patty liked the sound of that even less. As the car hit the dirt with a bounce of the BMW's expensive suspension system, Wanda hollered for her to stop.

Patty stomped on the pedal and came to a jolting rest on the road's shoulder across from nothing but a wide dirt spot. Wanda rushed across the rutted road, kicking up dust as she went, and stood right in the middle of the dirt, her hands stretched out like question marks. "It's gone!"

"What is?" Patty asked, looking at the whole lot of nothing.

"The trailer! The eighteen-wheeler! The Lone Star flag and the chicken-wire fence! The sumbitch hooked up and just left." Wanda's face dropped. She was now hustling back across the road as fast as her boots would carry her.

"What? What's wrong?" Patty kept saying.

"Hurry! We got to hurry!" was Wanda's only answer.

Within a few minutes they had entered College Mound, Texas, population 2,241, and were making a circle around the little dried-up county seat square with its stray dogs lounging in the road, Chevy pickups with gun racks and mud flaps lined up in front of a corner café, and bevy of old men sitting out in front of the gas station/video rental/grocery store. As they paused at the town's one stoplight, Patty caught the eye of one of the old men. He was wearing a once-red baseball cap that read "Johnson Grain and Feed" and was chewing, bovine and toothless, on something. She looked away. In a moment she glanced back. He was still staring at her. It wasn't the kind of stare Patty was used to, the smooth stare men gave her as if she were still on the beauty pageant circuit. No, he was giving her and her fancy city car the once-over reserved for all those who had the misfortune of not being hometown folk. She looked away, then looked back. He was still staring. She looked away again, waited a beat and peeked back out of the corner of her eye. He was still staring. And he kept it right up until he rolled the big wad in his cheek into spitting position, let a nice brown arc fly into the street and began popping the contents of a box of Sweet Tarts into his mouth.

Patty had forgotten about these places. Actually she couldn't remember the last time she'd left Dallas to go anywhere but other places just like Dallas on airplanes or interstates that did their best to avoid these pockets of retro-time. She glanced at a horse trailer hitched to one of the parked pickups. A bumper sticker—strategically stuck right under where the horse's tail flopped out—said: "I'm Texan. Kiss My Ass." Here she was, Dallas-slick chic, in kicker country. Land of chicken-fried steaks and dust and cow pies and Lone Star Beer and covered-dish suppers and armadillos and mosquitoes the size of small animals.

The light changed; she glanced back at the ogling man as they rolled away. His chair was directly under what was left of a peeling, forgotten Holsum Bread ad painted on the brick wall, along with a faded poster of an old Clint Eastwood movie: "Rental available inside." When you get around to it. When it suits you. No rush. What a strange place for a Wanda, Patty realized. A strange place for someone to even consider having a donor-inseminated child. Or maybe not . . . after all, way out here in the country, she'd seen huge satellite dishes planted beside rickety mobile homes. To Patty, that always seemed as strange as a cowboy with a cell phone. How was it that the past, the present and the future could so easily coexist? People in these small country towns had DVDs and CNN, but barring news coverage of yearly Texas tornado destruction, the reel life they saw was rarely like the real life they led. Places where being called "old-fashioned" was a compliment, a clinging virtue. Except—she glanced at the hometown girl in her passenger seat—except for women who must have babies. Must.

She suddenly remembered a saying about Texas: It's just like anywhere else, only more so.

"Here. Turn here." Wanda was pointing now, trying not to look anxious. Patty turned in the direction of Wanda's finger and drove down an uncurbed side street lined with big unkempt yards and tiny box houses long past their short prime. As Patty slowed to swerve her new car around the road's impressive potholes, Wanda threw open her door. Once again, Patty was slamming on the brakes, watching Wanda sprint across the street, this time through one of those sprawling, weedy yards to a peeling gray frame house. The screen door of the tiny house was lying back on its hinges. The wooden door behind it was ajar.

"Granny?" Wanda called as she took the steps two at a time and pushed the door wide. *"Wild Th—"* But as her eyes caught up with her mouth, the rest of her words disappeared.

Patty came up beside her and gazed at the sight. The house was a wreck.

Wanda vanished down the hall as Patty stepped gingerly inside. She gave the air a sniff. The place had a smell of mildew and musty wood, full of an old, poor woman's accumulation of comforting things now scattered across the room-sized oval rug, the kind found in a 1960s J. C. Penney catalog. She made her way into the middle of the mess and picked up a china figurine, a fancy Mexican lady with a painted face and a shattered torso.

Wanda stumbled back in, looking as if she'd been slapped. "You're a sumbitch, Harley Dean!" she bellowed toward the road. "It's a fact now!"

"Helloooo?" came a lilting, sweet old voice. A bluish-gray head, looking freshly sculpted in the beauty parlor, popped inside the gaping door. "Gladys? You back home, hon?"

"Mrs. Yoakum!" said Wanda, whirling around. "Did you see him?"

"Well, now, how are you, Wanda Louise? Sorry for your loss, dear. Where's Gladys? I thought she was with you. That's what your stepdaddy said. He . . . ooh." The woman looked around the room.

"You saw him stealing Granny's stuff? Why didn't you call the sheriff, Mrs. Yoakum?"

"Oh my. Oh dear. Oh. Well. When I saw him pull that big truck of his up here, I did come over here, dear. I said, 'Hello, Harley. Sorry for your loss. Is everything all right?' And your stepdaddy, he said everything was fine and that he was just picking up some of Gladys' things for her, because she had gone away for a little while to commiserate over your mama's death. That would be only natural, you know, even if they didn't get along as everybody knows." The little woman laid a forefinger upside her cheek. "But come to think of it, it was a little odd. And he was a tad more surly than usual. He was always surly, you know that, Wanda Louise, not that I'm talking about him or anything. He was just always a bit brisk for my manners. He didn't look well, either, a little pale around the gills, something wrong with his foot, I think, him limping and cursing to bring down heaven with each step." She stopped to tsk-tsk. "I still say that young people can make the effort to be civil around their elders if . . ."

"What about Granny?" Wanda cut her off.

The woman stopped. "What about her, child?"

"Where did she go?"

"Well, she's with you, isn't she? I hadn't seen her since the other day when you came for her after your dear poor mother's funeral. You must forgive me, by the way, dear, for not attending. I just don't get around like I used to, but I did bring Gladys some tomato salad, fresh from my garden. Beefeater tomatoes as round as your fist, they were. I had a lovely garden this year. Gladys did eat it, I hope, didn't she?"

Wanda ran out of the room.

Patty looked back at the little old lady, who was now smiling ever so sweetly up at her. "And who might I ask are you, dear?"

"Excuse me." Patty backed out of the room in Wanda's direction.

Alone, Mrs. Yoakum crossed her arms under her bust and walked through the ransacked room, shaking her head at the awful wonder of it all, not missing a thing. When she got to the kitchen, she saw her tomato salad, sitting with its Saran Wrap untouched on the counter. "Oh my. Well." She picked it up and headed out the front door. "Such a pity for it to go to waste, you know."

Trying to find her way out, Patty found herself in a screened-in porch that ran across the whole backside of the tiny house. She pushed the screen door open, the hinge screeching, and stepped down onto the overgrown yard, the door slapping shut behind her. To the left was a clothesline of forgotten sheets stiffly flapping in the small hot breeze. To the right, down a path of not more than ten steps was a fallout shelter like the ones Patty had seen only in pictures, round and green, with a little pipe vent, the kind to save the All-American family of the Eisenhower era from godless Cold War communism. Its metal door was flung open. She stuck her head into the opening; she couldn't see a thing. "Wanda?" No response. She climbed down the ladder and waited for her eyes to adjust.

The shelter was very small and very round. One naked bulb hung down from the ceiling. Somebody had pulled the light bulb's cord because the bulb was shining, casting harsh shadows around the hole in the ground . . . Wanda, probably. Granny obviously had spent time down here, too. But this trucker stepdaddy, or whoever had made a mess of the house, had definitely been here. All that was left now was a broken rocker, a TV antennae, a hot plate, a shelf full of bottled water and freeze-dried food enough to last a millennium. That was it, that and a framed picture, one of those three-dimensional pictures of a long-robed Jesus standing in front of a door. When you moved, he moved—to the left, he knocked; to the right, he looked back at you, waiting for a response. *Gee,* thought Patty dryly, *I can't imagine why Harley didn't take that.*

As she turned slowly all the way around in this perfect circular hole in the ground, she had a sudden sad image of Granny sitting down here, feeling so very safe. Safe from what? What was the poor woman afraid of? Patty was beginning to think that Wanda might be right about her grandmother, and that made her worry even more about where the old woman might be. "Wanda!" she called up the ladder. Where had she gone? Patty stepped back and stumbled on something. It was Wanda's little notebook diary.

★ ★ ★

When Wanda had jumped down into the shelter a few minutes ahead of Patty, she'd gotten so mad at what she saw, she'd kicked the broken rocker, rushed back up the ladder and looked across this backyard of her childhood for something else to kick.

Instead she wandered over to the far edge of her grandmother's property. It was a little area with big sycamore trees separating it from the Yoakums' and with an old latticed grape arbor walk-through tucked in the corner, hidden from the rest of the yard and the world. Wanda peeled some of the soft sycamore bark off one of the trees, out of childhood habit, and moved slowly into the little arbor, bending down to pass under the overgrown vines. As a kid Wanda had hidden there, especially on the nights when her mama would sit like a statue on the screened porch with her big red Bible in her lap. Never reading it, just holding it, a ghostly presence in the far-off dark. From here all Wanda would see was the glowing ember of her mother's cigarette and the shiny ribbon hanging down from the Bible, reflecting bright from the yellow bug light at the other end of the porch.

"You treat that Holy Bible like it was a durn Band-Aid, Louise," she could hear Granny's voice calling, strong and healthy, from the open kitchen window. "Why not try putting it over your heart and get on with it?"

"Leave me alone, Mother Gladys," her mother would answer, as Wanda watched the ember move up to her mama's mouth and glow brighter and the reflected ribbon press closer to her yellow, ghost-gray body.

Wanda shook the memory out of her head and looked around her at the grape arbor, the vines on the trellis now mostly dead, the bench all but rotted through. She found the initials she'd carved with Granny's sewing scissors in the bench and ran a finger over them. Then her eyes darted up, searching for the cicada skin. It had been there for years, sticking to the paint-chipped wood when all the others had fallen off, and Wanda had prized it, stared at its strangeness as if it were a snakeskin instead of the product of an insect with a seven-year molt. She had read all about them that year. Her heart skipped, a little kid feeling, when she saw it was still there, and she touched the place where the insect had slipped from the shell's hold. With that she sat right down on the bench and glanced around as if she were back home.

For a long moment she wrestled with sudden feelings she couldn't quite get a handle on. Part of her wanted to be back here being little Wanda Louise Ledbetter, listening to her mama and her grandmama bicker. The feeling squeezed at her stomach, she wanted it so. But another part, the smart part, the part people called too smart for her own good, told her to grow up, to stop the mushy stuff, to remember they lied. And lied big.

Then it was as if she saw her mother at the far end of the bench among the shady trellises. She was shelling peas, her fingers working, working, working, her face shiny. And then Wanda saw why. She was crying, the tears dropping onto the peas. She heard her mother sniff and watched her take a forearm and dab at the tears. Suddenly inside Wanda, one feeling pushed through the smarts and the meanness and the hurting truth: She wanted her mother back. Just for a minute, just to talk, not even about her daddy, just talk. Like mother and daughters are supposed to, like crying makes you want to, without fights. Please. Please. Please. Her mama's bright, liquid eyes turned toward Wanda. She smiled at Wanda through the shadowy arbor. Then she opened her mouth and said, "Fetch me my cigarettes, will you, hon?"

Wanda choked. *The one thing I remember my mama saying is that?*

She had found something to kick. She kicked the rotted arbor bench with the shitkicker toe of her cowboy boots, kicked it and kicked it until it broke all the way through. Then she hurtled out of the grape arbor, breathing hard, her hair in her face, thrusting her hands deep and hurt and angry into her back pockets.

That was when she realized her notebook was gone.

★ ★ ★

Across the yard and down in the ground, Patty held Wanda's little notebook open in her hand. She hadn't meant to look. She felt like her spying mother. But it had landed face down on the floor. And when she'd picked it up, the page before her began with the words "Dear Daddy":

> *"Dear Daddy, I'm going to call you Daddy because I never got to call anyone . . ."*

Patty hurriedly turned the page:

> *"Dear Daddy, You might read about me in the paper . . . don't fall over dead. I'm a little low on relatives lately . . ."*

And then a letter fell out of the back, floating to the floor, its scotch tape gone dry. The letterhead read "Office of the Governor of the State of Texas."

Dear Miss Wanda Louise Ledbetter:

Congratulations on placing in the top 1% of the state's scholastic achievement tests. You have a bright future ahead of you and are an example of the quality of our public schools . . ."

Patty forced herself to stop reading.

She pushed the letter back in place with a squeeze of the tape, closed the notebook and set it gently back onto the floor.

Just as she stepped from the ladder into the sun, Wanda appeared, wild-eyed, hair flying, frantically eyeballing the ground. Patty felt her heart move again at the sight of Wanda's face. She had the definite look of any thirteen-year-old now, a thirteen-year-old worried that her deepest personal secrets might be seen or read or known by another—and one of those secrets was that she was not so tough or so old after all.

Before Patty could even speak, Wanda had popped past her down the ladder, then back up, wiping off the little book fastidiously with slim, nervous fingers.

At a loss for what to do next, and feeling a little guilty, Patty meandered over to the house, stepping high through the tall grass, and sat down on the back stoop.

Wanda eased the book back into her pocket, then just stood there, suddenly at a loss herself. She heard a sound from the street, the sound of an old car in need of a muffler. She jerked her head around, the sound growing nearer and nearer.

But it was only an old Ford pickup. Wanda's shoulders sagged as it rattled on by. She shuffled over and joined Patty on the steps, staring out at the backyard.

"Do you want to call the police?" Patty asked.

"No. Good riddance to stinky, thieving rubbish." Wanda paused, sighing. "Granny would croak if she saw it like this."

A few more moments passed. Mrs. Yoakum waved from her porch. A cat passed through the yard. Wanda swatted an ant off her tanned knee.

"Where could your grandmother be?" Patty murmured.

Wanda leaned a weary cheek on top of a fist. "Someplace probably talking to . . ."

Suddenly Wanda knew exactly where her granny was. Without even finishing her sentence, she was up and rushing toward the car.

# Chapter 15

At the far edge of the country church cemetery, a handful of retirees were pulling weeds, mowing grass, trimming hedges, picking up trash. Today was the cemetery's annual cleanup day—the last Friday of the summer. Just as it had been throughout the century since this black land valley was settled by the first Tennessee travelers, who were probably no more than one generation from Germany or England or Ireland but, after passing the state line, would be nothing ever again so much as Texans. Reborn. To live, worship, birth their babies and be buried right here.

You never knew who would show up at the Poetry Cemetery cleaning from one year to the next, relatives from several counties away, old church members returning since the church disbanded, and nothing much took these workers from their work. Cemetery cleaning was a comforting tradition, one of the oldest ones, left from pioneer days. You took care of your own, no matter if they were dead or not. It didn't matter that you never knew them. It didn't matter that you weren't quite sure who they were. They were yours. It was somewhat biblical. Abraham begat Isaac who begat Jacob who begat Joseph. Tennessee homesteader Will Deveraux begat beloved wife Luella Deveraux Pirtle who begat beloved husband John Belcher Pirtle who begat beloved child Willis John who died at three years of age of the pox, his gravestone with its sweet small angel smoothed by time standing along with the rest, telling the story to the ages.

In this way, in these country patches, these places yet to be overgrown with people and industry and the concerns of the pocketbook, you could still connect with the past through the present. Take care of your dead, and you take care of your living.

When these cemetery cleaners saw the long car clatter halfway into the churchyard and the old woman and her big dog wander down to the other side of the old cemetery and sit down under the dead tree, they thought nothing of it. The woman no doubt was a Blankenship or a Perry or a Belcher, one of those out-of-staters they hadn't seen in a while, here to keep up the tradition, just taking a cat nap after a long drive. At lunch they'd invite her over, but for now they would clean and think and connect, alone with their ancestral thoughts.

And that's what they were doing, all in their summer whites under the bright sun, when the second car, one of those foreign ones, came rolling up, crackling the gravel again.

"Dear God," they heard one of the two young ladies murmur, getting out of the car and heading toward the old woman. *How nice,* they thought, going back to their weeds. *They're praying.*

Wanda and Patty rushed down the hill from the parking lot to where Granny sprawled under the low-hanging tree. Wanda was afraid to breathe as she flung herself in front of her grandmother and began shaking the daylights out of her, shaking until her own teeth rattled. WakeupwakeupwakeupOhpleaseplease.

Granny's eyes popped open. "Ooww! Stop that!" she grumbled, slapping at Wanda's hands.

Wanda gulped, wrapped her arms around the big woman's neck and squeezed. "I thought you were *dead—*"

"Well, you know, I thought so, too. Maybe I was; I don't know, considering I've never been dead before."

Wanda jumped to her feet, flailing her arms. "I can't believe you ran off! I was scared shitless, you know! You could have died out here and I'd never known it, you know?"

Granny looked around, a little dazed. "Thing was, I coulda swore I heard ..."

"Don't ever do that again!" Wanda scolded. "Where's Wild Thing?"

"Ran off," Granny mumbled. "I think I kissed her." Granny squinted over at the people in white, out at the ducks on the little pond, then up at the tree, and turned very quiet.

*"Wild Thing!"* Wanda called. "Where'd she go?" She peered frantically over the brushy pasture, then the pond, then the stand of trees beyond. *"Here, girl!"*

"Wanda Louise," Granny said. "You see that plot right over there? That's mine. When they all died off long ago, I bought the last one just for me. Nobody left to tell. So I'm telling you."

"I don't see her anywhere! Which way did she go off, Granny?"

Granny wasn't listening. "I used to come here all the time, I did. Come to visit. I should've brought you here a long time ago, Wanda Louise. I should have buried your daddy here. Your mama, though, was better to be buried with her people."

"Please don't talk about burying, Granny. You can't go off and leave me, too!"

"Your mama didn't mean to go off. It was an accident."

Wanda whirled angrily around. "You think she fell off an overpass into that egg truck *accidentally*? She killed herself, all right? Okay? Go ahead and say it out loud in front of me!"

"You sure are hard on people, Wanda Louise. Children just hadn't had time to make enough mistakes yet, I guess. That's what it takes to really forgive. Time. And living. God's truth."

Wanda ran toward the pasture, hands cupped around her mouth. "Wild Thing, come back! Here, girl!"

"Hello, Mrs. Birdsong," Patty said, bending down.

"Well, hello, yourself." Granny answered.

"Are you all right?"

"Hey! Everyone all right?" they heard, coming like an echo, from the direction of the road. And Patty knew that voice.

"Hi," called Griffin LaCour, tromping down the hill.

Patty's hands landed on her hips. "How did *you* find us?"

"You're easy to track out here, Patricia. I was worried."

"Griffin, this is *not* a good time! Don't you have any couth?"

Griffin stopped in front her. "Now, cut it out, Patricia. I'm serious. What does it take . . ." He looked around. "Where's the kid?"

She pointed across the pasture plots to where Wanda had run out of the brush and was now making dog shapes and pointing to her ear as she talked to the people in white.

"Time to go," groaned Wanda's grandmother suddenly, getting to her feet and heading slowly toward the car. "I'm feeling rather melancholy now."

Wanda came running back toward them. "I can't find her!"

"I'll help you look," Griffin offered.

"She's gone!" Wanda collapsed and put her face in her hands. "Damn dog. Damn-damn dog. I don't need her, anyway!"

Griffin scanned the area from left to right, squinting. He put a hand over his brow to shield against the sun, hoping to catch a glimpse of yellow dog. Instead a glint of metal caught his eye close to where Granny had been sitting. He picked it up. "A buffalo nickel. Why, I hadn't seen one of these . . ."

But before he could finish his thought, Wanda had scooped it out of his hand and thrown it as far as she could. "I hate this! I hate it all! This isn't my family! I don't have a family! I don't have anything and I'm never going to be anything!"

"That's not true, Wanda," Patty tried. "You can be anything you want."

"Maybe rich people like you! Maybe people like my donor daddy! Not people like me! This is it. I'm going to end up as crazy as my mama and my grandmama! I can't even get a dog to stay with me!" She rushed up the hill just as her grandmother made it to the Cadillac. The old car roared to life.

Patty and Griffin both now ran toward the Cadillac, but by the time they made it up the hill, the Cadillac, Granny and Wanda had pulled loudly away, spraying gravel and dirt into the air.

"The kid's driving?" Griffin asked, waving at the dust. "Her nose is sticking through the steering wheel."

"Great, just great." Patty threw up her hands. She gazed back on the cemetery scene with its pond, its planted trees and people in white. She caught her breath.

"What?" Griffin whirled around.

"It's like Granny's dream. That's really odd."

"Second sight," said Griffin. Patty looked at him sideways. "My great-aunt Ida did that sometime when she was real old. Scared the pisser out of this little boy, I tell you that."

Patty fumed. "Griffin, what are you doing here? Just go away!"

"Patricia, will you let me be a human being?" Trying a charming smile, he took a step toward her, his voice softening. "I'm not the bad guy. I'm on your side."

Patty rolled her eyes. "You're on your own side, Griffin LaCour, where you've always been."

Griffin sighed and tried again. "I'm not the same guy I was seven years ago."

"You're not still hiding your dirty laundry under your bed?"

"Changed my ways."

"And your string of temp wives?"

"Okay, maybe I'm a little like the guy two years ago." Griffin paused. "That's a joke, Patricia. C'mon, you did call me, you know."

Patty cursed, threw up her hands, cursed again, pivoted and headed in a huff toward her car, with Griffin following. "I'm sorry I did!" she yelled over her shoulder. "It doesn't look like either of us has done poor Wanda any good. So just leave both of us the hell alone!"

Griffin stopped in his tracks, grinning deep and wide. "You still care."

Patty, throwing open her car door, shot Griffin a dirty look. "Are you out of your damned mind?"

Griffin laughed. "You do. You're cussing at me. I'm the only one Miss Texas ever cussed at in college, and I bet I'm still the only one. In fact, I bet I'm the only one you've *ever* just let go with. Wow. You must be about to pop from all that stifling. This job of yours has made you so nice you've turned into your mother."

Patty gasped, turning all the way around. "What a horrible thing to say!"

"I'm right about this, aren't I? That's *really* why you called."

"You are so wrong you don't know how wrong you are."

Griffin stepped closer, touching her. "Patricia, I've wanted to call, too. I still think we need to talk about . . ."

Patty jerked away. "I don't want to talk about that, Griffin. You understand? Ever."

"Well, maybe we need . . ."

"Damn it, Griffin! Just shut up!" Patty slammed her car door on the rest of his sentence, then roared away, popping gravel airborne.

"You cussed again! I heard you!" he yelled at the top of his lungs, rising on his toes to deliver it.

Across the cemetery, the workers looked up from their weeds at the echoing sound, in time to see, thankfully, the last member of the noisy clan drive away.

★ ★ ★

As darkness fell, Patty pulled up to the Motel 9. She had figured Wanda wouldn't have taken Granny back to the scene of her little house's crime without cleaning it up first, but she hadn't figured on the scene she was now seeing through the office windows.

Griffin pulled in behind her, still filling up her rearview mirror just like he'd been doing all the way back to the city. Patty did her best to ignore him as she ran toward the harshly lit office, where Wanda and Granny were hovering amidst their suitcases, and the manager was leaning over his motel counter. "Watch your mouth, girl!" he was yelling over Wanda's summation of his family tree. "I had to rent out your room. We're full up."

Patty came through the door. "What about the money I gave you?"

"Back payment, lady." He smiled, big and bad and black, full of teeth way past the point of dental return.

"Excuse me," Griffin interrupted, smiling, as he eased in behind the women. "Say, buddy, is it true what I've been hearing about the drug deals going down in this chain's motels around here? I should introduce myself. Griffin LaCour, *Dallas Tribune*." He held out his hand. The manager shook it, the rotting smile fading away. "Any comment on that? Tell you what. I'll get back to you about it. We'll be on our way now." Griffin grabbed up Wanda's and Granny's beat-up bags, pointed the three women toward the door and backed out behind them. Throwing the luggage into the Cadillac, he turned toward Patty. "They can stay with me tonight."

Patty looked strangely at Griffin a second, then said, "No, they're staying with me." She turned toward Wanda. "How about it?"

# Chapter 16

*Earthworms excrete a slimy substance
that keeps pairs stuck together until
fertilization is complete.*

—Wonderful World of Biology

The cat was lying in a ray of sunshine coming from the balcony door, warm, contented, patient. She hadn't moved more than a few inches either way from that table in two days just in case another feast from kitty heaven might appear. She was in the process of scratching an ear when a sound made her freeze, then hightail it to her hiding place.

"Granny, you take the guest bedroom," Patty was saying as she steered the old woman in the front door and down the hall. "Wanda can sleep on the sofa in there with you. My nurse friend is going to be here any minute, okay?"

The old woman waved her hands as the trio moved into the room. "Fine, fine. You go on now, Wanda Louise." She lowered her stiff self down to the bed and eased her feet up on it. "Time for a nap." Wanda slipped Granny's worn open-toed Sunday sandals off her feet and dropped them to the floor, then backed out of the room.

"I'll pay you back," she said to Patty as she stared back at her granny. "I'll pay you everything back."

Griffin came huffing and puffing down the hall, dragging the bags. Patty held the door open for him. As he passed by, her eyes settled on the back of his neck. On a cowlick, still curling the wrong way. She pulled her eyes away with a little mental shake and led Wanda back into the living room, a large area with a cathedral ceiling and an overabundance of expensive white furniture and designer touches.

"Where's your cat?" Wanda asked quietly.

"Somewhere. She'll show herself when she decides to." Patty studied Wanda as she gingerly touched the blue stained glass of the Tiffany-style table lamp.

"He staying the night, too?" Wanda nodded her head back down the hall.

"I'll tell him to leave now, if you want."

"Aw, he's okay." Wanda waved a hand. "He's just a mudpuppy."

Patty almost smiled. "A mudpuppy."

"This lizard that's still got gills, like you know, it never grows all the way up. Makes these puppy sounds when you try taking it out of muddy water." Wanda felt something warm and furry making figure eights around her ankles. She bent down, picked up the cat and began rubbing its full, perfect ears until from somewhere inside the cat came a contented vibrating sound. Which made Wanda feel sad. She put the cat down.

Just then the doorbell rang. Patty opened it just as Griffin reappeared from his back room bag-hauling. There, filling the doorframe from side to side and top to bottom, stood the widest woman in the widest nurse uniform the reporter had ever seen.

Patty put her arms as far around the big black woman as she could and hugged. "Thank you, Lucille, for coming by," she said. "We couldn't get her to go by the emergency room."

The wide woman smiled, which made her look even wider. As Wanda led her back to Granny, the only notice she took of Griffin LaCour, sole keeper of the Y chromosome in the room, was a disapproving arch of an eyebrow. Griffin, on the other hand, took extreme notice, and made way. After they disappeared down the hall, he stood alone in the room with Patty, his hands stuck in his front jeans pockets, shoulders hunched and awkward.

Patty pivoted and went into the kitchen.

"Nice place," Griffin called to her, slowly stepping toward her as she opened a cabinet and pulled out a glass. "Thanks, I could use something to drink. Before I go."

She paused, then loudly pulled out another glass.

Griffin picked up the dented mobile phone from the kitchen table. It rattled. "What happened to this?"

Ignoring him, Patty yanked a soft drink bottle from the refrigerator and popped it on the counter.

"Truce, Patricia." Griffin moved closer.

Patty cut her eye back at the man. "Would you have really taken them to your place?"

"I told you. I'm a changed man."

Wearily, Patty considered Griffin. She never could tell what was a put-on with him. "You're a mudpuppy, that's what you are."

Griffin cocked his head. "A mudpuppy?"

"Ask Wanda." With that Patty rubbed her face and gazed back down the hall. "I wonder what's going to happen to her."

"She does grow on you," Griffin admitted.

Patty filled his glass to the brim and pushed it his way. Then they both turned and leaned against the counter—several safe feet apart. For a few silent moments they sipped and swallowed, both staring straight ahead.

"So," Griffin tried.

They both took another sip.

"The story was good," Patty admitted, frowning into her glass. "You can still write."

Griffin shrugged, surprised at the sudden compliment. "Thank you."

More staring, sipping, swallowing.

Patty cut her eye toward him: "I'm not really like my mother, am I?"

Griffin waved the idea away. "I just said that."

Patty studied him a moment. "Well, at least you didn't say I looked beautiful. You never did."

"You want me to?"

"No. Not you."

One more round of long sips and careful swallows.

Griffin tried again, smiling awkwardly. "What's your husband's name?"

"Eric. Eric Little."

"You didn't take his name, hmm?"

"No."

"Modern guy."

"Yes."

"That's good."

"Yes."

"A stockbroker."

"Yes."

"Terribly successful, I suppose."

"Oh, yes."

Griffin scrunched up his lips in a judicial way, his eyes falling on the extremely large oil portrait of the two of them on the far wall. The guy had nicer hair than Patricia did. "Nice portrait." He squinted. "Although I don't think the artist got your nose exactly right."

Surprisingly embarrassed, Patty glared at her painted nose, at their painted smiles, at this, the most pretentious of Eric's ideas.

Griffin took her silence wrong: "But still nice," he backpedaled. "Everything's real nice."

Patty's eyes wandered away, unable to keep looking at that portrait. As they roamed around the room it occurred to Patty how much in their lives had been Eric's idea—every purchase from the couches to the wall-paper. Even the now-battered mobile phone had to be the "best" one on the market. Good Lord, she suddenly realized, the guy was preten-sion personified. Eyeing the monogrammed crystal glass in her hand, she almost gagged on the raw epiphany. How blind is love, anyway?

"I'm sure he's a great guy," Griffin was saying. He swished a few more chin hairs with a fidgety finger. "But I can't quite see you with a stockbroker."

Patty rolled an eye his way. "Griffin, look at me. I go perfectly with one. I work in public relations. I shop at Neiman's. I sleep on designer sheets and drink out of etched glass. I spend an hour each morning making myself beauty pageant presentable, and I like people noticing. You never did see me as I really am."

"Yes I did, and I still do, obviously better than you do. Admit it; you find it strange, too."

"I find it perfect." Her eyes went back to the portrait. "Oh, yes," she echoed, taking a big deep breath to fill a shallowness she seemed to have just discov-ered. And then with the tiniest bit of sarcasm, she added, "Exactly what I deserved."

Griffin heard it. Reran it. Listened to it again. Then he tried: "Why did you marry him?"

Patty's eyes hadn't left Eric's fine face. "Because of the way he danced," she said, more to Eric than to Griffin. Then she laughed very slightly, a little mocking, a lot dreamy. "People were watching him instead of me, he was so beautiful, so athletic and graceful, so poised and perfect." She paused, then added in a voice gone somewhere inside herself, "Seems I mistook a country club upbringing for a romantic soul."

"He danced," Griffin repeated, watching her.

"You know," she murmured, eyes still on her dancer, "you grow up believing the most unreal things: true love is waiting; beauty is forever; and life is this journey in happiness. It's as if you spend your time being young daydreaming, and your time being adult slowly, wrenchingly waking up." She breathed in.

As if just realizing she had spoken her thoughts aloud, she expanded her exhale into an incredulous, arms-out huff: "I can't *believe* I just told you all that." She turned and poured the rest of her drink down the drain. "Let's stop this old schoolmate thing, all right?"

"What thing?"

"The way people spill their guts with somebody just because a long time ago they walked across the same quadrangle."

"I think we were a little closer than that," Griffin snapped, then added, with an edgy, hurt voice: "Damn close. Close as two people can get."

*Too close.* Patty began scrubbing her glass, running hot—scalding hot—water over it as the ghost guilt came floating . . .

"And no, Patricia. Not too close," she heard Griffin say.

Patty's head all but swiveled off, whipping back at him.

"That's what you were thinking, wasn't it?" Griffin answered.

Patty turned back to the sink. "You do *not* know me that well."

"You're the one who hasn't changed," Griffin went on. "You still act like someone really knowing you is a big mistake."

It was. She knew that, knew that well. Reveal yourself and people get upset; people leave. Better to stay what you're supposed to be, what people want you to be, do whatever it takes to keep the image glowing. At all costs. She scrubbed the glass. "Stop this, Griffin. *I mean it.* I *know* where this is going. I won't talk about that."

Griffin's jaw muscles did a little jig. "Are you ever sorry?"

"I want you to go," Patty said evenly, over her shoulder.

Griffin set his glass down a little harder than he needed to. "I should be the one mad. It wasn't just your decision, Patricia."

Patty stiffened, seeing sterile hallways and long-ago Dr. Strake, the ghost guilt now fully formed. She squeezed the wet glass—it slipped, bounced, and shattered in the sink. With a curse scared out of her, she lashed out at Griffin. "How can you say something like that? I didn't have a choice and you know it! We were just children ourselves—stupid and naive and selfish—"

"You underestimated me."

"Oh god, Griffin! You've forgotten. You were relieved I did it! It was all over your face!" Patty held his eyes for a second, no more, then dropped her gaze back to the sink.

She felt a sting.

"Did you cut yourself?" Griffin asked.

She wiped away the red drop on her stinging wet forefinger, cleared the pieces of glass out of the sink, searching distractedly, desperately, for something to dry her hands with. "I . . . I really can't handle this now." She waved her wet hands in the air, then gave up and furiously rubbed them against her linen skirt. "Please go. *Please.*" And she pushed past him.

"Patricia—"

She opened the balcony door, went through, shut it solidly against any more of his words and prayed she could do the same against her own thoughts—that glassware was a dangerous thing to have in the kitchen; that talking to old loves was like picking at old scabs; that her Sunday school's Jesus was the only one guaranteed to be able to forgive and forget.

Someone's idea of a joke came to mind: The longer you live, the longer you live to regret it.

She pressed a trembling thumb against the sting.

Griffin stood inside with his arms in the beseeching position for a beat, then lowered them, studying Patty's back. He realized that he was in deep, deep trouble. Because he was pretty sure he was back in love with her. Or maybe he was never out of love with her. Now there was a concept. They'd both have to do a lot of scraping to really get back down to it, though.

He ran a hand through his thick fuzz of a goatee, fuming loud enough to spook the cat. It was almost seven, and he still had to write some "Brave New Wanda" thing tonight, something, anything. He turned and slogged down the hall in search of Wanda—just in time to see a glimpse of ponytail vanish the wrong way into the wrong door.

★ ★ ★

In the other room, Wanda had just pushed the window as high as it would go, and already had one boot over the sill, when the door opened and the reporter guy saw her. Before she knew it, he had a deathgrip on her T-shirt and was making a grab for her ponytail. "Ouch! Watch it!"

Griffin let go of the ponytail but knew better than to let go of anything else. "Where do you think you're going?"

Wanda turned those lonesome hazel eyes back at him. "I need to go look around again."

Griffin readjusted his grip. "At the risk of sounding like my father, I hasten to point out that you don't have a driver's license. So give me another story to write besides your premature death on the freeway in your vintage Cadillac, okay?" She made an attempt to pull out of his grasp, one boot still tucked up on the ledge. Griffin held on. "Look, I'll go with you out there tomorrow, if you promise to stay put. Your dog's probably smarter than all of us and has already bedded down nice and warm for the night."

Wanda studied him, trying to stare him down. She tested the strength of his grip; the scrawny guy was stronger than he looked. So she climbed back in, he let go, and they both plopped down on the leather couch beside the window.

Wanda leaned over her knees and rested her chin in her hands.

Griffin rubbed his face hard and settled his tired eyes on her. "I'm supposed to write something about you tonight for my column tomorrow."

"No more pictures." Wanda said. "And don't call me Louise."

Griffin studied her a moment. "I don't suppose you'd want to sue."

"I don't trust lawyers."

"But a judge . . ."

"I don't trust judges."

"Well," Griffin said, "that pretty much covers the civil court system. Look, can I at least write that you're thinking about it?"

"I'll think about it."

"So I can say you're thinking about it?"

"I'll think about thinking about it."

"So much for the story." Griffin ran a thumb and finger over his goatee with long, slow, deliberate strokes, then sighed. "Patricia just kicked me out."

Wanda pulled both of her legs up under her Indian fashion and studied Griffin LaCour. "You two know each other real well, huh?"

Griffin looked back toward the balcony, trying to see through walls. "Too well, maybe."

Wanda noticed. "You like her."

He forced himself to look out the window, in the opposite direction. "Liking ain't going to get the job done, I don't think."

"Dubby Mayhew likes me, but it doesn't get the job done, either."

Griffin smiled in spite of himself and shook his head. "You know, in a funny way you remind me of Patricia in college. I think she sees it too, whether she knows it or not."

Wanda horse-laughed, blowing spit.

At that, Griffin smirked. "Why do you figure she's going out on this limb for you? Your winning way with people?"

"But . . ." Wanda sneered. "She's so . . ."

"Nice." He stretched an arm across the back of the couch. "Blame her mother. I used to have this uncontrollable urge to pick my nose every time I was around the woman."

Wanda was still aghast. "But she's been in *beauty* pageants."

"The Queen Mother again," he answered. "Started her out at four, Little Miss Texas Preschool Princess or something. It's a way of life when you got a mama like that. Trust me on this: deep down, there's a nice simmering fire inside that woman just waiting to flame back up."

Wanda thought about that for a moment. "Well, if you're so goofy over her, why didn't you end up with her instead of this other guy?"

Griffin began to say something and thought better of it, gazing around the room. A steady hum was coming from the other side—a fax machine and a computer and stock gizmos littered the maple power desk against the far wall. Trophies and awards went to the ceiling. The place smelled of money and success. "For all I know," he finally said, quietly, "this husband of hers is better for her."

Wanda curled a lip. "He's an asshole." From her pocket, she pulled a wadded-up piece of fax paper she'd found on the floor.

Griffin flattened it out. For a second he was actually speechless, until he fell back on the only word, however overused, that seemed to fit: "That— asshole!"

She walked over to the sleek desk, pulled open a left drawer and handed Griffin the household's hospital receipts for the current year, all the attempts to become pregnant, in chronological order.

"Kid," he murmured as he glanced through the papers, "you ever consider a career in investigative reporting?" He studied the medical procedures and thought of Patty back on her balcony. Then he thought about them both back in their senior year, and a sad smile spread across his face. He felt a pair of burrowing kid eyes on him.

"Just so you know," she said. "I got a .22 on the premises."

Griffin looked hurt. "I'm the good guy, remember? Why do I have to keep reminding everybody of that?"

That was when they heard the voices, coming toward them loud and fast. Before they could get off the couch good, the door burst open and there stood smiling Eric of the expensive portrait, except he wasn't smiling. "Letting total strangers in our house is bad enough, Patty, but even back here? They're going through our personal papers!"

Patty grabbed the papers from Griffin, with a look that said: *You're going through my papers?* She turned defiantly back to Eric. "It's my house, too. And keep it down, Granny's asleep."

Nonplussed, Eric looked back toward the guest room. "Your grandmothers are both dead!"

Griffin popped him in the chest with the wadded-up fax. "Asshole."

Feeling that more emphasis was needed, Wanda added: "A shithead piss-ant asshole."

Eric guffawed. "You certainly have some classy friends, Patty." He grabbed up the fax machine, computer and stock market gizmos, unplugging as he went.

Patty stopped him by standing in the doorway. "Trashier than adultery?"

Eric hesitated.

"Did you know," announced Wanda, "that contrary to popular belief, the black widow doesn't eat her mate after mating? The mate is actually polyga-mous—doing it with anything that moves—until he's so worn out by the time it gets back to her, she just consumes him like she would any small helpless shithead piss-ant in her way."

Eric stared incredulously at Wanda.

"Little-known biological fact," Wanda added, chin out.

"Who is this child?" Eric spat. Arms full, he pushed past them and out the door. They followed.

Patty kept pace with Eric's stride. "Frankly, right now I don't know what kept us together all this time."

"Slime," Wanda suggested as the parade moved back to the living room.

Eric rolled an eye at Wanda and waited.

"Earthworms. They mate because they're stuck together with slime. Don't have much of a choice." Wanda wiggled her fingers slimily. "Another little-known biological fact," she pointed out.

"Would you get this irritating child away from me?" Eric turned his back on everyone but Patty; he sighed and leaned close. "Patty, I'm worried about you. There's some sort of personality change you've gone through. Perhaps this baby thing . . ."

"Me?" Patty laughed. "*You're* the living cliché. Your secretary? Congratula-tions on the winner sperm."

Eric's face dropped. He set the machine and computer on the edge of the sofa table, gently so as not to scratch its high gloss finish. Then grabbing Patty's arm, he moved her several steps away, but the two visitors followed. "We'll talk about this later. In *private.*"

Griffin yanked Eric's arm away from Patty. At that, Eric and Patty both shot him looks to decapitate. "Don't push it, friend," Eric snarled, jerking his arm out of Griffin's grip.

"Stay out of this, Griffin," Patty snapped.

Griffin pressed closer. "Fax anyone lately?"

Eric swung open the front door and grabbed up his equipment. "I don't know who you are, but if I didn't have my hands full, your mouth would be full of fist."

Griffin howled. "Who's writing his lines? Larry, Moe and Curly Joe?"

The cat appeared from somewhere, tail high, and trotted out the open door. Wanda followed, calling to it.

Griffin moved into Eric's face and gave an exposed patch of his sternum a rather tough poke with several outstretched digits. Eric stumbled back on the front door's threshold. "Watch it. I've got a bum football knee."

Griffin scoffed: "Right. You played football."

Eric took his best athletic stance, shifting the equipment to one arm, resting the load on a hip. "As a matter of fact I did play a little ball."

A light bulb all but appeared above Griffin's head. "Eric Little. You played split receiver for Rice! I remember when you got that knee busted, Texas game, end of the fourth quarter. Took you out on a stretcher. Guy came out of nowhere and . . ."

"Blindsided me. Who the heck are you?"

"Griffin LaCour, *Dallas Tribune.*" He stuck out his hand.

Eric shook it. "I read your column all the time."

At the sound of the sudden male bonding, seconds this side of backslapping, Patty let out a frustrated rumble of a shriek, pushed both of them out the door and slammed it good and rattling shut.

"Hey!" Eric shouted, but in the wrong direction. "Get away from the car, girl. I just got a wax job." He rushed toward his hunter green Lexus, equipment jiggling. Through the dusk, his voice came floating back: "Go wash that mouth out!"

Griffin turned weakly back toward the front door. He gave the door a half-hearted knuckle rap. All was quiet beyond it, though, and stayed that way. So he slumped down on the step, closed his eyes and began banging his head on one of the pillars.

"Doesn't that hurt?"

Griffin opened one eye and saw Wanda standing over him, holding the cat.

"Do me a favor. Go ahead and shoot me with that .22." Sighing, he gazed back one last time at the front door. "Tell her I'm sorry and I won't bother her anymore." And he was still without a story. Glancing at his watch, he jumped to his feet. "Man, the softball game!"

"Baseball?"

Griffin turned all the way around at the change of voice coming from the girl. It was the first time he'd heard anything but a world-weary sound from this kid. For some reason it made Griffin look at her, really look at her, for the first time. Past deadlines, agendas, the people's right to know and his right to a byline, he saw a girl who was into the goddamned mess of the adult world, way, way too early. How old was she? Thirteen? What was he doing at thirteen? Reading Superman comics, waiting for his voice to change, not giving his parents or his future a thought past suppertime. And playing baseball.

"You like baseball?" he asked.

She liked it. She liked it a lot. She let the cat go to say so.

"You any good?" he asked her.

"Dubby Mayhew lost his hundred-dollar glove betting I wasn't. Want to see it?"

"You have it with you?"

"I got everything with me."

The rest of the reality of this child's life sank in: Griffin thickly realized that all Wanda Ledbetter had in the world was in that cheap, ripped bag he'd lugged inside.

Wanda, meanwhile, was suddenly all careful boredom. "But I don't have time for such stuff." Shields up.

Griffin felt like giving himself a shake. Was this kid getting to him? He was just tired; that was it, he fretted, smoothing down his goatee. But he kept looking, not at the T-shirt, cutoff jeans or those beat-up boots, but at that expression on her face. It was a look that showed she'd be a kid for only another second or so, the way things were going.

*Oh, why not?* he thought. *It is a church team no matter how much they play for blood. How could they say no to an orphan?*

And then, another idea brewing, he rolled his eyes toward the door. "Hey, listen," he said, flexing his wrist. "My reporter buddy conned me into playing for him, but my wrist's acting up. How about doing me a big favor?"

Click. A little of the shield went down: The kid smiled.

He looked back at the house. "And there's just one more thing . . ."

★ ★ ★

Fifteen minutes later, Patty and Griffin were sitting in the ballpark, Patty working hard to get comfortable on the bleacher seat.

Wanda, ponytail swishing, was running back and forth, back and forth, out in center field, screaming grief at the batter, pounding her fist in her glove, kicking up dust in her worn-out sneakers.

"I can't believe we're at a ballgame in the middle of all this." Patty sighed. "But Wanda does seem to be having fun. And it was nice she wanted me to come." She looked around. Everybody had on fancy T-shirts with their church name written across the front: Holy Spirit Descending Pentecostal Church in blue; First Baptist Church, Dallas in red. Someone above them was waving a homemade sign: *All the Way to State Again! Behead 'em, Baptists!* She snickered. "I also can't believe you're playing for a church softball team, Griffin, even if you are just doing it for a friend."

"They didn't ask me to preach, Patricia. This is serious stuff. You can only push these Christians so far when it comes to softball."

Patty looked at him doubtfully. "Weren't you the one that said the problem with Baptists is they don't hold them under long enough?"

The aluminum clink of a bat and the crowd's screams made both of them look up. The ball was going back to center field. Wanda was coming up fast, coming, coming. "I got it!" she yelled, and just as she was on the ball, a boy about her age sailed in front of her and caught it.

"Hey!" Patty yelled. "You see that? Why isn't he staying in his position?"

Out on the field, Wanda shot the boy a fried look as the Baptist crowd roared. The boy waved his arms in triumph and flipped the ball back to the pitcher.

"That was Wanda's ball," Patty shouted, looking at the crowd clapping like crazy. She squinted. The woman clapping the loudest for the boy looked familiar.

"Patricia, I want to talk to you about something . . ." Griffin was saying.

Another aluminum clink, and the ball went airborne, this time toward where the boy was standing.

Wanda sprinted in front of the boy, and just as the ball was almost in his glove, she leaped high and came up with it. The crowd roared; Wanda coolly chunked the ball back to the pitcher.

"What if I father you a child?"

Patty's head jerked around at Griffin, as did the whole row of Pentecostal heads in the row below them. *"What?"*

Griffin stared down the row. "Mind your own business, will you?" He turned back to Patty. "I'm serious. And you know I can."

Out in the field, the boy readjusted his ball cap and eyed Wanda. Wanda punched her glove a couple of times and eyed him back.

Patty flushed. The old scarred-up ghost guilt this time was like a knife, and she turned the rush of anger onto Griffin: "Get another old girlfriend to further your career, *all right?"*

Griffin jerked her back down. "That isn't what this is about!"

Patty glared at his hand now gripping her arm. He softened his grip, leaving his fingers, soft, tentative, on her skin a moment longer than needed before letting go. He tried again: "What I'm *trying* to say is I'd do that for you. No strings. I'll sign anything."

Patty studied him under lowered eyelids. She was rather taken aback by the look on Griffin's face.

"I'm kind of surprised myself," he added. "But I'm truly willing to do this for you."

The old pain turned sideways. "You are certifiable," Patty mumbled, uncomfortable, shaking her head and looking away. But she could not deny she was rather touched, finding herself resisting an uncharacteristic nudge of actual feeling toward him.

"I know about you two trying," he was now whispering. "I can't say I'm sorry if it's what broke you up. But if you want a baby so bad, I'm a pretty good bet."

Patty's heart slowed, skipped, started up again. What did she want? She'd thought she wanted Eric. She was wrong about that. She'd thought she wanted lots of money and security. It hadn't done much for her. She'd thought she wanted an important job. From every indication, she was trying to sabotage that herself. And she'd thought she wanted a baby. But now she wasn't so sure why she wanted that, either. Or at least why she had wanted it so desperately such a short time ago. She felt so very tired.

"That is what you want, isn't it?" Griffin was asking.

"I don't know; I really don't," Patty murmured.

Another aluminum chink. A weak little grounder, out at first.

"Thank you, Griffin, but no." Patty smiled, full of sighs and absurdity.

The side was changing. The boy jogged over to Wanda and they walked slowly into the dugout together, chatting cheerfully. And everyone was clapping except for the same woman on the other end of the bleachers who had been clapping so hard a few moments ago for the boy. Patty looked at her more closely. "Oh, my lord," Patty murmured. She knew her all right. As she watched, the woman swiveled her head around to Patty, then back to the teenagers, then back at Patty, a stricken look growing across her face.

Then to Patty's horror, the woman pushed down the bleacher bench, crawling over Baptist and Pentecostal knees and toes alike, heading right for her. Patty braced herself.

A second more and the woman moved within inches of Patty's nose, so close no one else could hear, and said: "You keep that girl away from my Charlie. You understand, Ms. Hightower? Keep-her-away." And she was gone as fast as she came.

Patty groaned. "I *knew* I shouldn't be seen with you two. I'm going to be fired."

Griffin looked back and forth between the two women. "Who the hell was that?"

Patty closed her eyes. "Dr. Youngblood's ex-wife Lorraine."

Confused, Griffin frowned. "But what was that about Wanda talking to that boy?"

Patty looked at Griffin, suddenly just as confused. "What *does* she have against Wanda talking to her son? She can't be that much of a snob."

"Her son?" Griffin stared down at Wanda and the boy talking and punching their softball gloves below. A coyote grin spread across his face. He just loved a good coincidence. "And here I thought the story was dead," he said under his breath, his thumb and forefinger making thoughtful circles in his goatee. "Patricia, couldn't you say it's at least possible Wanda and that boy bear a small resemblance? I mean if you look at them just the right way?"

# Chapter 17

*The male fiddler crab dances the
female along in the crook of his
single enormous claw arm.*

—Wonderful World of Biology

Granny opened her eyes in the shadowy room and saw someone standing over her with an extremely large hand. "Who's that?"

"Patty and the reporter guy, they took me to a ball game," Wanda said, punching the hand. "I helped out. They needed a good girl player."

"Well, now, isn't that nice?" Granny mumbled and drifted back to sleep.

"We won." Standing over her, Wanda fidgeted, still full of the story. Finally she shook off her glove and stood a moment in the dark. Then, pulling the stolen vial and her notebook from where she'd hidden them in her beat-up suitcase, she set them both neatly on the room's desk, turned on the lamp, opened her little book and wet the tip of her pencil with her tongue:

> Dear Daddy,
> We won.
> I feel good. Things haven't changed much, you know, but I still
> feel good. Why is that? I have noticed that bad thing after bad
> thing happens, shit piling up so high you got to put your hip boots
> on, and then finally, this small good thing bobs up. And instead of
> being surprised, you're like, hey, right—I've been waiting for you . . .

"Wanda Louise, that you?"

Wanda stopped, turned toward her grandmother's shape under the sheets.

The lamplight revealed her old face, drowsy, full, flushed with forgetfulness.

Wanda hesitated. "Hello, Granny."

"Hello yourself. That nice Lucille was so interesting." Granny's voice trailed off. "I have high blood pressure."

"I played in a ballgame. We won."

"That so?" Granny patted her chest as she yawned. "You know, I am dead-dog tired."

"I had a double and a home run. You should have seen me."

"That . . . so?" Granny's voice fell away as she dozed off once more.

Wanda began writing again:

> *It was a double and a home run, I had five RBI's and I caught three flies. You should have seen me, all right. Good night.*
>
> *Your daughter,*
> *Wanda*
> *P.S. Bet you were some ballplayer.*

A few blocks away, Dr. Charles Youngblood sat in his apartment, lights out, staring at the last purple streaks giving way to dark. His thirty-inch TV was on, sound off, shadows from the pictures playing across the walls. Slow jazz coming from the stereo served as background for what was showing, one of those funniest home video shows. A slightly blurry kid in diapers was bothering a wiener dog in a party hat.

Dr. Youngblood, though, wasn't aware of any of it. Clutched in his palm was his mobile phone. A siren-loud, off-the-hook sound had been bleating from it for over a minute. At last he hit the off button and looked down at the piece of molded plastic, staring, contemplating: *Interesting how this technology works,* he mused. *Just an invisible impulse. Coming along a line and then through the air. Nothing to grab. At least you used to have the satisfaction of killing the messenger.*

His eyes wandered back to the darkness coming down. Shortly he was aware that the phone still in his hand was ringing; he tapped the Talk button and slowly lifted it to his ear.

"Dr. Youngblood? Griffin LaCour. Is it safe to say that you had some 'dealings' with Dr. H. L. Roddy while you were in medical school at Parkland?"

Gently Dr. Youngblood set the phone down, got to his feet, walked past the TV just as the television audience was laughing at a clip of a man being hit in the crotch by a baseball thrown by his son, and disappeared through the door.

"Dr. Youngblood?"

★ ★ ★

From a couch in her spacious, well-appointed living room several miles away, Patty could have seen the same falling darkness of evening. But she wasn't looking. She sat below the portrait of her and Eric, flipping absently through the pages of a magazine. She couldn't have told you the name of the magazine, nor anything printed on its pages, yet this was all she'd been doing for an hour, ever since she and Wanda had returned from Griffin's game. Griffin's crazy offer had shaken her a little. It seemed to be making her think. She wasn't quite sure what it was making her think, but she was definitely thinking, her mind doing exhausting flip-flops over something.

Was it Griffin? No. Definitely not; of *course* not.

It must be Eric. His dimples smiled down from their portrait at her. She glared back at him, trying hard to turn him bald and beer-belly bloated, as her friend Lucille had suggested. But there he was—no, there *they* were—eternally, depressingly, so very beautiful. And she hated it. Lord, how she hated that portrait. Why, she wondered, hadn't she ever said so? Because she was nice. Always so nice. Now that the worst had happened in spite of her niceness, she wondered why she hadn't said a lot of things. She squinted at her nose. No, the artist hadn't gotten it quite right, but Eric's nose, well, now, the artist had sure gotten his right, hadn't he? Gotten everything right. Everybody did with Eric. Real easy on the eyes, everyone said as they sidled up close to him. And, she had to admit, to her, too: the Football Hero and the Beauty Queen. Of such are fairy tales made. *What a pair you make. What beautiful babies you'll have. What a catch, what a lucky girl.* What a lucky, dimple-stupid girl. She frowned up at the portrait, tapping a forefinger on the slick magazine paper, swallowing down how mad, how sick, how not-nice she felt right now.

But what about all the baby tries? Wasn't that part of what was bothering her, too? She could still see Dr. Youngblood smiling down at her after yet another insemination. ("Lay still, knees high. We'll be back in thirty minutes.") Wincing at the memory, she was suddenly downright amazed what she'd been willing to do. Shots, tests, ultrasounds, drugs, laparoscopy, temperature charts, god-awful sex on demand. Why? Why had she wanted a baby so bad, so desperately? Had she been playing "Can This Marriage Be Saved"? Or "Keeping Up with the Fertile Joneses"? Or was she trying to fill gaps she knew not of—ones someplace higher and deeper than the one Dr. Youngblood's needle kept filling? Surely it wasn't just to have someone to care for her when she was old or, heaven forbid, to carry on the family line. And she would not let herself consider her past with Griffin, things that could never be changed, as some guilty motivation. So. What, then? Maybe this wasn't a logical thing, she thought, but something in the DNA women had no control over, a seminal response preprogrammed by the manufacturer. Cats prowl, birds fly south, rabbits burrow, dogs do that thing where they go around and around before they lie down. And women alternately torture themselves over not having and then having to have a baby.

That had to be it. There's truth in nature; her kid-genius houseguest knew that. Consider how all of creation seems to go into crazy mindless heat on a preordained schedule where nothing matters but a furious finding and blending of fluids. Put that way, what does love have to do with it?

Patty stopped flipping the magazine's pages and stared suddenly at a perfume ad: two gorgeous, wildly wet people were on the verge of something "scent-uously" erotic on a virgin sand beach . . .

She slapped the magazine shut. Who, she wanted to know, brought up love anyway? She felt her stomach turn again, sick, just as it had yesterday morning. Dear God, had everything happened just yesterday?

The phone rang. Without thinking, she snatched it up with her free hand.

"What did you do?" the voice abruptly demanded.

Patty paused. "Mother."

"Do I have to learn about something like this from others? What did you do to run off that wonderful man? Eric dropped by. He's very worried about you."

*Eric dropped by?*

"What did you do, Patricia Ann Hightower? He was too much a gentleman to go into it, no matter how much I asked. He just said you hadn't been yourself. And what's this about some white trash people and that scruffy Griffin LaCour person staying with you? My heavens, not him again!"

"*I* didn't do anything," Patty sputtered.

But before she could say another word, her mother was talking again: "You call that beautiful boy up and straighten things out. And get those people out of your house. Don't you know this could affect your position with the hospital? Not to mention the pageant world." Her mother hung up without even a goodbye.

Crushing the magazine in her fist, Patty slammed down the phone, wishing she could have hung up first. At that moment all the emotion she'd been pushing away, pushing back, back, back, came at her in a rush. Steeling herself against it, she stood up, skidding the magazine across the glass coffee table. Without a moment's premeditation, in glorious, angry, unthinking instinct, she stepped over to the painting, lifted it off its hanger and let it drop with a dramatic bounce behind the antique liquor cabinet dear Eric loved so much. And oh, the tiny dark pleasure she took at the scrape it made across the delicate woodwork on its way down.

Then the fleeting pleasure flipped over. Before she knew what hit her, she was crying, one of those all-out, blow-out, gasping cries that take over from beyond understanding. She slipped to the floor, and for a few blind, stand-still moments, she heaved with the weight of it all. Heaved as if parts of her soul would stream right out with her sobs. It felt like grieving, it was coming from so deep. But how can you grieve for a marriage that never was? And how can you grieve for a baby that never was? How do you grieve for dreams?

The room echoed with the quiet sound for a few long, dark minutes. Patty lay alone with feelings so deep she couldn't recognize them, forgetting her houseguests, forgetting even the reasons she was crying, forgetting the whole world.

Until the doorbell rang.

Patty froze in mid-sob and blinked at her watch: 10:15? She jumped to her feet and hurriedly straightened herself, blowing her nose into a tissue, grabbing a kitchen towel to mop her face, checking her red nose and eyes in the mirror. With a sniffing, give-up roll of her eyes, she blew one last time into the tissue and went to look through the peephole.

There, wiggling the fingers of one hand at the peephole and pushing his hornrims back up his nose with the other, was Dr. Charles A. Youngblood.

Patty slowly opened the door.

He took an unsteady step inside and lurched toward the matching white sofa and loveseat. Patty stood there, staring, as her gynecologist settled onto her furniture.

"Hope I'm not intruding," he called over a shoulder, his arms spread across the back of the sofa.

Patty sniffed into her tissue. "Well, actually . . ."

"Oh, do you have the sniffles? I could give you something for that. I'm a doctor."

She closed the door. "Why are you here, Dr. Youngblood?"

"So formal," he scoffed as he discovered a lock of wayward hair on his forehead and pushed it back into place. "Call me Charles. Or I'll call you Ms. Hightower."

Patty sighed and slowly came to rest in a chair across from him. "I think I'd rather keep the gynecological part of my life formal, if it's okay with you," she said.

"That's it," he mused. "Gynecologists probably hit the patient intimacy level right above proctologists. But we have feelings, too. Don't tell Eric, but I've always found myself attracted to you."

Patty found that thought revolting, wondering just what parts of her he was taking under consideration. "Dr. Youngblood, I'm not sure this is really appropriate."

He interrupted, a finger in the air. "Of course I have always found you a physically beautiful woman, but more importantly, a highly evolved person. Highly, highly evolved."

Patty sat straight up at that one. Two come-ons in two hours? She sniffed at herself: what, was she in heat?

"Yes, well," she finally stammered, "how nice, but . . ." But, she started to say, there's no way in this lifetime she was going to go out with someone who's looked at her private parts and thought of them in medical terms.

Dr. Youngblood frowned importantly. "I've always thought myself highly evolved, too." He nodded, and kept nodding as if waiting for Patty to join in. "Highly."

Patty sniffed at him. "Dr. Youngblood, have you been drinking?"

With a snort, he turned a doomed-looking grin her way, then held up two fingers on each hand.

"Peace to you, too," Patty said.

He shook his head, correcting her: "Twenty-two." He was now giving it a ten-finger flick twice and then fumbled to get one of the original twos in the air again. "That's how many." His hands dropped at about the same time his face did. "It's only natural to wonder, isn't it?" He waved an arm from shore to shore. "They're out there, all over Texas, California, Florida. Hell, one's even in Alaska. All these nearsighted, skinny teenagers who will soon be in need of major orthodontic work. Half my medical school class was doing it. Bowman was doing it every afternoon. I didn't donate but about thirty times total. Damn, my sperm must be super little swimmers."

Patty breathed in sharply: "Did you find records?"

"These days, of course, that's nothing. Sperm count may be lowest in recorded history, the American male's donation looking mighty anemic overall and getting worse everyday, but—no matter." He snapped his fingers. "We can spread those wiggly suckers across a month of females. Do you think I have to tell Lorraine? The woman can be so unreasonable."

Patty was about to pop. "Dr. Youngblood, have you found records!"

He squinted sagaciously. "We try to control everything. Big American can-do. Big fatal flaw's more like it. I always thought I could . . . Just smile, soothe, smooth over everything. Hmmph." He let out a snort at the idea. "The French, they know how to live, c'est la vie. Life is chaos. Enjoy. I didn't really want to be a gynecologist. What I really wanted was to sail around the world, be on the cover of *National Geographic*. Sail la vie!" He laughed at his clever quip. "You know my boy Charlie? Hates the water. Probably because it is my very soul, right?" He held out his two fingers again, rotating them as if examining his cuticles. "You think any of them sail?"

Patty reached out and grabbed his sleeve. *"Dr. Youngblood—"*

Then the man's face dropped to the center of the earth, scared, intense. "We have to talk. You being a professional in this publicity business, and me in my position, and all of them out there . . ." He went sickly pale, as if finally contemplating all the variations of disaster. His beeper went off. He didn't seem to hear it for a moment. Then as if coming to, he fumbled for Patty's phone and called in.

For the next solid minute, she listened impatiently as Dr. Youngblood kept saying "Yes" into the phone. She did not like the way all signs of his alcohol ingestion were vanishing before her eyes, posture dramatically improving, shoulders tightening. No, she did not like it at all. He was looking as sober as death.

"There's an emergency at the hospital," he told her as he calmly set down the phone. "The reporters have already arrived. I'll fill you in there." He looked at her a moment. Then before she could stop him from driving, he was out the door.

Patty stood in the middle of the room, staring after him. Then she rounded up her purse and keys, threw some powder on her red nose, wrote a quick note for Wanda and her grandmother in case they should wake, and headed for the garage.

Halfway down the street, Patty glanced in her rearview mirror.

Wanda looked back at her.

Patty grabbed at her chest. "You scared the bejesus out of me!"

"You should always look in the backseat before you get in, you know."

Patty began to give her a good talking-to, then stopped: "You heard us, didn't you?"

Wanda nodded. Patty saw her ponytail swish in the mirror. "Is Smiley Face my daddy?"

Patty opened her mouth to say something, but nothing came out. She closed it, then opened and closed it again. *Like some ridiculous goldfish,* she realized. Finally she just said, "Wanda, I'm sure this emergency has nothing to do with you."

"It was that bald guy, Dr. Crouch. Something about a baby."

Patty began to ask how she knew, but considering Patty and Eric's well-thought-out home in which every commode had a phone extension within reach, it seemed superfluous. "I have to take you back home. Granny's alone." She began eyeing the road for a place to turn around.

"No."

Just as Patty began to brake and turn the car, Wanda leaned over and held out the dog-eared hospital file. "Here."

Even in the dark of the car, Patty recognized the hospital file markings. She swerved and pulled to a halt on the shoulder. With a wary glance at Wanda, she turned on the overhead light, opened the old file and scanned its contents.

"These are hospital records, Wanda. If you give them to me, I'll have to keep them."

"She had the insemination done. She had me. Here."

Patty closed the folder and set it on the seat with a sigh. "But that may be all you ever find out. You know that, don't you? It was all set up that very way."

"Dr. Smiley Face knows something."

Patty turned off the overhead light and pushed the file back into Wanda's hands. "Here. Keep this a little longer. And don't argue. Griffin may be the better person for it; I just can't think this through right now. I should take you home."

"I'm staying. I won't cause trouble."

Patty didn't like it, but she didn't have time to go back.

A mile rushed by in silence. Then Patty heard from the backseat: "Bet you liked your daddy, didn't you?"

Patty paused, started to answer—

—then her cell phone beeped. "Yes," Patty said into it. "I'm on my way. What is this all . . . ?"

Wanda sat silent for another mile as Patty nodded into the phone, finally putting it down without even a goodbye. And although Wanda tried to get her to talk, Patty said nothing for the rest of the drive.

Inside the entrance nearest her parking space, Patty saw Dr. Crouch, his assistant and Dr. Youngblood murmuring and gesturing until they spied her. Out of habit, she turned the rearview mirror to check her face. But this time her eyes did not see lipstick need or misplaced hair or smeared blush. In fact, she was suddenly, utterly quite sick of that face. She pushed the mirror away. "Stay in the car," she commanded Wanda. "Unless you want me to lose this boring suck job."

As soon as Patty came close to the three, they began to move as a unit. Dr. Crouch grabbed her arm and pulled her into their powwow as they all marched toward the hospital's lobby. Once there, though, the men stopped dead, leaving Patty alone to thread her way through TV crews and reporters ganged around the entrance.

Patty took a breath as she moved into the scene, and the media crowd began shouting their questions. Griffin was standing on the edge of the crowd. She did her best to avoid eye contact—and found herself making eye contact instead with Miss Wanda Ledbetter, bobbing up and down on her tiptoes in the back.

Within a sound-bite second, though, Wanda was the last thing on her mind.

"How about a picture of the baby?" someone yelled at her.

"What's the hospital going to do with it?" shouted someone else.

Behind the crowd, still bobbing on those toes, Wanda noticed that all the gesturing seemed to be aimed at the far wing's doors. A group of whispering nurses were headed that way. Wanda squeezed through the crowd and followed them. They passed through the swinging doors, went down the hall and entered a window-encased room, closing the door silently behind them.

Wanda looked around her. She was surrounded by people butting their noses against the windows, making silly precious sounds at tiny newborn babies lined up behind the glass. Wanda watched the nurses head toward a corner of the room where there were no gurgling lookers. She eased up close to the glass in time to see the nurses join two others who were standing around one of the babies. They seemed to take turns shaking their heads over the baby. Wanda began to worry about it. She moved over close to see if it was okay.

That was where Patty found her thirty minutes later. She glanced at the newborn infant Wanda was watching. It looked perfectly healthy and normal except for a fuzzy, rose-colored birthmark the size of a golf ball on its neck.

"What's wrong with her?" Wanda mumbled.

"Not a thing," Patty answered. "Her mother died suddenly during delivery on Tuesday. An hour ago, the father decided he wasn't going to take the baby home. And it seems someone called the press."

Wanda did not look up at Patty. "She's a donor baby, isn't she?" she asked quietly.

"Yes," Patty answered just as quietly. "The woman's ignorant husband said he would have nothing to do with it, since it wasn't 'his.' He's filed a suit to disprove his paternity and responsibility to support. Maybe he's just angry out of grief and he'll change his mind. He did sign documents, so perhaps the court can force him to—"

"No." Wanda's face turned a bright, hot red. "Let him go!" She stalked away, breaking into a run.

Dr. Crouch and Dr. Youngblood pushed through the doors just as Wanda rushed through them.

"Ms. Hightower?" Dr. Crouch called as Patty walked slowly to meet them. Dr. Youngblood was shooting her tiny, pleading glances from behind the old man. "Ms. Hightower," Dr. Crouch repeated, looking back at where Wanda's ponytail had swished by, "wasn't that the Ledbetter girl?"

"Yes," she heard herself say. "It was."

"Well, what was *she* doing here?"

Patty raised her chin. "She's with me," she announced and pushed past them.

She found Wanda in the car, staring out the passenger side window. She did not look around. She did not speak. How late was it? It felt late, Patty thought, bone-weary of this day.

As she opened her door, Griffin emerged from a shadow. "Are you two okay?"

Patty glanced at the silent Wanda. "I guess you have your story."

As Griffin opened his mouth to reply, Patty just raised a hand, a small, tired stop motion, then closed the door, started the car and pulled out of the parking lot.

*Dear Daddy . . .* Wanda gazed out at the streaks of night rolling by her window. *Dear Daddy. Dear Daddy. You are not like that. You are not. You are not.*

★ ★ ★

Back at Patty's townhouse, Wanda tiptoed into the guest bedroom where her grandmother was snoring clear and contented. She eased under the sheets she and Patty had tucked into the corners of the sofa, laid her head back and tried to close her eyes. But they wouldn't close. They were pulled toward the window, to the moonlight, what little there was. She just stared at the slice of light, feeling no longer too mean to live, but too mad and sad and mixed up. As if she could stare long enough to make it illuminate all things between her and sleep.

"Wanda Louise, where am I?"

Wanda sat up. Her grandmother's voice had a vulnerable, bewildered sound that made Wanda shudder. Flinging her sheet back, she rushed over to the bed.

"We're in Patty's house, Granny. The nice, pretty woman from the hospital?"

"Hospital?" The light playing off the puffy, lost features of the old woman gave her granny so near the look of rest home women gone into themselves that Wanda could barely breathe.

"Oh, yes. Oh my, Wanda Louise." She grabbed the girl's arm hard enough for Wanda to feel the strong, rough old fingers down to her small bones. Then they softened, letting go, and Wanda—propelled by all the mad and the sad and the afraid she was feeling—threw her arms around the big woman's neck and hugged tight.

"I felt like this before," Granny said. "Under the tree. I've been gone a lot, haven't I? I wonder where I go."

Wanda straightened up, forcing her hands to smooth her grandmother's cover, to keep busy, fighting the wet swelling behind her eyes.

"I must remember, Wanda. Nobody's nothing without their memories."

Wanda begged: "Go back to sleep, now, okay? Please, Granny?"

As if she'd uttered magic words, her granny was back asleep. Wanda stood over her a little while longer. As she moved back under her sheet, she realized she was trembling. Her eyes went back to the window's light again and stayed there.

"HEY!"

Wanda bounced straight up from her pillow, eyes jerking open. Somebody very large was hovering over her in the dark, with hands on very big hips.

"Are you bleeding yet?" her grandmother was demanding to know.

Wanda groaned, pushing her bangs out of her face. "What time is it?" The moonlight was gone.

"You're old enough, you know. It's about time."

Wanda blushed herself hot there in the darkness. "Granny, no! Geez! Why do you say stuff like that?"

Granny grunted. "You know what to do when it does happen?"

"Yes, yes, I promise. We saw a video in health class. Stop it, okay?"

She studied Wanda a second, then sat down on the edge of the sofa. "I'm sorry, Wanda Louise."

"For what?"

Granny heaved a big sigh. "I never wanted to talk your mama down in front of you, but she done you no good. And I've been way too old to be much use to you. But you're almost there, almost grown. And I can at least get you on your way with this."

Wanda flopped back onto her pillow. "Well, I'm in no rush. Hadn't seem to do much for Cookie Belew or Trudy Sue Busby except make them crabbier."

"I'd like to tell you what it means," Granny went on. "But honest to the Lord God Above, I still don't know."

"I know what it means, Granny."

"Would you listen up, Miss Know-It-All? I'm talking about its deep meaning. I don't know why we got to bleed to keep the world going. I expect He's got his reasons. Seems He's always got his reasons. But it ain't no curse, like I was taught as a little girl. More a reminder we're just like the rest of creation, I suspect. Now the cramps, that's a whole other thing. You ask me, that's just plain spiteful. You listening?"

"*Yes—*"

"Yes, what?"

"Yes, ma'am."

She saw the big shadow finally shuffle away. "Good night now."

Wanda let out a sigh of relief. These little talks were flat taking it out of her.

"Where's that dog?" her grandmother was now saying as she crawled back in bed. "Lordamighty, I planted a big one on her. Outta my head."

Wanda looked at the ceiling, where rays from a nearby streetlight now reached flat like fingers across the sparkly tiles. Waiting for the peace to descend again, she watched the tiles sparkling like stars in a gray man-made night. Then, in a voice thin with quiet, Wanda murmured her deepest secret. "I found out Mama did have me with somebody else's sperm."

Granny was silent so long that Wanda was sure she'd fallen back to sleep. But then the creaky old voice said, as sad as the world, "Puts me in mind of the parable of the seed."

At that Wanda rolled her eyes, groaning quietly.

"You too good to hear the words out of the mouth of Jesus Christ himself?" Granny said. "Don't tell me you don't remember that story where the farmer is careless throwing those seeds around."

"I remember!"

"Yes, what?"

"Yes, ma'am. Can we go on to sleep now?"

The absence of Granny's rolling way with words made an empty space in the room for a few seconds. When the old woman spoke again, it was with a melancholy voice heavy with the meaning of more thought: "How do you know this for sure?" she asked Wanda, this child she'd always believed was her own blood.

"I saw records."

"Lord help us all," Granny murmured. The old woman wondered if she had heard right. *Seeds here and there and everywhere, upon the rocks, upon the weeds. My poor sweet boy-child, and my Wanda Louise. What kind of world? Who would want to live forever? Old age cures such thoughts. I'm so very tired. I do need so to sleep now.*

But these were Granny's thoughts, and Wanda couldn't hear them. She listened, her ears ringing with the silence, wanting, straining to hear something more from the prone, shadowed shape across the room.

Then just as Wanda thought there would be no more, just as she had began to surrender to the comfort of thoughtless slumber, she heard the cracked voice float across the darkness to her. "Doesn't matter who you think you are," it said. "Doesn't matter how you got here or why. You're still your own, baby. And still my little Wanda Louise. You remember that. You never forget."

# Chapter 18

$\mathcal{G}$ riffin LaCour was leaning back in his squeaky chair, arms folded across his chest. He had spent the last hour just like this, staring at his terminal screen, the blankness of the newsroom computer too much like how he was feeling himself. Every few seconds he'd rub his goatee with finger and thumb, this way, that. Then he'd move a little just to hear the chair squeak. Ordering thoughts had always come easily to him. And he usually loved the pressure of a good deadline. What was the problem tonight?

"Shit or get off the pot, *LaCour*—" barked a silver-tongued voice from the copy desk across the floor.

Griffin gave a little push-away wave. Okay, he was late, even later than he'd planned after the game and his attempt to talk to Youngblood, because he hadn't come straight here. Instead he'd found himself ringing the doorbell of the loft apartment of Cassandra, his first wife. The model. She answered the door in silver silk pajamas. "Griffin, what are you doing here?"

"Let me in. Just for a minute. I need your help."

Cassandra's sculpted eyebrows went straight up on hearing that. The door swung wide in the same motion as her hips. "This I've got to hear." Cassandra turned on a practiced bare heel and went into the kitchen. "I'll make some coffee."

"Cass," he began, calling after her, "would you consider me romantic? Even . . . unselfish on occasion?"

He heard laughter from the kitchen. "Griffin," she called back, "you didn't remember our anniversaries—*either* of them."

Griffin followed her into the kitchen, then leaned over the counter. "I'm not joking. I did something today . . . and I need some perspective."

Cassandra put a hand on her small waist and cocked a not-unaffectionate look his way, then went back to digging out coffee cups from the pantry. Watching her, Griffin was struck, like a jolt to the gut, with how much she looked like Patricia Ann Hightower, in fact, how much both of his wives did.

"You don't want the truth," said Cassandra.

"Yes, I want the truth."

"Okay," she said, closing the cupboard. "The truth is when we made love—which wasn't that often with that precious job of yours—I sometimes felt you would at any moment call out someone else's name." She turned her eyes toward Griffin to deliver the rest: "And Griff, dear, I always felt it would be your own."

He winced: *Ouch.*

"I told you that you wouldn't like it." Cassandra set the cups down and smiled slightly. "You have good qualities, Griffin. God knows I married you for some reason. Selflessness just wasn't one of them. But so what? However bad this thing is you've done, she'll forgive you. It's what we do best. You and I both know your commitment gene didn't make the leap across the missing link. You don't look good, sweetheart. I have an early morning car dealership shoot out at Texas Stadium, but if you need to stay . . ."

"Thirty minutes, LaCour—or we run the vacation piece about roadkill!"

Griffin popped out of the daydream and glanced up at the clock sitting on top of his monitor. It was digital. He just realized he hated digital with all that stand-at-attention exact perfection and wished for the old-fashioned, laid-back, approximate messiness of a face clock. He made a mental note to replace the hunk of modern junk. Then, blowing a big breath through puffed-out cheeks, he put his hands on the keyboard, rested his fingers over the keys and began:

Griffin LaCour/Column

I am curious about the mysterious force in the universe that creates relationships—that spurs us to choose whom we choose to fill our lives.

Theories abound.

There's the Earthworm theory, held by a young friend of mine with an impressive knowledge of animal husbandry, in which we are brought together at random and stuck to each other thereafter through a naturally produced slime.

There's the Narcissus theory, held by my Greek Aunt Leona,

spoken loudly at each of my weddings, in which we choose those who are reflections of ourselves.

And then, of course, there is the Love theory which the consensus of dead poets and soft rock songwriters have missionaried now for long enough to have become a part of our collective Western consciousness—at least until enough divorce lawyers make us wise beyond iambic pentameter.

A buzz of truth swarms among these three honorable theories: I must believe in Love. Why else would I have bought a tux to save wedding rental money? Aunt Leona must be right or else why would she feel it a sacred duty to keep showing up at my weddings to remind me? And slime must have been the stuff I happily kept smearing between the current female "thee" and me. What else could account for such sticky messes?

As a man of the modern world, of course, I would have said each time that there was no such force. I was only exercising my God-given, all-American, modern right of choice, to be choosy in whatever fashion I chose.

But here on this side of wisdom, I now see this choosiness as a modern madness. Because the madness is not confined exclusively anymore to the area of significant otherness alone.

Oh, no.

Now, dear reader, thanks to science, we can be just as choosy about the next generation of relationships . . . or just as modernly cavalier.

For those of you in the last remaining pockets of Father-Knows-Best-Land oblivious to the new millennium reality, "Brave New World" is no longer just the name of an overwrought perennial favorite of college required reading lists. We now have relational choices amazing only for the nonchalance with which we seem to be embracing them.

We are renting wombs, buying and selling our sperm and eggs, we are popping embryos as if they were popcorn and then freezing them like dead meat, we are reblossoming mothers out of menopausal grandmothers, we are contemplating a future when we will be able to copy ourselves a cloned baby, and right now we are screening genes for perfection (a practice which, I must admit, makes me shudder at the thought of what Adele Johnson LaCour might have chosen to do with her imperfect baby boy today).

No problem, right? It's just medical science at its best, offering us, the well-balanced, mature members of this modern society, the alternatives we deserve.

Okay. Take an average American couple, a bald, soft man who logs most of his time living vicarious video athletic glory in his Lazy-Boy and his frustrated, overweight wife who yo-yo diets between SlimFast and Sara Lee pound cake straight from the freezer. When procreative things go wrong and they are offered a chance to go shopping for their future generations in the neighborhood's sperm bank catalog, which product do you, dear reader, think they would purchase? The semen from a bald, dumpy man whose first love is pizza? Or that from a blond, blue-eyed surfer with a degree in astrophysics?

I don't know about you, but I shudder at the surplus of blond scientific surfers in our near future.

Because, tell me, how long will it be before we all demand the choice to be so choosy whether "things" go wrong or not?

Yesterday you read about orphaned Wanda Ledbetter, the donor insemination daughter asking Parkland Hospital for the identity of her "sperm father." Today you will read about another donor insemination baby, a no-name newborn baby girl entering this world with a mother dead and the husband/would-be-father who now rejects the child as if the rose birthmark on her tiny throat had been put there as a mark of hereditary ownership by her real father, her "sperm dad."

In the biological and/or ethical sense, they are all fathers: the unknown man who sold the seed that created Wanda 13 years ago, the unknown man who did the same 9 months ago to create the newborn girl, and this father-by-contract who now is refusing to bond with his dead wife's daughter for reasons reserved for his future psychoanalysis.

And father knows best.

But what about our relational theories? Well, the dead mother certainly believed in the maternal corollary of the Love theory so deeply she would do anything to have what her chosen mate couldn't give her. Even if it killed her. As for these "fathers," they seem to have taken a few too many cues from that Narcissus mirror, says a man who knows the look. And with apologies to the Earthworm theory, these guys just seem like slime to me.

Lover or child. Everybody's searching for someone, like the song says. Someone perfect, that is. If perfection is possible, we will surely pursue it.

I'm beginning, though, to understand the intrinsic value, even wisdom, in old-fashioned, messy, natural imperfection.

Griffin raised his fingers a moment, then languorously added: *And some old sweet slime . . . for its own slippery sake.*

Staring at that last line, Griffin wondered momentarily where it had come from, and then knew quite well. He screwed up his face, highlighted the line and hit the delete key, sending it into vapor.

"LaCour!" came the gravel growl from the copy desk. He threw up his hands for the benefit of the growler. Without another look at the column, he punched another key and sent it on its electronic way to print. *Not bad,* he thought. *Not bad at all.*

Stretching, he got up from his squeaky chair and headed through the stuffy copy room to the elevators, the electronic hum of the room fading away with each step. When he looked up from the small funk he'd gone into during the quiet elevator ride, the doors had opened onto the *Tribune*'s high-rise parking garage. Framed by the doors, the lights of the Metroplex went on forever.

Midnight. *Now, this was a day,* he thought.

He stepped over to the rail to stare out at the Dallas skyline and wished he hadn't given up smoking. He coughed for old times' sake.

A bass beat followed by a screaming electric guitar, loud enough to make his bones quiver, hit him firmly in the back.

Griffin thought he yelped, but since he didn't hear it, he wasn't quite sure. A couple of rows away, one of the paper's college interns had climbed into a truck with oversized tires and stoked up his quadraphonic stereo. Griffin found himself walking toward it as if in a trance, even though the volume was blowing his ears back against his head. Now he remembered why he used to stand right in front of the speakers at frat dances.

At the sight of Griffin LaCour drifting his way, the young intern popped the stereo off and stuck his head out his window. "Oh, Mr. LaCour, I'm real sorry. Usually I'm the only one up here this time of night, and the acoustics are outstanding!"

Griffin stopped, allowing a thought to make its way through the aftereffects of the din. And up from behind it, he felt an old sweet smile coming on.

BOOM BA BOOM BOOMBOOM BA BOOM WAAA WAA BOOM.

Patty bounced straight up in bed before she knew what had hit her. Throwing her silk robe over her Dallas Cowboys T-shirt, she ran to one of the windows at the front of the house.

With a mighty heave, she pushed the window up and yelled out at Mr. Griffin LaCour, who was standing in the streetlamp spotlight with a smirk on his face.

"Turn it DOWN!" she yelled. "THE NEIGHBORS!"

Griffin cupped his ear: *What?*

Giving up, she ran to the front door, swung it wide and rushed out to this lunatic from her past.

"DAMN IT, GRIFFIN! WHAT ARE YOU *DOING*?" she yelled, inches from his face.

Beyond him, parked outside the circle of light, a boy behind the wheel of a jacked-up oilfield truck waved a couple of tentative fingers at her through the crush of sound. Patty pulled the robe tighter around her T-shirt.

"MAKE HIM TURN IT DOWN," she screamed. "THIS NEIGHBOR-HOOD IS PRACTICALLY WIRED INTO THE POLICE DEPARTMENT!"

"IF YOU'LL DANCE WITH ME—" Griffin yelled back.

Patty gaped at him a second. Shooting him a shriveling look, she glanced frantically around at her neighbors' houses. Lights were coming on.

"OKAY!" she screamed. "JUST TURN IT DOWN!"

Griffin put out a hand, Patty snatched it—painfully, she hoped—and Griffin pulled her into the soft halo of the streetlight, nodding to the boy. The volume immediately dropped to close range, the song changing to quiet, mellow, sexy. And as songs sometime do, this song brought with it other things.

*The first time ever I kissed your lips . . .*

Patty stiffened. She loved this song. Why, she hadn't heard it in years, since . . . She looked up at Griffin. "Oh, this is too much," she suddenly said and turned to stalk out of the circle. The volume went back up. Patty pivoted, narrowed her eyes at the grinning Griffin and joined him back in the light. The volume slid down to where it played only for them again; Griffin pulled her close.

"Griffin, why are you doing this?" Patty asked, chin stiff against his shoulder. "Are you trying to drive me crazy?"

"Senior year," Griffin said. "Don't tell me you don't remember." He squeezed her hand. "Always makes me think of October nights."

Patty felt the warmth of the street's asphalt under her bare feet. Despite herself, the song was wrapping itself around her.

*. . . I saw the stars fall from your eyes . . .*

"This is so out of character for you," Patty said, not lifting her head. "Are you feeling all right?"

"You know, I don't know." He pulled her closer, his hand pressed against the small of her back, the cool of the silk robe feeling quite nice. "But I've got this odd feeling I'm going to keep doing things just like this."

A sweet summer breeze played across Patty's face, and the soft feel of Griffin's cheek against her forehead was not unpleasant. She felt her eyes close.

"Patricia, do you think it's possible some forms of slime never quite unstick?"

*. . . And we will last till the end of time, my love.*

"Oh, shut up and dance," Patty murmured, laying her head close to his neck. They began turning in a slow circle there in the middle of the halo's faint light, in the middle of the street, in the middle of the night.

"Hey," he whispered into her hair. "Want to try a dip?"

★ ★ ★

Granny's eyes opened.

*What's that noise?* she wondered. *Singing?*

*Well, how nice. Who's there?*

*Johnny? Why, why hello yourself . . . Can't quite make you out. Turn down that light a bit. Hurting my old eyes, and you are a true sight for these sore ones, such a lovely one, my Song of Solomon Beloved One! And my—look at you shining! Getting brighter, it is. So bright I'm all but bat-blind, might fall, break an old hip.*

*Where're you going? Wait up! Bright bright bright . . . Let me get my shoes on.*

*Such a sweet sight.*

*Such a sweet sound: Who else is that calling so nice?*

*Oh. God.*

*Why. Hello yourself.*

# Chapter 19

$\mathcal{W}$anda was dreaming of the little baby's red birthmark. It was growing. Just as it flooded over the little girl's whole neck, Wanda jerked awake.

Opening her eyes in the early morning light, she felt something sticky on the white sheet under her. She held up her cut finger, checking Roscoe's Band-Aid for leaks. Realizing it wasn't her finger that was bleeding, she jumped to her feet, threw back her covers and rolled her eyes at what she saw.

*Oh no. Hello, Cookie and Trudy Sue.*

Grabbing up the sheet, she rushed into the bathroom, slammed the door and plopped down on the commode to ponder this new development, her school video come to life. The bright white row of little bulbs around Patty's fancy wall-to-wall mirror irritated her; she squinted at her reflection, then leaned over, stuffed the sheet into the sink and turned the tap to gush. Over the noise, she thought she heard a voice:

*Wanda Louise, will you be all right?*

"Just a second!" she called to her grandmother. After she'd done all she told Granny she knew how to do, with the help of Patty's well-stocked bathroom, she flung open the bathroom door onto her brand-new world and slunk back into the room in a fine snit. "Well, you'll be very happy."

Her grandmother was in bed. Wanda looked closer. The big hump under the covers hadn't stirred. She was still fast asleep, her old cheeks bright, her feet kicked out from under the cover . . .

. . . and her shoes on?

Wanda began to say her grandmother's name but found she could not. There was a quality of silence in the room she could not bring herself to break. Instead she moved, slow, dreamlike, to the bed and, with the dread one reserves for the stillest of mortal moments, gently shook her granny's shoulder.

★ ★ ★

Patty had left her townhouse early that morning for two reasons. First, to dodge her agile young houseguest, and second, to catch Dr. Charles A. Youngblood and catch him good.

So as Dr. Youngblood swung his door wide and marched in at 7:00 a.m. sharp, coffee cup in hand, he found the hospital's Public Affairs Director sitting in one of the big chairs in front of his desk. He sloshed a bit of coffee on his sleeve at the surprise.

Patty smiled. "Good morning, Dr. Youngblood."

Wiping at his sleeve, he stepped back to the door. "Thank you, *Carla,* for informing me of my visitor!" Shutting it firmly, he pulled himself into perfect posture, his face now flashing his biggest authoritative smile as he stepped over to his leather office chair and sat down. "Good morning."

"How are you feeling today?" she began.

His smile went just a little tight as he tapped the chair's arm nervously. "Fine. You?" he answered, tapping faster, his smile a little lopsided, his eyes doing the mambo.

Patty sat up. "Dr. Youngblood, are you Wanda's father?"

"No!" he blurted, as if the word had been surprised out of him. Then he sighed and stood up.

"Well, then, who?"

"Not me." He caught her eyes and glanced away. "Not her."

He fidgeted for a beat. Patty waited. Finally he hazarded looking back at her: "About last night. I began worrying about publicity after I found out about my personal situation, and I thought of you. I hope you'll forgive the . . . intrusion."

"What did you find out, Dr. Youngblood?"

His eyes did another definite shift, down and away. "The findings do not concern the girl. I can't tell you any more. I have to consider my professional ethics." He made a wiping slash at the air. "You can sit there all day, Patty, and I can't." He turned toward the window. "There are policies involved. You should be able to understand that."

Patty let a moment linger. Then she tried: "You said the first day Wanda appeared that there were no records. Were you lying?"

"There are records, but none that will help her. That's all I can say."

She watched his back. The guy's posture was so straight, she thought with the right chop, he'd snap in two. "What are you going to do about your twenty-two?"

"There is nothing to do."

"But what if they show up in the parking lot?"

"They'd thank me, that's what I think," he said, turning back toward her defiantly. "It's *really* none of your business."

The silence dangled for a few seconds in the air between them, until Patty stood up. "No," she said curtly. "But I am a part of what we're doing now."

A tired, vulnerable look washed over his face. "We're doing good, Patty."

"I hope so," Patty murmured.

He adjusted his horn rims, the look now gone detached, doctorly, his posture again stiff. "About last night, I *can* rely on you to be professional." His jaw muscles were now dancing a nice, nervous jig. "I'm sure you value your work here, don't you?"

For that second less-than-subtle threat in as many days, Patty had a response, all right. Several pithy comebacks came clearly to mind, all of which she knew would contribute to an unemployed status. Yet she was surprised at how tempted she was to use them all. She stood there a moment, trying on the temptation for size. It was rather nice. No, she wouldn't say them. But she could have. She really could have. As she backed out of the room, she made as much noise as possible. Just to do it. And she enjoyed it, oh yes, very much.

By the elevator, she glanced out the floor-to-ceiling window panel. At the hospital's front entrance below, a protest group had already formed, the same one from the day before. She took the elevator down to the first floor and crossed the lobby to the nursery. She wanted to check on little Baby Jane Doe before she began to prepare the statement she'd have to make concerning the poor thing.

Going through the swinging doors, she found herself behind a slow-walking woman in a raincoat. She frowned. It wasn't raining outside, was it? "Excuse me," she murmured and went around the woman, thinking absently how black and long the woman's hair was. It was rather like Cher's in her Sonny days.

Patty whirled around. She gave the woman the once-over, from her Birkenstocks to her heavy makeup to her black, board-straight wig. And on the second glorious impulse she'd had in as many days, she grabbed a fistful of hair and yanked. The whole thing lifted up and off the woman's head.

The woman howled and made a move to run for it. Patty dropped the hair, grabbed  at the woman's arm and hung on like a tick, calling for a nearby nurse to contact security.

The woman grunted, pulling against Patty's grip. "My rights are being violated!"

"We have a mutual friend, Ms. Sperm Warrior," Patty said into the pale, powdered face.

"I haven't done anything!" the woman declared at the top of her voice, frantically patting down her dull fuzz of thin real hair with her free hand. "Just walking down a free corridor in a free country! Somebody should be doing something, but *I* haven't done anything."

"What exactly were you considering?"

The woman yanked at Patty's grip again. "I don't like to be touched."

"Tell me what you were doing here and I'll let go."

The woman tried to throw up her hands. "This poor, poor baby is a warning shot for all the problems coming. Can't you see?"

"Look, Miss . . ." Patty began.

The woman, though, had her speech prepared: "We aren't even asking if this is right or not, leaving it all to the doctors and scientists! Today it's creating children the way we think we want them, tomorrow it could be creating them the way they tell us to, *less* control over our bodies as women—not more!" The woman jerked again, trying to free herself, then thrust herself into Patty's face. "And you're part of the problem, Ms. Patricia Hightower!"

Patty reeled back. "How do you know my name?"

Free from Patty's grip, the woman rubbed at her arm, whisking the wig off the floor. "You'd think someone who'd survived a youth of swimsuit competitions would be wiser about the evil way of the world." She dusted at the hairpiece prissily. "Just look what you did to my wig!" Shaking it out, she patted it back in place, straightening it around her ears just as Leon came bouncing through the doors.

Leon popped his Stetson down over his brow. "This lady giving you trouble?"

Patty stared at the woman a moment, then quietly said, "Would you escort this woman outside, please?"

When the big guard had vanished through the doors with the wigged woman who was loudly questioning the hygiene of his filthy hands, Patty turned and made her way into the nursery to see the little lost baby. The nurse who was tending to the newborn smiled at Patty and began rocking the bundle in her arms ever so gently.

Watching the nurse's soothing rocking, Patty felt a tidal wave of rolling feeling, and the more she watched, the more she felt she might drown in it. She forced her mind away from it all and turned toward the elevators.

★　★　★

A few minutes later she got off the elevator and walked very, very slowly toward her office. Some blissfully thoughtless peace before all her official happy-talk work was what she desperately needed right now. The morning—the whole week—had already been far too filled with intrigue. She'd take a few moments, she decided, before starting work. Maybe lie down on the couch, get her bearings, just calm all the way down. She took a deep breath as she turned her office doorknob, pushed the door open and flipped on her light switch with a flourish.

There sat Nurse Stella Peabody in her starched bright white uniform and her polished white shoes, feet together at attention.

Before Patty could utter a word, the nurse said in a hushed, pinched voice, "Please sit down quickly, will you? And close the door?"

Patty obeyed.

Stella lifted her thick chin high. "Dr. Harold Roddy was one of the finest men I ever knew. You didn't know him; even the people who knew him didn't know him like I did. Everything he did he did to help people, help us all."

For a moment she let the testimonial linger in the air. Then she dropped her chin ever so slightly. "But there was a time when I thought maybe I should start keeping track a little of some things. For reasons we need not go into here." The chin dropped a little more, her hands now nervously adjusting her trifocals' gold chain. "Of course, it's nothing like an official list; just my scribbles, in case of emergencies, do you see? In those years before everything was so exact . . ." She looked back at Patty. "He was not himself at the end. So it seemed the thing to do at the time. And, well, I'd all but forgotten about it, so many years have passed." She sighed. "But then that sweet, lonely child showing up here like she did, oh dear me, my heart, it just sank, I worried about her so. And with what happened last night, well, what's a good person to do, Ms. Hightower?"

Patty was sitting on the edge of her chair, trying to appear calm. "Do you have it?"

The nurse crossed her arms as if she needed her body's help to support her words. "I told Dr. Youngblood of it two days ago. He ordered me to give it to him."

Patty sighed at that.

The nurse's strained face drooped, her eyes darting rabbitlike. "You must understand, Ms. Hightower. This job is my life."

Then Stella Peabody pulled a folded piece of ripped-out notebook paper from her pocket, leaned over and pushed it into Patty's hand. "This one, though, I did not give him—the child's. I didn't know exactly why at the time; now I know. But I just may be making things worse. There were three inseminations on the child's mother that month, yet I only have one of the donor's identities. I should have been more exact. Lord help me, I felt so guilty." Her voice caught.

She stood up quickly. "I mustn't be late for my shift. Ms. Hightower, please—never bring this up with anyone, even me, ever again. You *must* promise me that."

Patty was staring so intently at the contents of the small piece of paper that the old nurse had scurried out and was gone before she realized it.

Just as she started after the nurse, the phone rang. She hesitated, and that seemed all Stella Peabody needed to vanish. Patty sighed, reached over her desk and grabbed at the receiver.

"Yes! . . . Wanda?"

# Chapter 20

Dear Daddy

    I'm not crying.

    I'm not. Understand?

    I'm not filling up with snot and sadness and thundering lonesome again.

    I'm not.

    I'm not thinking either.

    Just for awhile.

    Because sometimes, most times, thinking is just this side of crying.

    I hope you are real.

    But I'm not

    I'm not crying.

# Chapter 21

*P*atty sat with Wanda on the edge of the white couch in her townhouse's living room. The ambulance and its paramedics had already come and gone, taking their time. Time was not a thing that meant much any longer. So they had moved in and out of the house doing their work, just part of the background, part of what it means for life to go on.

Wanda, still dressed only in the old T-shirt she'd slept in and her cutoffs, sat barefoot, hands folded, her eyes on the rug. Patty sat in almost the exact same position beside her, studying the same patch of carpet. "We have to inform your relatives, Wanda," she said. "For the funeral and the arrangements."

"Not any."

"No aunts or uncles? Cousins?"

Wanda shook her head.

"Granny didn't have any sisters or brothers with living kin?" Patty pressed.

Wanda shook her head again. Her hair fell in her face; she raised a hand and absently brushed at it. One strand stayed on her cheek.

"Wanda. It'll be okay," Patty tried, hating the false sound of it.

"How do you just die?" Wanda murmured faintly. "Just close your eyes and never open them again? How do you just up and decide to die?"

"It was a good way to go."

"She went, all right. Just like everybody else."

"Wanda, she didn't choose to leave you." Patty's eyes went to the empty portrait space on the wall.

"People are full of crap." The back of Wanda's eyeballs were on fire. "People go and they go and they leave you all ... all ..." The last word stuck to her tongue. She looked up, the unspoken word turning her face desperately soft, fragile with pain. The sight made Patty's eyes well up. She caught Wanda's gaze just long enough to see once more beyond her eyes into the powerful, huge, hulking hurt, back to the hurt before this one and the one before that, and the one expected to come after this. She wanted to hug her hard, squeeze the toughness soft and the wounds healed. But she didn't dare. Not even in this small moment when Wanda's guard was down. When it looked as if she wanted it just as desperately as Patty wanted to give it.

Then the moment was gone, the survival reflex settling back around Wanda so quickly that Patty could have sworn it made a physical sound as she watched the girl frown down again at the same piece of carpet.

So they sat there in silence.

The mantel's antique Swiss clock ticked, tocked, ticked again. It seemed loud. A little too loud and dead-sounding, Patty thought for the first time in all the years it had been ticking there on the mantel. She sighed, wanting not to have to do this to Wanda, any of this. But the business of wrapping up a life couldn't wait. "Wanda, are you sure you don't have any family at all? Think hard. The authorities will ask. And Granny would want them to know."

"Nobody Granny'd care to see." Wanda screwed up her face. "There was this sister-in-law of Granny's last dead husband, Aunt Beulah, that Granny never said died. She just said she wished she would."

"Well," Patty said with a quiet sigh, "we better call her."

Wanda set her jaw. "I don't see why. I never laid eyes on the woman. And I'm sure as shit-fire not going to live with her. And I'm not living with Harley wherever he is, and I'm not living in any foster home, either. I'm going to find Wild Thing and we'll just take off. Circumnavigate. Hit the road, Jack. Never come back. Never."

The clock had now become quite irritating. Tick Tock. Tick Tock. Patty fingered the folded piece of paper in her jacket pocket. Tick Tock. She hated these moments in life when it was impossible to know whether knowledge unknown could be better than knowledge known. Tick. Especially when she was the one who had to make the decision which it would forever be. Tock. Patty got up, stepped to the mantel and stilled the clock's arm. Why, she wondered, are the odds always so heavily on the side of disappointment over joy? And why do we feel the need to keep on betting anyway—for ourselves and for everyone else?

"Wanda," she said, listening to her own words as they hit the air, "I know this may not be the best time for this. Perhaps this should wait until after the funeral. But . . . I think I have something to show you."

She drew the folded paper from her pocket and handed it to Wanda.

★ ★ ★

An hour later, Patty's BMW stopped at the well-groomed curb of a wealthy Ft. Worth suburb. The red brick and stone Tudor-style house sat well back on a sculptured hill, its brick drive one of those serpentine ones, weaving its way up to where a new, gold Jaguar was parked. Under the front lawn's spreading maple tree sat a pure-bred Irish setter, perfectly color-coordinated with the house.

*Good grief,* Patty thought, rolling down her window. The place looked like something out of a child's fantasy. *Child's fantasy, nothing,* she corrected herself—*my fantasy.* The sight made her remember drives she and Eric had taken through such neighborhoods when they were first married, planning the house-on-a-hill future they had had no doubt was theirs. The same kind of drives her mother and her father had taken when she was a child, pointing to the left, to the right, showing little girls what little girls might one day have. And her heart hurt suddenly, not for dreams lost, she realized, but for years lost dreaming the wrong dreams, other people's dreams.

"What kind of doctor is he?" Wanda mumbled.

"A heart surgeon."

"You know him?"

"I've heard of him." Patty looked tentatively back at Wanda, thinking now of Wanda's dreams. "He's supposed to be very good." Patty paused, staring at her for a long moment. "Wanda, you did hear me explain how Dr. Ford was just one of three who donated for your mother's last inseminations. His name is just the only name we have. The odds are only one in three he's your biological father—you *do* understand that? A DNA test would need to be taken to know for sure."

The house's heavy front door opened, someone whistled, and the setter romped inside.

Wanda swung her car door wide.

"Maybe I should go with you," Patty began. *Maybe the stranger you know is better than the stranger you don't know,* she wanted to say. "Maybe I should help explain." *Or blunt the blow.* She suddenly wanted to curse. What had she done? This was wrong. "Wanda, you know, maybe . . ."

But Wanda was already out of the car and gone. She had eyes only for the carved oak door up the hill, and in a moment she was standing in front of it.

*Dear Daddy*, she practiced. *Dear Daddy, here I am.*

She raised a finger and pushed the ornate lighted doorbell. In, out. Some sort of chime played, the dog began barking, and a baby started crying. No one came. She pushed the doorbell again. This time, the door opened before her. There stood a woman holding onto the setter's collar, looking rather harried. "Yes?" she demanded.

Wanda's voice caught, and she cleared it: "Is Dr. Ford here?" The dog kept barking.

"Watson!" she called down the hall. And she led the dog back out of sight.

Nervously, Wanda shined her boots on the back of her jeans, smoothed down her hair, then shifted her weight from one boot to the other, tugging at her clothes. She'd put on her good jeans and a T-shirt with no writing on it. *Dear Daddy.* She eased her hand into her pocket and pressed her fingers around the small stolen sperm-bank vial she still protected, still kept close, safe, warm. *Dear Daddy, here I finally am.*

"Lenina, do something about that baby," she heard a male voice say, coming toward her. Then, a short, paunchy man with brown hair, brown eyes and a big nose was standing in front of her. "I'm Dr. Ford," he said, taking off his glasses. "What is it?"

The dog started up again from somewhere. Wanda felt herself about to stutter. She took a big breath. What had she expected? Blond hair? Hazel eyes? And a pug nose. Yes. Pug. "Hi, I'm . . . I'm . . ."

"I'm sorry, I can't hear you. Lenina!" he yelled down the hall.

Wanda's throat was so thick she couldn't swallow. She looked up at that frowning face and did not feel anything like she thought she would. No. No, she didn't at all. *Dear Daddy, it should be like this: You would see me and you'd say oh my god, you must be my daughter. You've got my mother's eyes! You've got my father's nose! Look at you! . . .*

"What do you want?"

*. . . Look!*

"Look, I'm very busy," he fumed.

"You want to b-buy some cookies?" Wanda heard herself gurgle at the frowning face.

"Cookies?" the man said, first surprised, then irritated. "No, I don't think so." And he closed the big door on her.

Wanda did not move.

"Lenina, it was about cookies for godssake," she heard from beyond the door.

The voice drifted away, beyond the barking. Wanda listened until the sounds trailed off, the quarreling, the barking dog and crying baby, blending, rolling together, far, far away behind the brick and stone.

Wanda backed off the porch, boots scuffing against the cement, then turned and rushed down the winding driveway, all but stumbling down the hill.

Patty, seeing the speed with which she was returning, started the car and, under her breath, uttered that curse.

"Let's go, okay?" Wanda threw herself into the passenger side. "Let's just go."

# Chapter 22

It had been twenty years since there had been a new grave dug at the Poetry Cemetery, the little community of Poetry having dried up years before. It wasn't that the place was full up; it was just that the younger kin of all those old souls resting in peace, who'd gone and bought marble markers and family plots big enough for generations of forever family togetherness, had moved their lives and their deaths a long way from this ghost community. Within another generation or so, even these graves would be all but forgotten, that being the way of the living who know not the dead.

So all the ruckus over at the little country cemetery was enough to get the remaining few old people who lived in the area down to see the goings-on, most of them rather proud the cemetery cleaning had just been done. The hole the two men from down the road had been hired to dig was in the Ledbetter plot, a family thought to have all gone and died off forty years ago between the war, childbirth, cancer, polio and normal farm accidents. They were an unlucky group, all right. Curiosity was high. Although the country air was heavy with the threat of a summer shower, the locals came.

Yet even with these curiosity-seeking old folk, the whole group attending the graveside service, not counting the gravediggers and the funeral director, barely hit double digits. The funeral party, from all the locals could see, consisted of only the pretty young woman who'd driven up in that rattling Cadillac wreck with the blond girl dressed in that boxy velvet black dress (and cowboy boots, Lord have mercy); the trio of older ladies who'd gotten out of the black funeral limousine that came with the hearse, and that hippie-looking young man with the facial hair who'd shown up late in that foreign car. That was about it.

The funeral itself had to be held up a while, until the child—a girl who didn't look like any Ledbetter they remembered—had been lured back out of the woods after spending a good long time making just a real rowdy racket. Like most young people today, she had no respect for the dead.

But when the service got going, well, it was right nice, everyone agreed. Remember this God-fearing woman, the nice young preacher had said. We are but the good we do, the stuff of memories we leave this side of eternity. Ashes to ashes, dust to dust; there's a time to be born, a time to die. A time to sow; a time to reap. Yes, in my Father's house are many mansions; but for now, until we slip this mortal coil, we have our memories. And "Amazing Grace." Shall we sing all four verses? Oh, my yes. Real nice. After that lovely of a service, why, they all wished they had a memory of the woman themselves. And such a nice afternoon for it, too, although it looked like rain.

Patty and Griffin were now standing under the funeral home's green tent, shaking hands with all these old people as if they knew them. Tugging at her borrowed dress, Wanda, hair combed and face scrubbed, edged away from the people to stand by her grandmother's grave. The cut flowers' stagnant sweet odor made her nose itch, and all Wanda could think looking at them were that they were dead and they didn't know it yet.

She swallowed hard. She sniffed.

She felt like cocking back her head and screaming till her throat hurt. Everything was pressing too near. Even the air was heavy on her, so heavy she could hardly breathe. She wished it would go ahead and rain, just go ahead and come on down.

The pastor, a middle-aged man whose face showed he'd spent more than a few afternoons this way, had moved close to Wanda. "My, Wanda Louise. You've grown into a young woman since I saw you last."

Wanda tugged at the too-big black velvet dress Patty had loaned her (without telling her it was from one of her teenage pageant days). "It's just Wanda now," she informed him.

The pastor nodded. "Your grandmother was quite a woman."

Wanda took a big breath. "She didn't like you, you know. Said you wouldn't visit her in her fallout shelter."

The pastor paused. "We all worried about her when we found her down there, Wanda. It wasn't normal. Even for your granny."

"Worry wasn't the point. Visiting was." Wanda moved a pebble around on the fake grass the funeral people had laid out under the tent.

The preacher was talking again. "Your friends are nice. It's rare to have such friends. And I just had a chance to meet your great-aunt, too."

Wanda shot a dirty look at the short, squat woman with yellowed gray hair and a low-hanging pair of Double D's chattering like a durn magpie behind her. "She's not my aunt."

"Wanda, have you thought what you're going to do?" the pastor began. "Perhaps you should come home with . . ."

"Well now, Wanda Louise!" the squatty lady interrupted. "How we holding up, young lady? Come to your old Aunt Beulah." She had popped Wanda's head into and out of her cleavage before Wanda could do a thing about it, and she came up with a snoot full of talcum powder. "My, hasn't she grown up fine? I haven't seen her since she was just a little thing at her mama's breast, God rest her soul. Such a pity about her mama. Poor dear girl's an orphan now, aren't you, sugar? Lord, Lord. Ain't it the funniest thing, preacher? There ain't anything left of the whole family. Except her and me. God works in mysterious ways, he does." She waved back at the two other ladies standing behind her. "Wanda Louise, I just met *your* nice friends, so I want you to say hello to my two friends from the retirement village that were kind enough to ride down with me. Say hello to Pearl and Martha May."

Hello, hello, smiled the two ladies, nodding.

Wanda looked down at the pebble by her foot.

"They were sorely disappointed that you wouldn't ride with us in the lim-o-zine. But we forgive your bad manners in your time of grief." She glanced back at the grave hole behind the tent and the coffin hovering over it, waiting on its metal gurney, then clucked her tongue. "I find it right sentimental she would want to be buried here by the Ledbetters. Went out of her way, since she's got no legal claim to do so."

Wanda stiffened. "What?"

"I'm just saying, sweetie, she was never married to that Ledbetter boy." Beulah clucked again. "But she was a brave woman, she was. Putting her life back together the way she did after the terrible indiscretion and the boy dying a soldier's death. She was a sight, I imagine, people being like they were about such things back then. Till that traveling salesman came along and married her, gave that boy a proper father, and took her away from here. Of course, if that salesman hadn't taken her away and then died so soon, why, she would have never ended up marrying my big brother Cecil and we wouldn't be standing here, would we? My, my, mysterious ways."

"But . . . our name is Ledbetter!" Wanda sputtered.

Beulah made a smug face. "Child, child." She flipped a wrist so chubby her Spiedel watchband looked as if it were cutting off circulation. "Back then all you had to do was move off a nice ways and you could call yourself anything you wanted. She sure made a point of calling that boy of hers a Ledbetter till the day he died, though, didn't she? And why not? He probably was. Oh, by the way, I'll be dropping by this afternoon over to the house to help clear out her things. I got a realtor real interested in listing it."

Now Wanda found her tongue. *"Granny's* house?"

"Oh, sweetie, don't you know? That house belongs to the Birdsongs, not to your grandmother. Our mother's old maid aunt Lila lived there till she died at the age of 103. When poor Cecil fell over dead with that aneurism and left your grandmother without a home, she moved in with Great-Aunt Lila. Then when Lila finally went to Jesus, my mother—that saint of a woman—said your granny could live there rent-free as long as she lived, considering how good she was to Cecil and all. Of course nobody figured that would be close to forever! Bless her heart!" The old lady laughed, her partial plates clicking. "Now it's mine, since I'm the only one left. And I can sure use the money. Things aren't free at the retirement village, are they, girls?" She said back to her friends. "Why, I almost couldn't afford to make reservations for the fall foliage trip this year, it's true."

At that, Wanda pushed past the old woman. Patty, who had been talking to the funeral director, had overheard the whole thing and watched as Wanda stumbled to the far edge of the plot. Patty went to her. She was standing over a gravestone, an old rectangle marker from World War II, the kind the government sent back with each body. It read: "Corporal John Lee Ledbetter, killed in action, 1943."

"Everybody lies to me!" Wanda gasped. "My mother, my grandmother, everybody I've ever known! That's what you adults do, isn't it? Lie to us kids. Lie to yourselves. Lie, lie, lie! Well, good riddance then. I don't want to remember. I want to forget it all. She never loved me, lying like the rest of them!"

"Wanda, you know that's not true!" Patty answered. "Nobody loved you more than she did. If your grandmother lied, it had nothing to do with you."

"Lies have to do with everybody, okay?" Wanda snapped. "I'm *glad* I'm not part of this crazy family for real. I'm glad I'm not part of *any* family. If ol'

Beulah's what you get when you got nothing else, I'll just take my chances with nothing!"

Patty groped for the right words, but what do you say? What words are there that don't sound like lies? Where are the words? She *hated* this.

"Patricia!"

Patty turned to look toward Griffin, who was calling from the other side of the tent. He was standing by the dead tree they'd found Wanda's grandmother under . . . when? Two days ago? Three? She squinted. Griffin was waving something at her.

Then a sound made her turn all the way back around—the sound of the old Cadillac coming to life. Patty ran up the hill so fast she ripped her hose. But all she saw for her effort was the muffler of the Cadillac dragging behind a big dust cloud. For a second she stood there, gasping for breath, watching them go. Then she rushed back down the hill toward Griffin.

"Patricia, look at this," Griffin called to her. "I just found another buffalo nickel here where Wanda's grandmother was sitting."

"Griffin, give me the keys to your car! Wanda just took off in the Cadillac."

"You gave her the keys?"

Patty threw up her hands. "Of course not! She must have had another set hidden somewhere in it. I knew I shouldn't have let her talk me into driving her down here in that thing. She's been making noises about running off ever since Granny died. Give me your keys! You can ride back in the limo!"

"With those old ladies?" Griffin said, digging in his pocket. "I'm coming with you."

"Somebody's got to stay and see Granny in the ground who cares. Please. Let me handle this," Patty pleaded.

Griffin frowned, reluctantly chunked her his keys and watched as she disappeared. He sat down on one of the big roots of the dead tree, careful not to tear his one nice pair of slacks, and looked at the buffalo nickel in his hand. Maybe he'd drive back with the hearse. Or pay one of the gravediggers to take him back to the city. Be worth every penny.

A glint of metal caught the corner of his eye. He looked down. A piece of the dead tree had broken off near the old roots, and something was shining behind it. Griffin dug around it a little with a couple of fingers, and the glint became more pronounced. So he grabbed a part of the old bark and yanked.

And from behind it cascaded nickels—buffalo nickels.

Griffin croaked out a delighted gasp. He began to claw with both hands at the bottom of the hollow tree, and the nickels flowed over his knuckles to the ground, coming down with the sound of a slot machine, the hollow tree trunk all but full of them.

"Ooh! Get away!" he heard one of the little old ladies squeal. "Why, I never!"

"Get, dog!" yelled one of the gravediggers. "Get away from my crotch, you mangy yellow thing!"

Griffin's head snapped up.

"Whoop!" he heard the preacher yelp.

Hearing that happy sound, Griffin sat back on the pile of nickels and smiled, deep and wide.

# Chapter 23

The glass between Wanda and the sleeping, ruby-throated baby was fogging up from Wanda's breath. Wanda wiped it clear with the sleeve of the velvety funeral dress she was still wearing and watched as a nurse tiptoed around the rows of newborns to check on the little ruby-throated baby. She looked up at Wanda and smiled. Wanda smiled back. The nurse turned to a candy striper, gave some sort of instructions and came out the door.

"Is she okay?" Wanda asked her, scooting up close.

The nurse smiled beatifically. "She's just fine," she whispered and went on down the hall to the nurse's station. Wanda looked back at the candy striper. She wasn't much older than Wanda, and from the looks of things, she was being made to change diapers. Wanda curled up a lip at the thought of that, dropping her eyes back on the no-name newborn baby girl as the candy striper began working on her. The baby had just let out a wail, her face all big-mouthed. *The stupid candy striper better not have stuck her with a pin or something,* Wanda thought. *She just better not have.*

Three older candy stripers appeared in the room. Much older, as far as Wanda could tell. She could only see their backs. One of them, with hair as red as I Love Lucy's and all but busting out of her jumper, began pointing and waving until the young candy striper rushed out of the room. Then the three surrounded the little ruby girl's bassinet, scooped her up, placed her in a big basket and walked authoritatively out. Right past Wanda.

Wanda's eyes went wide. That big one was no candy striper. She was no redhead, either. Wanda'd know that wig woman anywhere.

The red-wigged Sperm Warrior was whispering to the others as Wanda scooted up behind them just as they pushed through the swinging doors. "I estimate we have two full minutes before anyone notices. We must hurry. To prepare for the media."

"Hey," Wanda called hesitantly.

Wanda's Sperm Warrior, not slowing down a step, waved Wanda to follow as if she'd known Wanda was there all along. Wanda looked frantically around, wanting to call out to somebody. But the group was moving too fast, across the lobby, to the doors and out. So Wanda rushed after them. "Hey—" she called after them again. "What are you going to do with her?"

But the bogus candy stripers didn't stop until they had disappeared behind an old gray van only a few rows over from where Wanda had left her mama's Caddy. A group was waiting, and if it were possible, they out-weirded Wanda's Sperm Warrior. Getting a good eyeful of the crowd, Wanda began to worry big-time.

"It was so easy!" one of the candy-striped accomplices crowed as the group drew near. "Bet they'll have all sorts of big security gates up after today."

"Hey!" Wanda tried again. "What are you going to do with her?"

"I didn't bargain for this," one short, roly-poly half-bald guy was saying, rubbing his head. "*Kidnapping.*"

"Hey!" Wanda tried once again, this time punching her Sperm Warrior's arm, "I'm asking you a question. What are you going to do with her?"

The red-wigged Sperm Warrior suddenly handed the basket baby to Wanda and moved into the roly-poly man's face. "It's called civil disobedience, you idiot! You go to jail. That's what you do."

Wanda looked down at the basket in her hands. The baby yawned.

The roly-poly man rubbed his head harder. "Maybe a little resisting arrest, creating a public nuisance. But *kidnapping*? You're talking the Lindbergh baby, you're talking serious jail time."

Wanda took a step back from the crowd.

The red-wigged Sperm Warrior was now giving a lecture on civic responsibility, on the power—no, the duty—to demonstrate in a free society when one believes that society's ills can no longer be addressed in the normal channels.

The roly-poly man responded by panicking. "We'll go to jail!" he shrieked. "I'll be some reprobate's special 'friend'!"

Another male voice yelped. "I call for another vote!"

As the group started fighting among themselves, the grumbling and the name-calling getting louder and louder, no one noticed Wanda, still holding the basket baby, take another step back, then another, and another and another.

And to her amazement, in a few more seconds Wanda had set the basket baby in the Cadillac's seat, had started the car and was bouncing over the parking lot's speed bumps onto the road.

Away.

# Chapter 24

$\mathcal{P}$atty flung her townhouse's door bouncing wide, punched her blinking answering-machine message light and willed Wanda to speak from it.

She had five messages:

1. Her mother.

2. A carpet cleaning company wanting to rid her of filthy, ground-in dirt.

3. Greenpeace. The whales still need help.

4. Her mother. Again.

5. Eric. He'd stopped by and was very upset about the scratch on the ...

Popping Eric silent, Patty dropped to the couch with a frustrated groan.

*Okay, think,* she told herself. *Think! Think!* Wanda wasn't at her grandmother's house or fallout shelter. And she's not here. Where would she be? Patty saw an image of Wanda in her black dress and boots, on some godforsaken stretch of highway halfway between Dallas and Hollywood, thumbing down a tattooed pervert of a trucker ...

Patty stopped thinking.

She laid her head back on the sofa and closed her eyes. What had she done to this girl? She'd thought she'd done the right thing. Since meeting Wanda, she had flouted the "correct" thing, the rules, the regulations, the expectations of everyone at home and at the hospital, the correctness that was set up around her like fenceposts, and had been so sure that doing so was "right." Why did she have so much trouble with the difference between what's correct and what's right? She'd taken this one stand past what others might think and look what had happened. Just look. If she hadn't decided to go on a sudden crusade that probably had more to do with herself than with Wanda, the old woman and the girl would probably have gone back to College Mound that first day, Granny might still be alive, and Wanda would not be without family or home. And except for Eric, her own life would have gone on its dull, plodding yet safe way. If she hadn't stuck her neck out and her nose in. If her world hadn't blown up at the same time this girl's had. If she hadn't tried to be something she wasn't. If. If. If.

The house's silence was stifling; even the cat wasn't showing itself. Patty thought she might just pop from the quiet, two-ton guilt of it all. Up from behind it, the little ghost "if's" came dancing, going a lot further back than a lost kid and a weak-hearted, big-souled grandmother—a lifetime further. She could trace them back past Eric, past baby attempts, past Griffin and the young scared awful choice, all the way back to mother-mannered nice-girl lessons, hand-me-down expectations and a spurting little girl spirit stomped flat. She could "if" all day. And what would happen then? They'd come right back at her, popping with the sting of a rubber band from hell.

Life was constructed with choices, she realized; every choice is planning your future for you, no matter what you are told, no matter what you think. Yet no one prepares you for this simple, central, magnetic thing. No one tells a little girl that the choices made around her, for her, by her every day of her life are what's creating the fences she'll keep bumping her knees on forever. No one tells her anything but what everybody else is doing, wanting, planning, dreaming, so often that the little girl thinks it must be what she should be doing, wanting, planning, dreaming, too. Until this crazy week, Patty had expected nothing less, accepted nothing less, wanting it all and planning on having it better. Then this scrawny, wild country kid materialized loud as a sermon in her shaky vision. This kid too smart for anybody's good and too self-possessed for little girl fences. And suddenly here was Patty Hightower, Miss Perfect Role Model Beauty Queen, making choices she didn't recognize: Reaching back for people she thought she wanted left behind. Making stands for people she hardly knew. Telling a doctor to sit on a tack! And enjoying it! What was going on? And what the devil did she want now?

Truth was, her knees were raw from the bumping, and she had no clue what to do about it.

Except stop thinking.

She grabbed the remote for the comfort of noise, punched on the television and began flicking channels, the louder the better.

One of the local channels caught her eye: SPECIAL BULLETIN flashed across the screen, and the Eyewitness News van appeared with hair-sprayed Tiffany standing in front of Parkland Hospital.

Patty fumbled with the volume:

*"Tiffany Yu coming to you from Parkland, where we have just received a tip that there may have been a kidnapping of the little Baby Jane Doe of our news story yesterday."*

Patty all but dropped the remote. She punched the television's volume higher: *"We have a group of protesters calling themselves the 'Sperm Warriors,' here behind me, who are taking credit for the kidnapping in protest of what they call the dangerous, one-sided, unregulated aspects of the assisted reproduction programs . . ."*

*"We are not!"* yelled one of the faces behind her.

*"We are too! Sperm is forever!"*

*"And as you can hear, there is some dissension in the group itself over the admission. But no one seems to be able to produce the baby itself. I have here with me Mr. Leon Quattlebaum, head of hospital security. Can you tell us anything, Mr. Quattlebaum?"*

*"Well, Tiffany, not much. These people I know got a constitutional right to be here, but half of 'em don't seem to have the sense God gave a goose."*

*"IS the baby missing? The tipster said that three rather mature candy stripers were seen walking out with the baby in a basket."*

*"Well, Tiffany, I'm not at liberty to say one way or another."*

*"Have the police been called?"*

*"Well, Tiffany, all's I can say is I can't say."*

*"We also have an eyewitness who saw a young blond girl with such a basket sneaking away from this group."*

*"Well, Tif—come again?"*

*"We are told that as soon as Parkland Hospital's Public Affairs Director returns from the funeral of her grandmother later today, we will receive . . ."*

*"Excuse me there, Tiffany, but did you say . . . ?"*

*". . . the hospital's response to these rumors. In an Eyewitness exclusive, though, we have this home video taken by Mr. Ray Bob Digger this afternoon. Ray Bob, tell us about this as we show it to our viewers."*

*"Well, Tiffany, we were here picking up Auntie Thelma from her gallbladder*

*operation and decided to commemorate it on videotape. That's my converted van on the left there, and as you can see, here comes Auntie through the front electric doors, being rolled out by my wife Pearl. That's Pearl waving."*

"Thank you, Ray Bob. To the right, you can see that Ray Bob has captured the movements of three rather mature candy stripers carrying a basket into and out of Ray Bob's frame. And if you look closely, the blond girl in the black dress and cowboy boots behind them does seem to be following the three. Well, there you have it. Has there been a kidnapping? Are those our kidnappers? What is the fate of Little Baby Jane Doe? Those are the questions of the hour. Back to . . ."*

Patty all but swallowed her tongue. She sank onto her soft white sofa in awe and let the real reason for this whole week settle down to rest—this girl, this scrawny, stringy-haired, foul-mouthed, amazing child who seemed to know the difference between correct and right, all by herself.

A piece of Patty flopped over, throbbing, sudden and sad. She caught an image of herself in one of the large mirrors across the room as she let an idea grow. She could have sworn the sofa, the room, shifted as she did. Because she now knew exactly where Miss Wanda Ledbetter, this anything but safe, brave new Wanda, would be.

And she knew, now, exactly what she wanted, very much, to do about it. If she were crazy brave enough herself.

★ ★ ★

On the seventh floor of Parkland Hospital, Dr. Charles Youngblood was waiting to begin a consultation

"Good afternoon, Dr. Youngblood!"

The couple walked in excitedly and sat down. "We're going to do it," announced the woman.

Dr. Youngblood was standing at his window, staring at the crowd and the TV crews congregated around the entrance below.

"Dr. Youngblood?"

Looking around at the couple, he adjusted his horn rims, moved behind his desk and eased wordlessly into his leather chair.

"We've decided," the woman repeated brightly.

"Just so long as we can keep the donor out of it," said the man, with a decisive wave of his hand. "Forms signed, all rights waived. That's what you said."

"Yes, of course." Dr. Youngblood leaned over his desk. "Unless . . . you'd like to try one of the assisted reproduction procedures again. Or even perhaps consider the possibility of living without . . ."

The woman cut him off. "But isn't this what you recommended?"

"Yes."

"So," the woman asked expectantly, "when do we start?"

Dr. Youngblood fingered his ship in a bottle gingerly, absently. Checking the cork.

# Chapter 25

*A sea star reproduces by regeneration.*
*An arm pulls itself away. And the arm*
*becomes a new, a different, sea star.*

—Wonderful World of Biology

Dear Daddy.

Wanda had written the same thing three times in her notebook and had crossed out each with big black straight marks.

~~Dear Daddy~~
~~Dear Sperm Father~~
~~Dear Donor Daddy~~

None of them looked right anymore. And Wanda wasn't quite sure why.

She sat in the Cadillac parked on the wrong side of the Ft. Worth street, tires hugging the big house's high curb. She'd been sitting here over two hours, no one in sight, fancy car gone.

She squinted around at the glum afternoon. It had turned out to be one of those rare gray summer days in Texas, the kind that creep out from behind all that relentless hopeful sunshine as if to remind everyone of things as they really are. As they've always been, as they always will be, ancient or modern, past or future: ugly. The more gloomy and looming the sky seems, the smaller the world feels and the deeper the feeling goes. Especially for a thirteen-year-old, when you're a runaway from your grandmother's funeral parked in your dead mama's Cadillac at the curb of the fancy house of the man who may have made you. And you're packing a hot baby to boot.

A drizzle was coming in the rip of the Cadillac's convertible top, and Wanda just sat there letting it dribble down her scalp and through her hair. She could swear someone was spitting on her—and for once, Ms. Too Mean to Live didn't even feel like fighting it.

But she got out of the car anyway, rummaged in the trunk and laid one of her mama's mildewed blankets over the tear in the ragtop. Her granny's yellowed handkerchief, which she'd found in the car, was now too damp to keep the baby's face dry, and she wouldn't want the baby to get wet. Not *her* fault, any of this. Wanda plunked down behind the steering wheel, slammed the long door and wiped at her face with the sleeve of her borrowed funeral dress.

*Phwew.*

She glanced at the basket beside her. The baby was smelling to high heaven. Like pukey milk or dead flowers or wet dog. That made Wanda even more melancholy, lonesome for grandmothers and dogs gone. People die and they leave holes. That's the way things are. And the hole inside her right now was yawning at her, getting bigger, not smaller. "I got so many holes, Ruby," she gasped, wiping at her eyes with the back of a hand. "I swear, I've got to be the Human Grand Canyon."

Blowing a sigh out her nose, she gazed at the new trouble she was toting. "I just thought the law was going to be pissed over me shooting Harley," she said, quietly watching the newborn. She frowned. The baby was sure still. Real still. Even with the raindrops on its cheek. Even with the slam of the car door. Wanda reached over, took hold of a bit of the baby's plump arm and pinched.

The baby yowled, loud, healthy and very much alive.

*Sorry, sorry,* Wanda patted, cringing, relaxing. The baby went straight back to sleep. "How do you do that?" she asked it. Oh, man, if she could do that. What a trick.

Not know. Not care.

Not know that the people who have to love you don't.

Not care that people who do love you die.

Not know or care that learning such things has nothing to do with how old you are, or how smart you are, or how determined you are. Like shit, it just happens, like it did for her mama, for her granny, for little babies, even for pissants like Harley, and surely, sometimes, for fancy doctors who live on hills in fine, tall houses, who might have your genes, who could be your blood. Who could make things right.

A car passed. It was the fancy car. It pulled into the long, curving driveway and ascended the hill to the house. Wanda Ledbetter had been waiting the whole afternoon, the whole lifetime week, for this moment, for the someone who could be the intimate stranger she'd been hell-bent to find. From her rolled-down window, she watched the Jaguar's door open and the big-nosed man she'd all but touched yesterday stride purposefully into the house's side door.

And she began writing again furiously, the pencil whispering on the cheap paper:

*Dear Dad—*

No. Scratch.

*Dear Dr. Ford,*
*I don't sell cookies. But you sure sold yours . . .*

Erase. Start again:

*You don't think you know me, but—put it this way—you double-jointed?*

This time, Wanda ripped out the page and threw it to the floorboard. Then writing big, black and hard, she scrawled:

*Dear Dr. Watson Ford. Are you my fucking daddy?*

Are you? She gazed up at the red, orderly bricks and saw his impatient eyes, felt him slam the door, heard his voice trailing off, full of snit, full of itself, full of Harley sounds. Harley with good grammar.

No, she realized:

You wouldn't want me, would you?

You do not know, do not care, do not dream that I exist. Do you?

You will look at me with those same eyes, but this time with fear around their edges like some cornered possum, won't you?

You . . . you could be little Ruby baby's real father, too, could be father of a tubful of us, one by one, introductions all around, and it would be no different, would it?

Sperm, that's all you were, all you are.

And sperm has no feelings. Sperm doesn't love. Basic stupid biological fact. All right? Understand? Stupid? Stupid little dumb kid *Wanda Louise.*

Leaning her head back against the top of the old seat, Wanda squeezed her eyes good and tight and shut against the knowing, the knowing too much.

It was beginning to do more than drizzle. The raindrops, big as bombs, splattered the windshield, and the wind was blowing them in the window. Wanda opened her eyes at the assault. Vacantly, she wiped at her cheeks and the sad, slow storm blowing in from behind her eyeballs as she turned her head toward the Cadillac's passenger seat, wanting more than life itself to see her big granny filling it full, waving that yellowed hanky, wiping and griping, complaining about her bladder being full, her feet being swollen, her granddaughter being smart-mouthed and weed-stubborn. Wanda wanted to talk to her, fight with her: *You just had to go and die, too, didn't you?* she wanted to yell. *You had to go like everybody else, just when I know what I know.* Wanda squinted hard, desperately, wanting to see the hanging fat jiggle on her granny's old arms, wanting those sagging old cheeks to purse together and those eyes to sparkle and hiss as the old mouth ran on.

But there was no squint between heaven and earth that powerful.

The rain blurred the window. The baby yawned. Sniffling, Wanda pushed her wet bangs back off her forehead, looked down at the newborn riding in her basket seat and wrinkled her nose. Holding her breath, she cracked her window and shook the edges of the little blanket to clear the air. "You sure do stink, Ruby Red. But if you want to stink, you go right ahead and stink. Nobody has a hold on you. You are your own. You remember that. You never forget."

As the noise of the rain battering the ragtop filled her ears, Wanda tried to salvage some leftover meanness, to stop the stupid sniffling, to think clearly about what was going to happen to her. Only thing she knew for durn sure, there'd be no Harley, no Aunt Beulah, no Baptist preacher or foster family. No sir, not in this life.

But—what *was* she going to do? And what was she supposed to do with this baby? *Think!* She was supposed to be smart, so gotdam stupid smart. *Thinkthinkthink!*

But all her thinking only made Wanda gaze back up the hill. And a wave of deep lonesome passed over her so sudden and rough that all she could do was gulp it back, squeezing her eyes shut once more.

When she opened them, a BMW had rolled to a halt by the curb across the street. From it came the beauty queen, holding a newspaper over her head and running toward the Caddy.

She stopped by the cracked window; Wanda sat up.

"Hey, there." Patty smiled. "You okay?"

Wanda shrugged, pawing at her eyes.

Hurrying around to the passenger side, Patty opened the door, picked up the baby's basket and eased into the seat.

Wanda could barely look at her. "I . . . shouldn't have gone off." She ducked her head. "That was not right. I'm going to pay you back. For everything you've done for Granny and for me." She looked back at Patty and held her gaze. "I promise." An image of the new granny hole in cemetery dirt loomed up dizzily in front of her eyes. She felt something hot and smothering rise up her throat. "Is Granny . . . ?"

"Things went fine." Patty delicately checked out the sleeping basket girl in her lap. "Hey, little girl. People are looking for you."

Wanda took a big, nervous breath. "I guess you're wondering what she's doing here, huh? Well, I just couldn't leave her with that crowd, okay? You never saw a goonier group, I swear, ya know?" Just then, a car turned the corner; Wanda took one look around and almost choked. It was a police cruiser. "Am I going to jail?"

The cruiser rolled to a halt right behind Patty's BMW. After giving the gas a little punch, a muscular cop turned off his horsepower, detached himself from the car, placed his cap on his head, then glanced at the BMW with approval before focusing his attention on the rusting Cadillac. He adjusted his cap and sauntered across the pavement toward it.

"Afternoon. Got a call from a couple of homeowners." He leaned in the window. "About an unusual vehicle out here for a long time. Improperly parked, I might add." He looked straight at Wanda. "You ladies have business here?"

Wanda, who had stopped breathing, opened her mouth to answer, only to feel a fingernail poke her in the ribs. "Oh, it's all my fault, officer!" Patty was suddenly bubbling. "I told my niece—this is my niece, Molly Ann; she's visiting me from the country—I told her to wait for me here on the corner because she didn't know the way to my new home and then wouldn't you know, I was detained! It was a bad idea, I know. She had to wait *hours*. Without any way of my contacting her since I had the cell phone. That's my BMW right over there." Then up from the end of the sentence sprang Patty's blinding, pageant-winning smile, attempting through sheer brilliance to blot out any patrolmanlike questions of drivers' licenses and ages and home addresses and other sticky subjects.

The patrolman stood up straighter. Patty went on, quickly reading his name tag: "We'll be moving right along—Officer Jenkins, is it? I promise, Officer

Jenkins. By the way, my name is Patty Ann Hightower. I am *so* sorry to have put you out. Really. On such a dreary day, too." And she punctuated it all with an instant replay of The Smile.

The officer smiled back this time, pausing in The Smile's glow. As Wanda held her breath and Patty held her smile, he responded, "No, no, that's fine. No bother at all. So, you're named after your beautiful aunt?"

He was talking to Wanda.

"Now wasn't that just the nicest thing?" Patty replied, slow and sweet.

"Well, you have a pretty baby there, Ms. Hightower. Don't let it get it wet. Drive careful." He had leaned as far into the car as professionalism allowed to deliver this last line, received another Patty Smile as reward, then tipped his hat again, strutted back to the cruiser and pulled away.

Wanda breathed.

"And you thought beauty contest skills had no value." Patty turned The Smile toward Wanda, thoroughly pleased with herself.

"He bought it all. Even thought Ruby Red was your baby," Wanda said in awe.

The baby gurgled and yawned. Patty reached into the basket and smoothed the baby's black crop of hair. Taking a deep breath, she picked up the baby and pulled it right into her arms, feeling its warmth, its softness, and feeling something else she couldn't quite name, but something she knew wasn't exactly what she had expected.

Wanda watched Patty rock the baby gently, noticing the strange way she was looking at it. "What's going to happen to little Ruby?"

"I'll tell you what's going to happen," Patty murmured. "This little baby is going to have a wonderful life. She'll be strong in the ways that matter. And she'll be beautiful in the ways that matter. And she'll grow up smart and wise and savvy and she'll take on the world—in all the ways that matter."

Wanda thought about that, then added, "But won't be nice."

"No, she won't be nice at all."

"And won't take shit off nobody—"

"And won't take shit off anybody. But most of all, above everything else," Patty added, pulling her eyes from the baby girl to smile at Wanda, "she'll be loved and she'll be wanted by one of the dozens of couples lined up waiting just for her."

Wanda narrowed her eyes. "How do you know that?"

Patty put the baby gently back in the basket, pulling the blanket around it for its ride to the future. "Somebody's got to have the happy ending."

Wanda chewed on that a moment, brightening and nodding. "Law of averages." She grabbed the steering wheel with both hands. The air was so thick it seemed to hover between them, Wanda squeezing the wheel, Patty trying not to notice.

Patty took a breath and stole a glance Wanda's way. Taking another breath, she turned her gaze out the front windshield and said: "Wanda, remember when you asked me if I liked my father?"

Wanda looked around.

Patty stole another glance at Wanda. "The truth is my memories of my father are all about phones and doors—he was always on the phone, leaving the table to talk on the phone, closing the door to talk on the phone. Until one day he wasn't even on the phone anymore or behind the door, because he had left to be with the person on the phone. And it probably wouldn't surprise you to know that phone person was a former beauty queen." She put a hand to her temple and rubbed a moment. "What I'm trying to say is, it doesn't matter."

Patty paused, gazed at Wanda, not knowing how to get out the rest. Wanda's face was breaking her heart, it was so fine, so strong. *Don't you know*—Patty ached to say—*that it doesn't matter who your father is? Don't you know whoever he is, he doesn't deserve you?* She had turned all the way around in her seat, trying to get the nerve to say all this to this incredible kid. And she just couldn't get the words to come. Finally, in frustration, she fell back into her seat and blurted the only thing she could: "Sometimes don't you just want to rear back your head and scream till you croak?"

With that, Patty gave Wanda a look that would have made Wild Thing bark and run. Then, right then, right there, the beauty queen laid back her head and screamed to bust a lung.

Wanda's jaw dropped: *Whoa.* The beauty queen sounded like a stuck coyote.

Just then a stroke of lightning pounded the distance, and, as if in harmony, Patty smiled the most satisfied smile of her life and started right up again, this time shaking it out from so deep, so close to busting a vocal cord that Wanda's heart began to throb from the sound. The throb went so deep, so suddenly and harshly, that Wanda felt a crush in her chest. She felt the thunder she'd tried to bury with her mother rumbling up from inside, pressing her breathless. She felt it make her throat thick and her head hurt from holding it in so very long and so very hard. And it pressed and pressed until finally Wanda couldn't hold it in any longer. And she laid back her head and joined in, too, screaming the hurt, the hard, heavy internal thunder, into the open. Loud enough for people in houses high on hills to hear through the storm, loud enough to bust through the fences encircling them both. Loud enough to hear it deep, deep inside themselves.

And that was the moment Ruby Red joined in, wailing as only a baby can, surprising silence then laughter out of them both. Patty scooped up the baby and began rocking and soothing, rocking and soothing, leaning back into the old car's seat. And finally, so did Wanda.

The orphan and the beauty queen felt good, bad and washed-out spent, glancing sideways at each other like partners in crime, thinking about absolutely nothing at all for another moment—another fine, pure, empty moment—as the rain filled up the silence between them and their separate thoughts came racing back. Then they were still. And even little Ruby Red was once again sleeping like a baby.

Except for a gentle sleeping whiff of baby sour, the air was now full with that charged, electric, after-the-rain atmosphere. Patty placed the baby back into its basket and breathed in deeply. She could actually feel it inside her skin, as if the current were passing straight through her. She sneaked a look at Wanda, then at the sky beyond. "The worst, I think, is over. Look at those clouds racing off."

Wanda looked.

Fumbling for the damp newspaper she'd brought, Patty unfolded it and handed it to Wanda. "I saved this for you."

Wanda sat up, taking the soggy newsprint in both hands. She stared at it until she saw her name again and then read the column slowly. She stared at it deep in thought for a handful of quiet seconds. Then she folded her arms over it and held it close to her chest. "Least the mudpuppy got my name right."

"Yes. He did."

Wanda frowned. "You think, then, maybe I should think about letting him do more stories?"

"It's something to think about."

"I think I might. Think about it, that is. I mean, after I find Wild Thing. And after I decide what I'm going to . . ." Wanda clamped down, unable to finish the sentence. She glanced up the hill, then forced her gaze back on the baby. Looping the sleeping baby's fingers over one of hers, she felt the little reflex, the built-in blind grab. "There are tests, aren't there?" Wanda mumbled. "Tests to see if he is my . . . you know."

"Yes," Patty assured her. "Lawyers may have to become involved. But we can make him do it, if you decide that's what you want."

Eyes now firmly on Wanda, Patty began drumming her fingernails on the baby's basket, the images of what she was about to suggest flashing through her thoughts: Suck job in jeopardy. Cowboy boot scuffs on the Spanish tile. Dog hairs on the cream sofa. "Wanda . . . does Wild Thing like cats?"

Wanda, staring at the baby, was lost in her thoughts.

"Wanda, listen . . ." Patty tried, louder. She sniffed at the charged air, feeling brave. "How would you . . ." She paused. "What I'm trying to say is I have this idea about you and me. I think it's a good one, not that we wouldn't have some problems, but I think it could work. It's certainly something else to think about . . ." Patty lost her nerve. This was insane. It would never work.

Wanda pulled herself out of her funk and looked up at Patty. "What?"

Gazing up the hill, Patty pressed her lips into a line: *Just ask her!*

Wanda sank back into her own thoughts without a ripple, her eyes trailing back to the house up the hill, her one-out-of-three chance house; Patty was talking again, but she couldn't hear a word. She was reaching one more time with all her might and all her energy and all her blind and deaf and wounded will for the power of the meanness that started her journey here, for the power enough to finish it.

With a slow, jaw-jutting breath, Wanda pushed the big, squeaking door wide and rose from her mother's Cadillac. Slamming it behind her hard enough to rattle the whole car, she turned and took another breath. Patty went silent, watching.

Then Wanda was all boots. She clomped up the long driveway, stepped up on the covered front stoop and once more stood contemplating the rich, ornate doorbell. She raised a finger toward it, ready to ring, ready to tell. But still hearing yesterday's barking dogs, far-off babies and strained, strange voices, she plopped down on the step instead and squeezed her eyes shut. Because on top of those sounds, louder than them all, came the sound of Harley screaming the secret, her secret and her doctor donor daddy's secret.

With her last measure of meanness, she forced her eyes open again and realized she was clutching her mother's wallet picture of the old movie star James Dean. She had placed the crinkled thing, along with her little notebook and other important stuff, into one of her velvet funeral dress's small pockets. (She had made it very clear that any dress she wore had to have pockets.) She had crushed it beyond recognition, squeezing it so hard, and now gazing at it, she saw everyone and everything at once in the cracked face: She saw Granny and her nickels, Wild Thing caught in the trap, Harley and the trailer, her mama and her cigarettes in the dark, but most of all, bigger than everything else, she saw her first daddy—a daddy dead long enough to have turned into her impossible dream.

Gently, she laid James Dean on the step beside her, pulled out her notebook and her stub of a pencil, wet the tip with her tongue and began to write:

Dear Dr. Watson Ford,

There's this Sunday school story, maybe you heard of it. About this sloppy farmer who had lots of seed to just throw around anywhere. So one day he did. Some fell on rocky soil and dried up right there, some fell on good soil and grew tall and healthy. But one fell on rock scrabble soil where it grew but had a real hard time of it since it didn't have any roots to speak of. And finally, it withered way before its time.

I know the original meaning was real different from how I'm thinking of it now, but isn't that the way with stories? They mean what you need them to mean.

So here it is: I'm too mean to live, but I'm too mean to wither, too, you hear. Just so you know.

Hey, you don't know what you're missing.

Wanda

With a big, black flourish, Wanda finished signing her name and tore the page from the notebook. Then, without another thought, she was tearing them all out, all the letters, every one, until she had folded and stuffed them all inside the fancy curved mailbox by the fancy big door, wiped her face with the back of her sleeve and stared at what she'd done. She heard a dog bark beyond the door and a muffled male voice silence it.

"Maybe you are my father," she said toward the sound, "and maybe you aren't." Then, in words low, like a beat-up benediction, she added: "But you *ain't* my daddy."

She felt something shake loose in her, loose and free and gone.

The last of the drizzle had stopped. Back down the hill, a car door slammed. She glanced toward the noise. Patty had placed the sleeping baby basket in the backseat and was now standing in front of the Cadillac, looking up toward her. Wanda took a deep, long, steady breath. Then, reaching again into her velvet pocket, she slipped her hand around the stolen sperm-bank vial, still full of its milky contents. With a last warm squeeze, she opened the fancy mailbox and set it gently to rest on the stack of torn and folded letters.

As she did, she heard one of those sweet sounds that can suddenly make your insides feel calm, steady, safe. It was the sound of a familiar rattling old car being gunned to life. And she turned to see it barreling up the winding driveway, coming her way.

*Photograph Credit: L. Clay*

# About the Author

$\mathcal{L}$ynda Rutledge, a native Texan, has always been fascinated with the big, wide world, and that curiosity has led her here, there and a big chunk of everywhere as a writer. She's hang-glided off a small Swiss mountain, swam with endangered sea turtles, petted baby rhinos and dodged hurricanes. She's been a ghostwriter, a copywriter, a film reviewer, a book club director, a university writing professor and a travel writer. And she's lived to tell about it.

Her articles (under Lynda Rutledge Stephenson) have appeared coast to coast and around the globe in the *Chicago Tribune,* the *Chicago Sun-Times,* the *Houston Post,* the *San Diego Union-Tribune, Poets & Writers* and the European *Die Woche,* and her books have been reviewed in the *Washington Post, U. S. News and World Report,* the *Chicago Tribune, Publishers Weekly* and *Library Journal.* She's also taught on the faculties of Baylor University, Texas Tech University and Columbia College, Chicago.

*Brave New Wanda* has earned writing awards and grants including an Illinois Arts Council Prose Fellowship Finalist Award, Ragdale Foundation and Atlantic Center for the Arts residencies, plus Ropewalk Writer's Retreat and Squaw Valley Community of Writers' Screenwriting Program scholarships. An excerpt from *Brave New Wanda,* entitled "Granny's Ravished Heart," was published in *Emergence II* women's anthology, and another excerpt was part of an NWU Reading Series.

Her writing career has allowed her to wander down roads in Australia, Europe, Hawaii, Mexico, much of the Caribbean and the continental U. S. —even back to Texas. But her husband Don, her dog Brazos and her thirteen-year-old Miata convertible keep her coming back home.